He fought for king and country, but that battle was nothing compared to the one he'll wage for a woman's heart.

Still reeling from the news of her father's death during the Norman Conquest, Isabel Dumont is unprepared when trouble arrives at the castle gates. Alexandre d'Évreux, a Norman knight with close ties to England's new king, has arrived to secure the land and the loyalties of the Dumont family. Desperate to protect her people, Isabel strives to keep the confounding knight at arm's length and hide the truth about her father's death.

For Alexandre, the spoils of war come with more than just a generous gift of land. They come with Isabel Dumont. Vowing to marry only for love, Alexandre finds himself in a difficult situation as a conqueror granted dominion over the land and its people. Isabel is the one person capable of helping him win the regard of those living in the war-torn country...if he chooses to accept her.

Just when Alexandre finds a spark of hope that he and Isabel have a chance at love, she vanishes. His quest to find her plunges him deeper into the conquest's fallout. Was she taken? Or did she leave?

# Siege of the Heart

*By Elise Cyr*

**KENSINGTON BOOKS**
Kensington Publishing Corp.
www.kensingtonbooks.com

**LYRICAL PRESS**
An imprint of Kensington Publishing Corp.

*To Shirly*
*thanks for*
*being there from*
*the beginning!*
*Elise Cyr*

# Chapter 1

*December 1066*
*Northern Gloucestershire, England*

At least she now knew the truth.

It was little comfort though, as Isabel Dumont watched the messenger ride out of the bailey. She let out a breath, a feathery cloud on the cold air. The messenger had declined her offer of hospitality, and she did not ask him to reconsider. Instead, she had seen to it his horse was watered and had pressed a gold piece into his palm to ensure his silence.

Snow had threatened all morning. Now it fell around her in fat flakes, but she did not move. She did not think she could. Her limbs felt heavy, almost waterlogged. Like the time Julien had knocked her headfirst into the river in a moment's foolishness. And then pulled her back to shore.

That had been ages ago. Her brother's message now had the same effect, leaving her winded and frozen in place.

Captain Thomas, who handled the training of Father's men-at-arms, stamped his feet beside her. "My lady, if you wish it, I will make the announcement—"

"No!" The word ripped through her chest and rang in her ears. "No. You will say nothing. To anyone."

His eyes widened. "But this cannot be kept secret."

His disapproving tone cut through the numbness that suddenly filled her. She twisted away from him and looked out past the gates. The graying countryside swallowed all sign of the messenger. If only his words were as easy to erase.

"Your father—" Captain Thomas began.

She balled her hands into fists. "Do not say it," she whispered.

Captain Thomas shook his head. "I must. Your father is not coming home. I know it was not the news you hoped for, but Julien's message…"

He lifted a hand toward her shoulder, and she gave him a sharp look. He stopped mid-motion, his fingers dangling awkwardly, before resting his hand on his belt. She turned on her heel.

Captain Thomas hastened after her. "Wait!"

She wrapped her woolen mantle more securely around herself. She would not discuss it further. She could not. Not when she could scarcely think.

"My lady, please—"

She slipped her hand to the hilt of her sword—one of her father's cast-offs—and the brush of the leather-wrapped handle against her palm made it easier to rein in her breathing. "You said there were reports of the Welsh attacking tenant farms to the west?"

"Yes. I was going to have Kendrick and some of the other men scout the area, but—"

"Good. I will join them. Tell the men to make ready."

Captain Thomas's mouth tightened. For a moment she thought he would disobey her, but he slowly turned toward the castle to do as she bade. Lord Bernard Dumont, thane to the king, had fallen. Now it fell to her to ensure the safety of the Dumont lands. Captain Thomas, of all people, should know what that meant.

Isabel thrust a bow and quiver of arrows from the armory over her shoulder and ducked into the stables, waving off the groom before he assisted her. She led her mount outside and fastened the leather saddle straps. Hardwin flinched when she drew them too tight and kicked his hind leg out in protest.

"Shh. I am sorry, boy." She ran her hands over his sleek flanks. "I was careless."

Kendrick and four more trusted men-at-arms filed out of the stables. Strong, steadfast men who should have been fighting by her father's side in York. Not ordered behind to protect her.

Her father...

Isabel took a deep breath and pulled herself into the saddle. Captain Thomas's gray head appeared next to Hardwin.

He tugged on her stirrup. "My lady, I must protest." He threw a glance at the other men and kept his voice low, his lips barely moving as he glared up at her. "I am responsible for your welfare."

She squeezed her eyes shut. Her welfare was the least of her concerns. She turned to the fair-haired Kendrick. "Ready?"

He nodded. If he observed her exchange with Captain Thomas, he gave no sign of it as he ordered the other riders ahead.

She pressed her heels into Hardwin's sides. Captain Thomas trotted along with them, the stubborn man still clinging to the leather stirrup. She grimaced but kept her horse's speed in check.

"Isabel..."

Before Captain Thomas had the chance to chastise her again, she leaned down as far as she could without losing her seat. "I need this," she said through her teeth. "Can you not understand?"

His hand dropped away. She spurred her horse

and did not look back.

Kendrick led the party west, past snow-covered fields and into the forest that served as their primary hunting grounds. The bare beech branches overhead hampered the falling snow, but the bitter wind still found her and her five companions. Isabel gave up trying to keep her hood in place, and her braids whipped out behind her as they rode.

Trees grew sparse as they neared the end of the hunting trail. After a few more strides, the horses emerged onto an open field.

Kendrick called for a halt. He kneed his mount around. "My lady, there has been no sign of the Welsh."

She scanned the area. Only tumbling snow interrupted the stillness of the field. "Captain Thomas reported holdings to the west were raided less than a fortnight ago. The Welsh will not ignore an opportunity to strike now the Normans control England." She met the gaze of each rider, ending with Kendrick. "We must be vigilant."

Kendrick straightened, his golden curls dull in the leaden afternoon light. "We will, but I do not believe your father intended for you to lead a scouting party when he left you in our care."

"Mayhap not." She was certain her father had not intended for many things to come to pass. "But I will not compromise the safety of Ashdown. Not with so many of our men pledged to Harold's army." She yanked her hood over her head to escape the unrelenting snow and gave Kendrick a hard look. "And I would not be left behind, knowing I could be of use."

"Your quarrel is with Captain Thomas, not me," Kendrick said.

Looking between her and Kendrick, Godric snickered. "Indeed. We know well how persuasive you are when you want something," the man-at-arms said to her. "I remember a certain young maiden who talked me out of my winnings at dice." Godric quirked his bushy eyebrows, waiting for a response.

Isabel pressed her lips together as she cast about for an answer. "You should have known better than to gamble on a feast day."

She could not muster a smile to soften her words, but Godric just laughed.

"So that is why you turned my coin over to Father Joseph? He's been praying for my soul ever since."

"What's this? Not even a grin?" A touch of concern sharpened Kendrick's voice. "What news did the messenger bring this morn to make you so foul tempered?"

Isabel's head snapped up. The men stared at her.

They could not know. Not yet. Not when she could hardly believe it herself.

She breathed deep. Winter air lanced into her lungs. "I am fine, in truth. My father sent word of their victory at Stamford Bridge." She spoke slowly, as if uttering the words could make it so.

"No new tidings then? We heard rumors of that battle and then Hastings weeks ago," Kendrick said.

"The messenger's mount went lame outside of Cirencester, delaying his travel here. At least my father sought to get word to me. He will return to Ashdown in a few days' time."

Her swift dismount silenced any more questions. Eagerly, the men followed her example. Isabel could not blame them. It had been a long, unfruitful ride and they would miss the midday meal, thanks to their outing. She straightened the padded tunic she wore over her kirtle, eager to stand after sitting in the saddle so long.

Kendrick ordered the two youngest, Edgar and

Cuthbert, to scout ahead on foot while the horses rested. Blinking rapidly, Isabel looked to the cloud-choked sky and prayed they would be quick.

"I bet they did not have an easy time of it in Yorkshire," she heard Martin say to the others, his hushed voice clear on the crisp air.

"They say one of Harald Hardrada's Norse barbarians slew fifty housecarls before he fell defending the bridge," Godric said with wonder. "For the army to march south to meet the Normans pressing from the coast so soon after the battle..."

"You heard the tales of the Normans at Hastings," Martin said. "A lake of blood surrounded the hill where they made their stand."

Isabel's gaze fell to the ground, frozen mud and snow marred by hoof prints and booted feet. Better than blood.

"That is enough," Kendrick said. "We still have miles of hard riding."

Isabel looked her horse over, glad to find he had not gotten any scrapes from the trail. Kendrick broke away from the others and reached her side. "I am sure your father will return safely," he told her quietly. "You need not worry."

She patted Hardwin's neck. Just as well he thought her merely worried. "Do not tell me that. You heard the reports of the Normans' victory as well as I."

"Yes, but once your father returns, he will set things aright."

Isabel's mouth twisted at his words and the earnest look on his fond face. Snowflakes clung to his beard and hair. She itched to brush the snow off him. "It may not be so simple," she only said. Once, she would not have hesitated to tell Kendrick anything, but the time when he did not tower over her was long past.

Edgar and Cuthbert hastened across the field.

Red-faced and out-of-breath, they slid to a stop in front of Isabel and Kendrick.

"What happened?" Kendrick asked.

"Tracks, heading toward Ashdown from the northwest," Edgar said.

"Perhaps five or six riders passed this way," Cuthbert added.

Kendrick had the men mounting their horses with just a look. "Mayhap this has not been a fool's journey after all." He nodded at Edgar. "Lead on."

The tracks skirted the northernmost boundary of her father's lands before heading south, deeper into the holding. Unease gathered in a tight knot in her stomach. The Welsh did not usually travel so far east. At least not since the Confessor bestowed these lands upon her father so he could train a force in Norman horsemanship to repel the Welsh. They must be feeling more daring since the Norman invasion left so many areas unprotected. That did not bode well.

After an hour of riding, Isabel and her men broke from the forest and onto a large field with a small rise to the north. The snow had lessened, but flakes still fell, partially covering the ground. The last man had just cleared the tree line, when an arrow glanced off the shoulder of Edgar's horse. The animal reared in fright.

Isabel's breath left her in a rush. Coming around the hillock toward them, five heavily armed Welshmen rode into view. Ambush.

Before she could react, the Welsh loosed more arrows. This time they aimed for Cuthbert. He hauled his circular shield in front of his body just in time to deflect them. Startled, she and her men wheeled their mounts away to avoid careening into the oncoming Welsh raiders. Their ability to fight from horseback would not help if their mounts were cut down before they formulated a strategy.

Returning to the tree line, Isabel reined her horse to a stop and slid to the ground. Their attackers must have heard them coming as they crashed through the forest. It was too late to wish they had been more prudent in their pursuit.

Men on both sides readied their blades. She swiftly nocked an arrow and let it fly at the Welshmen as Kendrick and the others prepared to charge.

Edgar regained his seat. He raised his shield and urged his horse forward, brandishing his sword to scatter their attackers. He caught a Welshman with his blade, and the wounded man fell to the ground.

Breathe, she told herself. She took aim again, careful to avoid her men. Steady now...

The Welshman's shoulder jerked back as her arrow dug into his chest. She bit her lip. The exultation she normally felt after hitting targets set against haystacks or tree trunks was absent. They did not scream in pain.

Edgar's mount reared again. Moments later a Welshman pulled him out of the saddle.

"No!"

At her cry, Cuthbert and Martin dismounted and sprinted into the fray, swords flashing in the dim light.

Her hand trembled as she reached for another arrow. Kendrick and Godric brought their mounts to a halt next to her. "I want you to get back on your horse and fly from here," Kendrick said. "It is too dangerous."

She barely spared him a glance. "You know I will not leave." Her father may have kept her away from past battles, but she was just as skilled in arms as the men. Her place was here. Now, more than ever.

Shooting again, she struck a Welshmen in the back before he landed a blow on Cuthbert. She wrenched her gaze from the man writhing on the ground. She could not hesitate to do what was necessary to defend her home.

Two Welshmen lay dead. In the next instant, an enemy's sword brought Edgar down. An angry cut ran the length of his torso, his blood melting the snow around him.

Kendrick cursed. "Promise me you will get away from here." His gaze found her before he spurred his horse forward. He and Godric urged their mounts toward their attackers, hacking at the three remaining Welshmen on the field.

Isabel stayed in position, firing arrows when she had a clear shot. She struggled to control her breathing as she banished Kendrick's censure from her mind.

Her horse whickered and paced fitfully, drawing her attention away from the battlefield. One of the ruffians had managed to get to the trees and sneak behind her. The bowstring smacked against her wrist, but the momentary sting was the least of her worries. The Welshman was almost upon her. His leer and the sword in his hand told her she needed to do something. Quickly.

Her bow crashed to the ground. She slapped her horse on his rump to get him out of the way. The last thing she needed was the animal used as a ploy in the ensuing fight. She pulled her sword out of its sheath just in time to raise it against the Welshman's steel as he bore down on her. He swung at her again.

She scrambled to block him. He was too strong.

The impact of the next clash of their swords rattled up her forearms painfully. Pivoting before he could land another blow, she slashed at her assailant and managed to cut through the crude armor protecting his chest.

Staying on the balls of her feet, she backed away from the man. Her chest heaved with each indrawn breath. Her arms shook from the effort of holding her sword in front of her as she waited for the man's next move.

Over the roaring in her ears, she heard Kendrick shouting. She hazarded a glance behind her and caught a glimpse of the arrow an instant before it lodged itself into the upper part of her right arm. Crying out, she clawed at her shoulder. Her blade tumbled away and hit the ground with a dull clank.

Kendrick rushed toward her and made quick work of her opponent. The dark look on his face momentarily distracted her from the pain as he retrieved her mount. "Get on," Kendrick demanded in a tone that brooked no argument. "Head back. We will follow."

Isabel gathered her weapons. Kendrick gave her a hand up so she would not place pressure on her injured arm as she mounted. "Tell Captain Thomas to make ready for Edgar." She followed Kendrick's gaze to the fallen man and nodded.

She kicked her heels into her horse's flanks. Hardwin responded with a burst of speed as she directed him south toward her father's castle. Her wounded arm throbbed too much to do anything but let it fall to her side.

Clinging to her horse with her other arm, she wrapped the reins around her wrist. Before she reached the trees, she braved one last look over her shoulder. Kendrick and the others lifted Edgar onto his horse like a sack of flour.

It was not supposed to be like this. Isabel swallowed the ache at the back of her throat. Captain Thomas would know what to do.

She and her horse dashed through the forest. She didn't realize she was crying until the frigid air lashed against her wet cheeks. At least no one would see her tears. Now, she could cry for Edgar, her father, her country, without fear of discovery.

Her gut churned as Hardwin lurched over a fallen log. Her stomach trembled with each stride, but soon enough she spied the palisade walls as her mount broke through the trees. Wiping her streaming eyes and nose on the sleeve of her mantle, she urged her horse on. She rushed into the bailey without bothering to check her speed and jumped out of the saddle. Her legs nearly gave out as her feet touched the frost-hardened ground.

Clutching her horse's neck, she bellowed for the servants to fetch Captain Thomas. "Hurry! Edgar is hurt."

She brought her hand to her shoulder and winced. Flames licked up her wounded arm. She looked down at her fingers and nearly fainted at the blood clinging to her like tree sap.

It was all too much.

She called again for Captain Thomas. Through a haze of pain, she sensed someone approaching. Instead of Captain Thomas, with his gray hair and strict bearing, an unfamiliar man stared down at her with ice in his eyes.

# Chapter 2

*Earlier that day*

Alexandre d'Évreux commanded his men to a stop at the crest of a small hill. The rolling countryside stretched below them like a quilt, gray with age. Old snow dotted patches of tenant farms, and still more snow fell, hushing sound. A cluster of buildings along a quicksilver river marked the village of Ashdown. In the distance, on another hill, was the Dumont castle.

At last.

Hugh de Roche, his shield bearer, followed his gaze. "Good vantage in all directions, leagues of farmland..." He turned back to Alex. "You're a lucky man."

Alex grimaced. "*Non.* Nothing is for certain yet. And it will not be until we return to London with Lord Dumont and his family."

"I do not understand William's interest in them. Scores of English nobles have already traveled to Berkhamsted to bend their knee to him, strengthening his rule over this land. What is so important about this thane?" Hugh asked.

"William expected his support. Perhaps not at Hastings, but certainly once the battle was decided. He could be a powerful ally and make things easier with the English. At least that is what our king hopes," Alex said.

Hugh's brows drew together into a single sooty

line. "What if they have gone into hiding?"

"Then we will wait in Ashdown until they can be found." Alex grinned at the disappointment filling his shield bearer's face. Only a few years separated them, but Hugh still had the patience of a child. "Come," Alex said. "We should change into our mail before we make our approach."

"There's a likely spot." Jerome de Combrey, another of his men, pointed to a clearing skirting the road ahead. Large enough for them to dismount and don the armor that had kept them safe at Hastings.

At Alex's nod, the men urged their mounts toward the break in the trees. As they traveled the eerily quiet roads west from London to northern Gloucestershire, they had taken to wearing their lighter padded leather tunics in lieu of the heavier mail. Alex would be a fool to draw near an English castle without taking precautions—even if Lord Dumont was once a countryman.

Jerome's frank gaze found Alex as Hugh brought them their mail. "Do you think William knew how extensive the Dumont holding would be?"

Alex looked back through the bare trees and glimpsed the castle once more. "I believe he did. He would reward me for my service, but since he is still unsure of the extent and nature of his holdings, he is unable to grant me the property outright." Alex did not envy his lord the task of sorting through decades of English legal documents to account for his hard-won kingdom.

The familiar weight of his knee-length hauberk settled over his shoulders, iron links shining dully in the fading afternoon light. Hugh fastened the plate greaves to Alex's legs before he pulled on his own waist-length hauberk.

Alex looked over Hugh, Jerome and the six other

soldiers his father had granted him when he first pledged his sword to Duke William. They were dressed for battle, eyes gleaming with possibility. A show of force in case Lord Dumont proved difficult.

"Approaching the gates in plain view is rather direct," Jerome said as he smoothed his surcoat over his mail.

Hugh looked up from fastening his belt. "And unexpected."

Alex shook his head. "We have every right to be here. No need to lurk in the shadows."

Jerome lifted a shoulder. "Would you answer if a party of strange knights showed up on your doorstep?"

Hugh chuckled. "One look at us and they will beg for mercy." He patted his scabbard. "If not, there's an answer for that."

Alex raised his hand for silence. "*Non*. We have our orders. We must give the Dumonts every courtesy until we learn more." He made eye contact with each of his men. "Do not risk their goodwill because you did not get your fill of killing at Hastings."

Satisfied with what he saw on his men's faces, he put on his helmet. "*Bon*. We ride." Without another word, Alex mounted his horse and led his men down the hill.

He kept his eyes trained on the Dumont castle. Wooden palisade walls encircled a large number of outbuildings. A huge mound of earth rested in the center, on top of which stood a timber watchtower. The motte and bailey structure seemed out of place in England, where so many lords and men of might made their homes in hillside forts, living little better than animals. The Dumont castle was more reminiscent of those of the homeland Alex had left behind when he crossed the channel. The thought eased his mind only slightly.

The sentries were not ignorant of their advance and had drawn the gates shut well before Alex and his men came within range. No arrows, though. Instead, Englishmen up on the walls argued in their harsh tongue, their mutterings carrying on the frigid air.

With the collective strength of his men behind him, Alex took a steadying breath. Time to see what they faced. He removed his helmet—a sign of good faith—and hailed the sentries in French, the only language he knew. "On behalf of William, Duke of Normandy, defeater of Harold, I, Alexandre d'Évreux, request an audience with Lord Bernard Dumont."

His voice faded, and only silence was his answer.

From behind his helmet's nose guard, Jerome gave Alex a look.

Hugh exhaled noisily, his breath a white plume on the air. "Do you think they understand?"

Alex tucked his helmet under his arm and kept his eyes on the men on the walls. "We will find out."

"We should have strapped that cleric to the pack horse, ill or no," Jerome said. A cleric had been charged to accompany them to aid in translating their words into the barbaric English tongue, but a fever had taken him two days into their journey, and they had left him behind.

Snow clung to Alex's hair as the minutes trickled by. His hand closed reflexively over the hilt of his sword. If they were not granted entry, Alex had few peaceful options to fall back on. He didn't want to disappoint his liege, but if the Dumonts resisted, Alex would not have much choice.

His horse stamped impatiently. Alex had to agree. Time to change tactics. They would retreat a safe distance and decide their next steps.

He was ready to give the order when a new face appeared on the wall. A man with graying temples and the squared shoulders of a soldier. He gave Alex a long, inscrutable look, then gestured to the Englishman next to him.

The gates groaned, then slowly opened wide enough to admit horses and riders single-file.

Alex gritted his teeth. Would he and his men be picked off one by one as they entered the courtyard? He reminded himself their arrival had probably taken the Dumont household by surprise. Perhaps they were simply being cautious—as much as they could within the bounds of courtesy.

Before he forgot his courage, Alex tapped his horse's sides with his heels. He passed into a strangely empty courtyard for a castle this size, offering up a silent prayer when no swords or arrows confronted him.

Small but stout, an old woman exited the hall and stood in the middle of the courtyard. He brought his mount up short. Her back was stiff, with fear or importance he did not know. He did not miss the keys she wore at her belt.

He nodded to her. "I am Alexandre d'Évreux, envoy for Duke William, soon to be the ruler of this land. You have heard such tidings?"

She finally nodded as Jerome and Hugh flanked him. "Welcome, sir." Her words were a crude imitation of his language.

Household servants and a few soldiers filed into the courtyard, unarmed and grim-faced. Tense, curious, wary. Since they did not attack them when they had first arrived, Alex felt certain they would not interfere now. It was enough to know Lord Dumont had taught his household to respect his Norman countrymen, even if the man in question was not there to greet them.

"I seek Lord Dumont and his family," he said to the woman.

Her brow pulled tight. In concentration or concern? "Pardon?" she asked.

"Lord Dumont. I would see him. At once."

She shook her head, her simple linen headrail brushing her shoulders. "He is not here."

"When will he return?"

"I know not."

"What about the daughter? The son?"

She held up her hands. "You speak...too quickly."

Forcing back a curse, he asked again, slowly forming each word.

She shook her head. "They are not here either. Come, you must be tired. A long journey, no?" Her offer of hospitality was unmistakable despite the poorly phrased words.

Jerome's raised eyebrows matched Alex's as he dismounted and let a stable boy lead his mount toward Lord Dumont's stables.

Alex tipped his head to the servant and smiled. "My thanks to you. We have traveled many days and—"

A high-pitched whinny pierced the air.

"You filthy cur!"

Alex whirled around just as Hugh backhanded a different stable boy across the face, knocking him to the ground.

For one tense moment, silence blanketed the courtyard. Then instinct kicked in. Alex took two steps toward the boy. An arrow lodged into the packed dirt at his feet. He jerked to a stop, his gaze leaping to the walls. A dozen archers with arrows nocked.

His men raised their shields, their naked blades ready to taste blood as they circled around Alex.

They had come so far, and now this? He held up his hands. "*Non*! Stand down. Now!"

Dimly, he could make out an Englishman's shouts along the walls. Then one archer relaxed his stance, followed by another.

Alex gave Jerome a stern look. He was the first to ease off, the rest of Alex's men cautiously following.

He would see this fixed. Alex leveled a glare at Hugh and kept his hands raised. "Your pardon," he called out.

Air aching in his lungs, he slowly approached the hapless stable boy, still sprawled across the ground. Alex helped him up, cursing the boy's wild eyes and the red streak across his cheek.

He dusted him off and led him to the old servant who had not moved, nor dared to breathe he guessed, based on her white cheeks. "Good woman, please give him my apologies for my shield bearer's conduct."

Her gaze darted to Hugh and the men on the walls before stopping on Alex. She gave him an uncertain nod. The boy scurried to her side and they exchanged frantic whispers before he sprinted toward the stables.

However, that was only half the problem. Frowning, Alex turned back to Hugh.

He spat on the ground. "He startled my horse."

Alex growled. All this over such a trifle? He grabbed two fistfuls of Hugh's surcoat and shoved him back a few paces. Hugh's heel caught on a half-frozen clod of dirt, and he fell back. Laughter sounded, but a harsh command silenced the Englishmen on the walls.

Alex loomed over him. "I care not what the stable boy did," he said through his teeth. "I care only that you have single-handedly threatened our mission here."

Hugh's gaze fell. "I just reacted—"

"And nearly got us all killed."

"It will not happen again."

Alex battled back a fresh surge of embarrassment and anger. He took a deep breath. "Do not make me regret taking you into my service."

Hugh swallowed and nodded.

Alex stood back as Hugh struggled to his feet. "You will see to our horses' stabling personally since you are so concerned."

He waited as Hugh slunk off to the stables before returning his attention to the Dumont servant. "Please accept my apology for this unfortunate misunderstanding."

The woman gave him a jerky nod. "The boy was more scared than hurt."

Perhaps all was not lost. Alex inclined his head. "It is kind of you to say so."

She hesitated, then squared her shoulders. "Let me show you where you'll be staying."

As Alex followed her to the main hall, he threw a look over his shoulder. His gaze caught on the gray-haired knight still up on the walls. The Englishman stared after them, an unreadable look on his face.

Bloodshed had been prevented this day, true, but Alex would need to watch his back.

\* \* \* \*

Alex set down his eating dagger and looked along the high table. Despite the difficulties earlier, his comrades seemed to be in good spirits, with food, wine, and revelry flowing. If only the rest of the dinner guests were so cheerful. Sharp looks were aimed his way whenever the Englishmen and women thought his attention elsewhere. Distrust imbued the air, as thick as the smoke curling up from the fire in the center of the room. What else could he expect?

"Alex." Jerome put a hand on his arm.

"I am sorry," Alex said. "I was not attending."

"*Non*, I gathered not," Jerome said with a grin. He followed Alex's gaze over the main hall. "It is an excellent castle."

The hall was soundly built, timber reinforced with stone. Horsemen on a hunt leapt across thick tapestries that kept out a great deal of winter's chill. Fresh rushes graced the floor and crumbs of feasts past had been swept clear from the tables long before the start of the meal. A well-kept home, and goodly-sized. Alex had been given a room in the living quarters located over the hall, while household staff made use of rooms off the kitchens. And the nearby lodgings for Dumont's men-at-arms were large enough to house the rest of Alex's men.

He leaned back as a serving girl set a platter of venison on the table. "*Merci*," he said, eyeing her closely.

The girl's mouth fell open before she simply nodded and gave a short curtsy. He frowned as she backed away from the table and hurried off.

"What's wrong? Don't tell me you are disappointed she did not swoon at your attentions," Jerome said with a laugh.

"Nothing of the sort. I was merely seeing if she recognized the word."

"Matilde told us the staff only speak English. We're lucky she knows as much French as she does." Jerome pointed to the old woman who had greeted them in the courtyard, now bustling around the room, directing servants. "She said her father was a merchant of sorts, and she learned French as a child before coming to serve the Dumonts."

"Yes, but is that not odd? I would think Lord Dumont would have retained a few French-speaking servants."

Hugh looked up from his cup. Still chastened when he had returned from his duties in the stables, his shield bearer had been quiet for much of the meal. "Are you suggesting they are refusing to talk to us?"

Alex nodded. "I can understand their defiance, but it bodes ill for our presence in England."

He glanced at all the strange faces taking the meal with them. Someone here had to know where the Dumonts could be found, but Matilde claimed she did not understand him when he had questioned her again before the meal. And now, the other servants and guests were keeping their distance from the high table where Alex and his men sat. He kept an eye out for the gray-haired knight, who had not yet made an appearance.

He rubbed his temples. "I am not sure how we will be able to find the Dumonts if they do not wish it."

"Worry not about the son. There's not much doubt he was at Hastings," Jerome said.

"Ha," Hugh said with a sneer. "He probably didn't even survive the battle."

A heavy clank momentarily drowned out the rambunctious voices filling the hall. Dread coiled tight in Alex's chest. The English surrounded them on all sides—it didn't matter the majority of the Dumont soldiers had most likely fallen serving in the English army. Alex and his men were still outnumbered. And after the confrontation in the courtyard earlier, he would take nothing for granted.

Hugh and Jerome gripped the hilts of their swords. Alex scanned the hall for the source of the disruption, for a sign they would need to defend themselves. If their hosts regretted their offer of hospitality...

His gaze landed on Matilde, a heavy-laden platter at her feet. She must have dropped it. Hardly a cause for alarm. He sank into his seat, his men following his lead.

The tray's contents had splattered onto the rushes, and a pair of hunting dogs snarled over the mess.

Matilde flushed as she shouted commands in English to the other servants to help clean up whatever the dogs left. The older woman scurried from the hall after a quick backward look at Alex. He could not shake the feeling the parting glance was a condemning one.

Drumming the table with his fingers, Alex turned to his comrades.

"The son forfeited any inheritance when he lifted his sword against us," Hugh continued.

Jerome leaned in, amusement twinkling in the depth of his eyes. "And I hear the daughter is a beauty. But she may be too high-spirited for you, Alex." Hugh and the others chuckled, the tension from a few moments ago now forgotten.

"She might be worth the trouble, if this castle is any indication. Lord Dumont must be getting on in years. You'll not have a long wait, Alex," Hugh said, a smug grin on his face.

"You'll marry that minx Dumont and be comfortable for the rest of your life, and us along with you," Jerome said.

Alex's stomach tightened, uneasy at coveting what William had promised when too many things remained unresolved. He pushed at the meat on his trencher with the tip of his eating dagger, all too aware of the hostile looks darting toward the high table.

"Dumont will see the advantage in having a son-in-law of William's choosing, I have no doubt," Jerome said when Alex remained silent.

Hugh surveyed the room with ill-disguised contempt. "Bah, William is too considerate of these English dogs."

"You forget Lord Dumont hails from Lisieux and was one of the Confessor's men. Surely this meal is evidence of that much," Jerome said.

Alex had to agree. In addition to plainer faire like

hearty stews and meat pies marking English cooking, the meal included elaborately spiced and sauced dishes reminding Alex of the grand meals he had enjoyed growing up in his father's hall in Normandy. Back when he could still stomach such feasts and his father's hospitality.

Hugh shrugged. "Mongrel then, if the Norman is such an important part of English society."

"William must tread lightly if he wants to remain king of this land. Allowing the nobility to marry their daughters off to Norman knights will ease the transition," Jerome said between bites.

"And you must not forget there are many other men William will need to reward," Alex said.

Hugh took a sip of the small beer they had been served. "I suppose we must be grateful to William for thinking of you for this holding."

"Yes, but not everyone can claim to have saved William's life during the battle," Jerome said. "No doubt he found Alex worthy of this estate, wife or no."

Alex shifted in his seat. He hoped for the same things they did, but hearing it spoken of so coldly... He was glad Matilde had not remained in the hall regardless of how much she would understand of their conversation. He shook his head. "The Dumonts may resent William's heavy-handedness."

He knew better than to assume the holding would be worth an unhappy marriage. His parents had taught him that much. However, William seemed convinced Lord Dumont would be receptive to the match. And Alex, having no prospects of his own as the third son of a Norman lord, was thankful his gamble in joining with William paid off, despite his misgivings about the marriage. Perhaps he would be pleasantly surprised in both Lord Dumont and his daughter.

"I do not want the possibility of my marriage

spoken of again." Alex waited until he heard the murmur of assent around him. "After all, we must still find them."

Jerome gave him a wink. "I hope you'll like what you find in the lady."

"Keep watch on your tongue, Jerome." Alex stabbed at a piece of venison and ate, while his men busied themselves with their trenchers.

The harsh murmurs of the Englishmen and women in the hall rose in volume. Then a handful of men left the tables and went outside. Alex looked at Jerome and directed his head toward the commotion. With a nod, Jerome excused himself to investigate.

Hugh looked up from his cup. "Probably nothing. The Englishmen are just tired of sharing a meal with their conquerors, no?"

Alex drained the rest of his beer and kept his eyes on the entrance of the hall.

In moments, Jerome returned to the high table. "They're opening the gates!"

Alex jumped to his feet. He had given orders he be informed of all comings and goings, but had not expected much activity, given the snow that had begun shortly before they arrived at the Dumont castle.

Jerome led Alex out of the hall. Hugh and the rest of his men followed. The sentries stationed along the palisade walls shouted back and forth in guttural English. What had raised such a commotion? Perhaps the Dumonts had returned. Alex looked at the bewildered faces of Hugh and the rest of his men, before turning to the opening gates.

"It's a wonder the English can even see in all this."

Alex ignored Hugh's grumble and peered past the gates. Through the falling snow he could just make out a horse heading toward them at a gallop. Pulling up sharply, a disheveled woman slid out of the saddle and shrieked out orders in English. Members of the Dumont household scurried about in response. Leaning heavily against the horse, she called out again. He didn't understand the words but recognized the urgency behind them.

Underneath her cloak, the girl wore a padded leather tunic over a woolen dress. She had a sword and a small knife strapped to her waist, and an empty quiver rested on her back. Another sword was fastened to the saddle. What would a mere girl be doing with such an arsenal?

Her eyelids fluttered when she found the blood that saturated her clothing and seeped onto her hand from her injured shoulder. She swayed, and Alex hastened his steps toward her. When she finally looked up at him, surprise and disappointment stained her features.

She shook her head as his arms closed around her. "No..." Her voice had lost all its frantic energy from before.

The sentries cried out again as more riders, leading a handful of empty mounts, streamed into the bailey. The girl pushed him away, but her feeble efforts drained whatever strength she had left and she collapsed against him. He disentangled her from the horse's reins and took extra care to ensure he did not aggravate the broken arrow lodged in her shoulder as he picked her up.

He stared at the men standing around him. "Who is this girl, and why have you admitted her?" he said, voice raised above their murmurs.

No one moved.

# Chapter 3

The air was thick with blood, sweat and horse. Alex clenched his teeth and tried to think of another way to communicate with Dumont's men.

Matilde ran out of the castle. The gray-haired knight from the walls kept pace by her side. The Englishman seemed to be very skilled at making opportune appearances. That warranted further investigation, but it would have to wait, as Matilde came over to him, her gaze locked on the injured girl in his arms.

"Know you who she is?"

Before she could speak, Hugh and Jerome tensed beside him in a way as familiar to him as breathing— the quiet moment before a fight. Both men had seized the hilt of their swords, intent on something behind him.

A cold blade came to rest none too gently against his neck. Tightening his grip on the girl in his arms, he kept still as a strong hand clamped down on his shoulder. From behind, an Englishman barked into his ear, but the meaning was lost on Alex.

Hugh and Jerome unsheathed their swords and took a cautious step toward him.

"Wait!" Matilde cried.

The fierce fingers digging into Alex's shoulder told him he would do well to call off his men even though his hands burned to take up his sword and fight.

The bastard pressed the steel more firmly against

his neck. His skin stung at the contact. Alex cursed to himself. It was no use. He gave his men a warning look, and they came no closer.

The gray-haired knight spoke harshly to the man holding the sword to Alex's throat and pointed at Alex and the girl in his arms. He did not know what the old man was saying, but he prayed the Englishman would listen to reason.

He held his breath and fixed his stare on Matilde. She seemed frozen in place, her face a mask of horror, as the sword dug into his neck. He barely noted the fact the Englishmen had stopped conversing over the roar in his ears.

Heartbeats later, his attacker finally pulled away with a growl.

The spell on his men broke, and they rushed forward to seize the Englishman. Alex squared his shoulders, the tension that had gathered in his frame slow to dissipate.

He knew his reaction to the attack would be crucial to his relations with the Dumont household. If he were too harsh, he risked angering Lord Dumont for disciplining one of his men in his stead. If he were too lenient, the English household might not respect his authority. And respect was already hard enough to come by.

First, though, he needed to see the man who dared to draw his sword against a Norman knight. He well remembered how fiercely the axe-wielding housecarls had defended Harold at Hastings. He expected some bearded giant, not the lad barely on the cusp of manhood who struggled in Hugh and Jerome's grasp.

The boy's blond hair was streaked with blood and grime, but the matted locks did not hide his glare as he locked eyes with Alex. That this young whelp had caught Alex and his men by surprise rankled. He debated the best way to punish the boy, when the young Englishman's gaze fell to the girl in his arms, his face filled with something stronger than concern. Interesting.

The boy held still as Hugh stripped him of his weapons. He spoke to the older knight again, gesturing to the girl and then the prone man on one of the mounts in the courtyard.

"What are they saying?" Alex asked Matilde.

The woman's wrinkled face slowly regained its color. "One of the men in the scouting party was badly injured," she said in halting French.

"Why did you not tell me half the household was away?"

"Your pardon, sir. I did not know when they would be returning. I thought—"

He could not stomach her excuses right now. He just thanked God the confrontation had not brought more carnage. He tipped his head toward the young Englishman. "Who is that?"

Matilde frowned. "Kendrick, one of Lord Dumont's men-at-arms. Your presence here... surprised him. You can be assured he will cause no more trouble. He understands the situation now."

Alex doubted that very much, seeing the hatred still simmering in the young man's eyes. "And her?" he asked, adjusting the girl in his arms.

"My daughter," Matilde said, hesitating for only a moment. "Let me take her."

Desperation haunted her careworn features, but he was three times a fool if he believed he held her daughter in his arms. Before he could reply, the gray-haired knight tried to lead Kendrick away, but Hugh and Jerome stood in their way. The man looked at Matilde and pointed to the injured rider, still unattended, and spoke urgently.

"They are only going to see to the wounded man's injuries," Matilde said.

"Then they will welcome my men's assistance." Turning away from her beseeching expression, Alex gave his men a nod. Hugh and Jerome would escort the two Englishmen to ensure they only intended to go to their comrade's aid.

"By your leave, I will take her to my room," Matilde said.

Alex gave her a curt nod. "Show me."

The old woman ushered Alex into a room off the kitchens. Female servants scattered as she motioned him over to a small pallet along the far wall. Alex laid the girl down gently. Heat radiated off her body. "We will need bandages and a poultice. She also needs dry clothes. It is a wonder she is not frozen."

Matilde relayed his orders to the servant who had followed them. The servant returned with supplies and heated the brazier set in the center of the room.

Alex felt the girl's forehead and brushed the hair back from her burning face. It was a pleasing color, a gleaming golden brown in the torchlight. He slid back her cloak.

Matilde gasped and pulled him away. "What are you doing?"

Alex looked at her sharply, and she dropped her hands. "The girl has a fever. Her clothes are sodden, and she is already chilled through. We must dress her wound."

"Yes, sir, but let me tend to her. You must be busy with your other duties."

"Your...daughter is in no danger from me. I have seen my share of arrow wounds."

Matilde put herself between Alex and the bed. "But, sir, it would not be proper for you to..." She worried her lower lip.

"This is no time for modesty," he said as he looked back at the pale, drawn countenance of the young lady. "Step aside. Now."

He waited until the old woman moved away before approaching the bed once more. Alex managed to pull off the girl's cloak and ease it away from the wound. Dried blood coated the right sleeve of her dress. The belt came next. The finely scrolled, double-edged broadsword and scabbard he had observed earlier, along with a well-made knife—a seax if he recalled the English name correctly—came with it. Their bearing and craftsmanship were exquisite.

He looked questioningly at Matilde before setting them aside. "How did your daughter come to possess such fine weapons?"

Matilde did not answer as she helped him peel off the girl's dress. Underneath, the girl wore a silk and linen shift, not a coarse woolen one, which bespoke nobility. Alex's gaze found Matilde's hooded one once more, but he said nothing as the shift too was removed.

He looked her over. Certainly more woman than girl. Pearly skin stretched over her frame, with hollows and curves in all the right places. There was just enough to her for a man to grab hold of.

He gritted his teeth. Now was hardly the time for such thoughts. He wrapped his fingers around the shaft of the arrow and pulled while Matilde held her down on the bed. The girl's eyelids fluttered open, her face screwed up in pain. She bellowed, shaking her head. Alex tried to work the arrow out further, but the girl wrenched her arm from his grasp with surprising ferocity.

This time the girl's eyes stayed open, muddy pools of fury and pain. She called for Matilde by her given name—not *maman*—but the rest of her words came out in a panicked rush. Matilde ran her hands over the sides of the girl's face and crooned to her in English to calm her down.

Alex grabbed her flailing arm. They could delay no longer.

"No!"

The girl tried to pull away again, but her strength was ebbing. He prayed the pain would make her sleep once more. It would be easier that way.

"No, no, no," she gasped. Her fevered gaze burned into him.

With a hard yank, he had the arrow out of her. The girl shrieked and mercifully passed out. Once Alex was sure he had removed all of the arrowhead and shaft, he helped Matilde bandage her shoulder and dress her in a clean gown.

After Matilde administered an infusion of herbs to allay fever, Alex pulled her away from the bed. "She is not your daughter." Matilde started to shake her head, but Alex cut her off. "She is the Lady Isabel."

"Th-that is ridiculous."

"I think not," Alex said with a dismissive wave of his hand. "Her clothing is as exceptional as her weapons." He paused, gauging her reaction. "Despite Dumont's generosity with his servants, I find it hard to believe such quality is bestowed upon a waiting woman's daughter."

Matilde shook her head, her gaze dropping to her gnarled, calloused hands. When she remained silent, he sighed and turned his back on her. "Watch over her, and be sure to get some rest yourself. If her health worsens, I will hold you responsible."

"I will keep her safe," Matilde said fiercely.

"I thought as much," he said over his shoulder.

He stalked back to the main hall. What business did Lady Dumont have participating in a scouting party? Did she have any knowledge of her father's whereabouts? He was relieved she had been found. Yet, a woman who would pull such a stunt would not be easily dealt with. He had heard tales of Englishwomen who fought like men defending their homes. William had not exaggerated when he had spoken of the young lady's spirit. No mild-mannered girl would leave the safety of her home with only the company of a few men and the steel she carried at her side.

Matilde's defense of her mistress was admirable, though. Perhaps she really thought of her as a daughter. The woman had answered his questions, though he could not help but feel she had not been entirely forthcoming with her short replies and uneasy bearing. However, one thing was certain. As they had conversed, Matilde's responses in French had become more fluid and rapid. She had lost her stutter.

Alex had just won a bet with himself.

\* \* \* \*

"Jerome leads the first watch," Hugh reported, joining Alex as they walked toward the main hall the following afternoon.

Alex nodded. "*Bon.* I do not want us caught off guard if more visitors come to Ashdown." He glanced at his shield bearer. "Any reports from the patrol?"

"*Non*, but Matilde's descriptions of the boundaries were most helpful."

Alex's mouth twisted. "I am glad, despite her reluctance to share the information with us."

He had badgered Matilde into describing the extent of the Dumont holding, and his men spent the morning monitoring the territory. They located a clearing to the north that had seen a fierce battle, and a handful of dead Welshmen covered the ground. It explained the sudden arrival of Dumont's men the previous afternoon and the extra mounts they brought back with them.

"Matilde did as you bade and sent out messengers to the neighboring thanes for news of Lord Dumont's whereabouts," Hugh reported.

"*Bon*, but I do not expect them to be much help."

"The last of the messengers returned but a few minutes ago," Hugh said.

"And?"

Hugh shrugged. "No word."

"Worry not. I am certain our new charge holds the answers to many of our questions," Alex said as they entered the hall. He surveyed the room. Although it was not quite time for supper, men had gathered and were arranging the tables. "Indeed, it is time I checked on Lady Isabel. I will rejoin you at the meal."

He stopped just outside the open door. The gray-haired knight from the day before stood at the girl's bedside next to Matilde. The man had managed to slip away from Hugh and Jerome yesterday, and they had not seen him since. The older man brushed a curl from Isabel's forehead with a familiarity that tightened Alex's chest. As soon as the pair discovered his presence, the English knight gave a curt bow and left the room.

"Who was that?" Alex asked.

"Captain Thomas trains my Lord Dumont's men-at-arms." A note of caution lit Matilde's voice.

He nodded and cast about the room. A captain... He must be privy to all of the Dumonts' comings and goings. Why was he not with his Lord? If Captain Thomas did not know some French, since he was in such a trusted position in the Dumont household, he would be surprised.

"Bring him to me at supper." It was past time he attempted to speak with Thomas. "You will translate."

"As you wish."

He motioned to the still-slumbering young woman. "Any improvement?"

"The fever has subsided only a little, but she is strong."

"No doubt," Alex said, thinking back to her numerous weapons. The old woman fidgeted with the folds of her dress. "Carry on then." He left, knowing his continuing presence would only distract her from her charge.

After the meal was served, Matilde approached him at the high table. "Pardon, sir, but I am unable to find Captain Thomas. The other servants have not seen him since this morning."

"I see." He gestured to Jerome. "My man here will help you locate him."

He dismissed them with a curt nod. He took a last sip of wine and thumped the cup down on the table. The English knight had no desire to be found. He rose to his feet. The young Kendrick had also been scarce since the confrontation in the courtyard, but that was probably because Hugh was keen to see the young man punished, if only for the nick on Alex's neck. The accursed thing still stung.

Alex once again stalked down the hallway to Matilde's room. Perhaps the knight was checking on his lady again. He stepped inside.

The room was empty except for the girl. A sheen of sweat covered her forehead. Her fever must have finally broken. She moaned and writhed around in the bed, blindly wrestling with her blankets. If she continued to thrash around, she would reopen her wound.

Someone had placed a water basin on a nearby chest. Alex grabbed one of the cloths set beside it and briefly let it soak in the cold water. After wringing out most of the liquid, he tried to place it on the girl's brow, but her flailing arms hindered his efforts. He caught her wrists, and as he held them in place, she quieted.

When the moist cloth touched her skin, the girl opened her eyes. She blinked, her pupils contracting the moment she found Alex's body leaning over hers. With a gasp, she struggled anew.

Alex let go and sat on the side of her bed.

The girl moved as far away as she could, her dark brown eyes wide. She looked down at the thin shift plastered against her with sweat. He could clearly see the outline of her generous breasts through the damp material. His fingers itched to touch her again as he took in her curved figure. She flushed at his attention and lifted her blankets to cover herself in a futile gesture, chin held high. It was all Alex could do to repress his chuckle.

"Sir?" Matilde stood in the doorway. "I..." Her voice died out when she saw her charge awake.

Alex stood. "See to it the young lady here has the opportunity to bathe and change into something more appropriate," he said as his gaze flicked one last time over the girl's body. He did not miss the look of relief flooding her face as she caught sight of Matilde.

"And Captain Thomas?" he asked. Matilde shook her head. "Very well. Once you have seen to your lady's needs, you will escort her to my room so I may speak with her."

Matilde bowed. "Yes, sir."

# Chapter 4

Horror rolled through Isabel in waves as Matilde engulfed her in a hug.

"Oh, my dear, you worried us so!" Relief and censure colored Matilde's words. The woman had served her family for as long as Isabel remembered, and despite her tart tongue, Matilde always gave her comfort.

Isabel swiped a hand over her face. "Have the men returned?

"Yes."

"What of Edgar?"

Matilde shook her head, the lines of her face deepening. "His wounds were too much."

Isabel hung her head and willed the grief away. "We were set upon by a Welsh raiding party. Edgar's valor should not go unrecognized."

She fingered her bandaged shoulder, thinking about the Norman knight who had dared to touch her. She remembered his eyes from her arrival at the castle. And then...nothing. After seeing the way he had ordered Matilde about, the way he appeared to have her home well in hand, the disturbing way he looked at her... "Who was that man?"

"Alexandre d'Évreux. He arrived two days ago and—"

"Two days! What do you mean?" She struggled to get up, but Matilde eased her back onto the bed.

"My dear, you have been with fever the last two

days. I scarce hoped you would wake again."

"I knew not."

"Yes. They arrived but a few hours after the scouting party left. Alexandre is one of William's knights, sent here to escort you and your father to London so you can swear fealty to William."

"And what have you told him about my father?" The words came out more sharply than she had intended.

"I told him naught. He thinks I know only the running of the castle. When the Normans arrived, Captain Thomas bid all the servants to speak only English and pretend they didn't understand French, what little they know of it. Captain Thomas has taken care to stay out of their way."

Isabel grinned despite the fear roiling in her stomach. She imagined the frustration of the battle-weary knights when they could not communicate with anyone. "Not one understands a bit of English?"

"A cleric was supposed to accompany them here, but he fell ill along the way and was left behind."

"Well, that is a relief." Isabel frowned suddenly, her brows drawn together. "Does he know who I am?"

"He guessed, but I told him not, I swear it. I had trouble enough explaining your arrival," Matilde said uneasily.

"Nay, you did your best." Isabel reached over and patted her hand.

"What will you tell him?"

"I know not."

"Remember you are your father's daughter. He cannot force you to do anything."

"Of that I am well aware." Isabel looked down at her shift and groaned. "I better get ready."

Once she reached her rooms above the main hall of the Dumont castle, Isabel changed into a fresh shift and a simple woolen overtunic. As Averill brushed and plaited her hair, the serving girl told Isabel how glad she was she had recovered.

Recovered. Not the word Isabel would have used. The dismay of finding her home overrun with Norman knights still coursed through her. Had she remained at the castle and not joined the scouting party, she would have the situation under control. At least she hoped as much. How could she have known William would seek out her family so soon?

Averill tamed her thick, chestnut hair and tucked it underneath her headrail. The servant made one last attempt to smooth the locks. "We should go. This way, my lady."

"Wait." Isabel picked up her mother's brooches from the table. "I would wear these too."

"Yes, my lady." Averill placed them on either shoulder to hold back Isabel's light mantle.

Isabel relaxed under the familiar weight of the golden bands passed down through the generations. Regardless of what happened in her conference with the Norman knight, she had something to remind her of heritage.

Following the servant across the hall, she reached for the seax, which normally hung at her waist, but the short, sharp knife was not there. Instead, only her leather purse and keys to the larder and storage rooms hung from her belt. Matilde had informed her their Norman visitor had seen fit to confiscate her weapons.

Another point they would have to settle.

Isabel grimaced as Averill stopped at the door to her father's chambers. Unfortunately, apart from her rooms, they were the only quarters befitting a man of Alexandre's station—the envoy of the man who would soon be the king of England.

The door opened, and Alexandre admitted the two

women into Lord Dumont's solar.

"Please sit." Alexandre indicated the chairs placed around a table covered in Father's correspondence and accounts. He signaled for the servant to leave them.

With one last pitying look at Isabel, Averill shut the door behind her. Isabel remained standing, warily staring down Alexandre. He stared back, his sharp blue gaze trained on her.

He appeared even more formidable in the flickering candlelight than he had when she first awakened. His thick, black hair was roughly shaped in the Norman tradition, and the knight wore it long, framing his angular face. He was several inches taller than she, an uncommonly tall girl herself. He had massive shoulders with such strength and power she could only assume they were the result of rigorous training and countless battles. William had brought his finest men to the shores of England.

They stood there like hunter and prey, but she would be no man's quarry.

"I am Alexandre d'Évreux. But you, my dear, can call me Alex."

He was clean-shaven, and she caught herself staring at the way his lips quirked. Englishmen, even her father, wore beards. Until now, she had not realized how much emotion the facial hair hid from view.

"I am here to escort Lord Dumont and his family to London, where he is to greet King William. While the lord is away, I am acting in his place. I chose to ignore your questionable arrival when you were with fever." He walked toward her with a decided prowl to his gait. "Now, I will wait no longer for answers."

Isabel lifted her chin, willing herself to ignore the fatigue already clamoring for attention. "I have questions of my own."

"I am sure. But first, Lady Isabel, you will explain to me why Matilde thought it necessary to hide your identity from me."

"I know not." Her gaze swept over him once more. "Perhaps she thought your intentions were dishonorable."

A muscle worked in his jaw. "Matilde is extremely loyal to you, no doubt. I assure you, I am acting under orders from William himself. No harm will come to you or your family, but I expect your cooperation."

She stiffened. "Am I a prisoner?"

"*Non*, not unless you refuse to cooperate. I only intend to be your family's escort to London. How easy or difficult that is will be up to you. Now, please, sit down." He gripped her uninjured arm gently above the elbow and led her to the chair. She finally sat, grateful for the reprieve for her tired body.

Alexandre took his seat across from her. "This is much more pleasant, is it not?" he said, seemingly oblivious to her hostility.

He thought he had won. She saw it in his twinkling ice-blue eyes. Well, let him think that. She was still in control of the situation despite whatever Alexandre might believe.

"You can speak French without even a hint of an English accent." He inclined his head toward her. "I am impressed."

"My father bade me and my brother to learn both English and French in our studies." Her scalp pricked at the careful way he watched her. Very well, she would play the humble maid for now. She ducked her head and folded her hands in her lap. "What else do you wish to know?" she asked with false resignation.

Under the veil of her eyelashes, she saw him relax slightly when he decided she was not going to make a

fuss. "To begin with, why were you away from home?"
"I accompanied some of our men to ensure our
borders were safe." That was true enough. She did not
want to lie to the Norman any more than she had to.
"There have been rumors of the Welsh making forays
into England."
"I see. How is your shoulder?"
"Fine. I thank you." She did not appreciate the
smug, self-satisfied look that had settled on his
handsome face. She forced her attention away and
concentrated on the harvest scene gracing the tapestries
warming the walls of the room.
"I am amazed your father would let you become
involved in such a dangerous situation."
"My father was not here to let me."
"And just where is your father? And your brother,
for that matter?"
"My father was called away to fight at Stamford
Bridge and has yet to return." She looked him full in
the face. "And I am certain you can guess the fate of
my brother," she said softly.
The Norman had the decency to look chagrined.
"I know we fought against him at Hastings, but I know
not if he survived the encounter. Has he sought to give
you word?"
Isabel firmly shook her head.
"Even if he does live, he made no secret of his
loyalty." He paused, his gaze searching. "Do you
understand what I am trying to tell you?"
She turned her head away for a moment,
swallowing back the bile in her throat. Her fingers
drummed against the keys fastened to her belt. "Yes.
Yes, I do."
"You say your father fought at Stamford Bridge.
Believe you he went on to fight at Hastings?"
"*Non.*"

"Was your father loyal to Harold?"

"My father thought Harold a fool," she said quickly. "Duty bade him to fight for Harold against Tostig and the Norsemen when the witan proclaimed Harold king."

"If that is true, where is he? He has had over two months to return here."

She shrugged. Her shoulder ached at the movement, and the sensation drowned out any attack of her conscience. "I wish I could tell you," she said, trying to keep her features as neutral as possible. "He said he would come home after fulfilling his obligations, regardless of what else Harold would ask of him. The roads further north may be impassable, which could have delayed his travel here."

He contemplated her for a moment, as if trying to make sense of all she told him. "How long will you need to make ready for London?"

"I, go to London? Impossible." She shook her head. "I will stay here. I will tell my father of your visit when he returns. I am sure he will be eager to renew his acquaintance with William."

He held up his large, thick-knuckled hands. "I must insist I stay here until he does so. I would feel accountable if anything were to happen to you."

"That is unnecessary. I can run the castle on my own."

Alexandre smiled like a man who just won a game of dice. "In your weakened state and the injury to your sword arm," he said, gesturing to her shoulder, "you need all the protection I can offer. Besides, as I said, William included you in his summons to London, and my orders are to remain with you and your family until you comply. Now, I ask you again, how long will it take you to make ready for London?"

Isabel nearly shivered at his cold gaze despite the

small brazier in the corner of the room. He was going to be harder to get rid of than she had originally thought. "Surely we will wait for my father to return?"

"Why, yes. I almost forgot," he replied smoothly. He smiled at her again and rose from his chair. He gave Isabel a small bow. "My lady, you would honor me if you would show me your family's home tomorrow. I am sure you will want to assure yourself that my men have not disturbed the castle during your illness."

Isabel rose, stiff from sitting so long. The meeting was almost over, and her spirit was stretched thin, like an overworked piece of iron at the smithy. "*Certainement*," she said, hating the suggestion and the thought of spending any more time in his presence.

Alexandre stepped closer. "My apologies for keeping you so late as you must still be weary. We shall continue this conversation tomorrow." He walked to the door and opened it for her.

The doorframe wavered in the torchlight as she moved toward him. Almost there. She forced herself to take another step. And another after that. With a sickening lurch, the room shifted under her feet. Her breath stalled in her throat. The Norman suddenly surrounded her on all sides.

In the next instant, Alexandre's strong arms drew her off the floor. His warm breath on her neck made her shudder. As soon as her ears stopped buzzing, she tried to wriggle out of his grip. This man always seemed to find her at her worst.

"Sir, put me down at once. I am quite recovered!"

He grunted as she dug her elbow into his stomach. "Save your strength, you foolish wench. I am a brute for keeping you here for so long."

He entered her solar and headed toward the adjoining bedroom.

"You are a brute! I command you to put me

down!"

He grunted again as her fist connected with his breastbone. "You, my lady, can only make requests, not commands." He growled the words into her ear. "And even then I do not have to heed them."

He dropped her onto her bed, and she let out an involuntary squeal. He grinned down at her. For the second time that day, Isabel found herself lamenting the fact he had taken away her weapons. "I will have some food sent up so you can regain your strength."

"That is unnecessary. I will—"

"*Non.* Rest is what you need. Do not make me post a guard at your door."

Isabel glared at him for what seemed to be an eternity, with the knight's sturdy frame towering over her. She felt weak and shaky inside like a newborn lamb, but it had nothing to do with fainting.

Alexandre's lips curled into a smile. "Tomorrow, then."

# Chapter 5

"So this is where you have been hiding." Isabel found her father's advisor staring out over the castle walls, a remoteness to his weary features.

Captain Thomas turned and smiled, and she impulsively threw her good arm around him. After a moment, he gently pushed her away. He studied her face and shook his head, clucking in disapproval. "It was a foolish thing to do, my lady, especially considering the messenger's tidings."

The messenger... She flushed under Captain Thomas's gaze and stood by the wall. The newly risen sun glinted off the rolling countryside still blanketed in snow. She tried to concentrate on the scenery, but her thoughts would not heed her. Captain Thomas would not be put off any longer. They would have the conversation she had avoided by running away like a child, with more disastrous results than she thought possible.

"Your father bade me to stay in Ashdown to protect you, and by joining the scouting party against my wishes, you have undone that," he said in a sharp voice. "Your brother is as good as dead if he is not already. And you already know your father's fate."

She let out a breath she didn't realize she was holding. "To think he was brought down by a fever..." Julien's message told her their father had been injured at Stamford Bridge and died of a fever two days outside of London during the army's march south to the coast, where William's forces waited. He had been so full of life when he left—he had patted her cheek and told her not to worry before he and his soldiers surged through the gates. "He deserved better. Now, I only wish Julien had decided to come home instead of going on to fight the Normans at Hastings."

Captain Thomas closed his eyes for a moment. "You mustn't let it trouble you. Your brother made his choice a long time ago."

Isabel grimaced. "I know." Julien had fully embraced his English ancestry. He spent much of his life at court, befriending many of the English thanes and housecarls. Julien had done everything he could to diminish his Norman background in the eyes of his fellow Englishmen to be accepted. Facing the Normans would be the ultimate test.

She shook her head. "Even if he lived, even if he could be pardoned, Julien would rather die than admit to his Norman blood."

"The same that runs through you," Captain Thomas said. "You will have to think of your future."

"I know."

"You should not have left the safety of the castle."

She shivered, but it was not because of the biting winter wind scouring the upper walls. "I needed to feel useful."

"Begging your pardon, my lady, that is no excuse. You should have known better." Seeing her frown, he added more kindly, "I taught you better, child. But none of that matters now. Whether you had joined the scouting party or not, Alexandre would still be here."

Her nails dug into her palms. "I know."

"You will have to go with him."

"I am needed here."

"That matters not. William has summoned you."

Isabel crossed her arms but stayed silent.

Captain Thomas sighed. "I will bid the sentries to watch for any suspicious activities. There have been no new sightings of the Welsh on our lands. That does not mean it will remain that way. No doubt they saw an opportunity to strike, with the Normans commanding everyone's attention."

"What else have I missed?"

"The son of Wilfred the candle maker has taken ill."

Isabel nodded. "I will visit them today." She looked up at Captain Thomas. "In the meantime, William's men, this Alexandre... He must not know about my father."

"I have not said anything to the Normans, nor will I until you grant me permission. But Isabel, you are a woman alone in this world. Any other girl would flock to this William the Bastard and throw themselves at his mercy."

"I am not any other girl."

"My lady, he could secure your future."

"By selling me off like chattel? I am Lord Bernard Dumont's daughter, and I have my rights."

"I am not denying your heritage, my dear, but your father's name will not protect you forever. You will have to face William soon enough."

"Nay, you are right about that. But until I get rid of these Normans, my father's death must remain a secret."

"What of your people? They have a right to the truth as well."

She breathed deep, her shoulder throbbing at the movement. "The loss of both their lord and their king would be too much right now. And I will not leave until I am certain the Welsh are no longer a threat."

Captain Thomas did not reply, but his disapproval

tinged the air around them.

"What do you make of Alexandre?" Isabel asked to break the silence.

For a moment, she thought he would not answer. "From what I can tell, he is a natural leader and is well-favored by William. His men will do anything he bids them."

"That may be true, but the man I met last night was an arrogant, churlish—"

"You are being unfair, my dear." Isabel snapped her head up. "Yes, you are," Captain Thomas said as he stared back at her.

"No, I am not. He treated me like a child." Even now, the overconfident curl of Alexandre's mouth and the corresponding twinkle in his eyes were sharp in her memory. "He thinks he can walk into my home and tell me what to do. He is insufferable and—"

"He is a different man from that of your father or brother, and you must learn to deal with him lest reports of your conduct gets back to William. Alexandre will see you as a lady and expect you to act like one." Isabel tried to interrupt him. "I am not finished," he said mildly. "And you know very well you do not act like a lady," he said with a hard look at the padded men's tunic she wore over her dress.

She smoothed the material over her hips. "This will serve me if I am going to tend to Wilfred's child."

"I wonder what Alexandre will make of your plans."

Her hand lingered on the quilted material. "He does not command me."

Captain Thomas let out an exasperated breath. "You have grown too wild. You must not provoke him with your boldness. I know you are strong and as capable as a man in many respects, but his upbringing will blind him to your unique qualities. You must understand that."

"I only understand there are people who need me."

\* \* \* \*

Alex circled the hall, his steps heavy and deliberate as the rushes crunched underfoot.

"There you are," Jerome said as he reached his side. "What is troubling you? You look like a caged animal with all this pacing."

Alex came to a stop and faced the fire pit in the center of the room. "I am merely impatient for our lady to grace us with her presence this morn."

"Ah, so her identity has been confirmed. Did she have any information about her father or brother?"

"Only that her father should be returning here shortly and her brother would have been at Hastings."

"We already surmised as much."

"I am well aware."

A calculating look stole over Jerome's features. "*Eh bien*, at least were the reports of her charms accurate?"

Alex thought about lying, then dismissed the thought. Jerome would have the truth out of him whether he willed it or not. "Her beauty is inducement enough to accept William's proposal," he said.

"You seem disappointed," Jerome said, undeterred.

"There is little else to recommend her at present beyond her appearance. She is defiant, stubborn, and, most importantly, unhappy with our presence here."

Jerome grinned. "You should be able to cure her of that. It is high time you met a challenging woman."

Alex shook his head. He did not have difficulty finding female company—something his men never tired of reminding him. Alex kept his encounters with the fairer sex to occasional brothel visits and brief trysts with obliging serving women. Things were simpler that way. He already knew in marriage, nothing was simple.

"Think on what is at stake," Jerome insisted.

Alex crossed his arms. "We both know my father will not welcome me back." He looked around the room and sighed. "I cannot walk away from this even if she never warms to me."

"What's this? The great Alexandre d'Évreux put off by a mere woman? I am in shock. I must meet this female terror."

Alex chuckled and for a moment the weight on his shoulders eased ever so slightly. Jerome, a comrade since Alex completed his fostering, was always able to make him laugh. "You will soon enough, I wager. I have not given up, but I will have to be my most charming. Starting today."

"Oh?" Jerome said, with a lascivious waggle of his brows.

"Yes. She has promised to acquaint me with her home, so we may be of service as we await her father's arrival."

"I see. That sounds promising."

"Only if she comes," he said grimly. "I have been patient long enough." Alex called for Matilde and ordered her to wake Isabel and bring her to him.

Jerome watched him as Matilde scurried out of the room. "Are you sure she is well enough to be up? Perhaps she is still recovering."

"Perhaps," Alex allowed, "but after my audience with her last night, I believe she would not meekly accept orders calling for rest. She needs to be active."

"Like you?" Jerome asked with a wry curl of his mouth. "I confess you have not told me anything that causes me worry."

Alex shook his head. "We shall see. Right now

she is ruled by fear. Of us. Of what will happen. She hid it very well, mind you, but I do not know how to convince her I am not her enemy." He stared into the fire's weak flames.

"You must remember, her brother is as good as dead and her country has a new king. Her trust of anything Norman is doubtful despite her father's connections." Jerome held out his hands. "Perhaps when Lord Dumont is found…"

Matilde reentered the hall, and he gave Jerome a tight nod, silencing him. "That is my hope."

She hurried over to them. "Sir, she is not in her chambers."

He studied the old woman's worried countenance, convinced for once she was ignorant of Isabel's whereabouts. "Search the area. I want her found immediately. Jerome, you are with me."

Matilde left to organize a search of the castle while Alex strode out to the stables. He wanted to see if Lady Isabel's mount was still in its stall. And, as he suspected, the stall stood empty. Curse the girl. He looked at Jerome. "What do you say to this?"

He shrugged. "The reports did say she was high-spirited."

Alex growled. All hope in getting to know the girl better vanished. Why had he not expected such trickery? Within moments, he, Jerome and two more of his men had saddled their mounts. Then they galloped through the castle gates to conduct a search of the grounds.

\* \* \* \*

Isabel cantered past snow-covered fields on her way back from the village.

Wilfred's son was indeed sick, with a chest-rattling cough that made his mother Hilda cringe each time the boy drew breath. Isabel had taught the panicked woman the precise amounts of herbs for a poultice they spread over the boy's neck and chest. Then she had taught her how to brew an infusion the lad should drink every day for a week.

The boy's breathing had already eased slightly when Isabel had taken her leave of the modest, straw-thatched home. Wilfred and Hilda's effusive thanks hardly made an impression on her as she had mounted and headed to the castle.

She rode past the sleepy homes of her people. Curls of smoke from their fires climbed into the sky. She was grateful they had not been exposed to the brunt of the Norman invasion. Thankfully, once word of the battle had broken out, her father's tenants had decided to do nothing without his consent. If they panicked and left the safety of the Dumont lands, her family's name would not protect them. Even now, even with a new king, they had enough trust in her father to see them through these turbulent times. She frowned at that thought and urged her horse faster down the road.

She soon let Hardwin have his head. With the wind in her face, she matched her movements to her horse's strides. He took her to the edge of a small wood. A stream, not frozen fully, wound through it. The soft tinkle of water made the forest less lonely in its snow-blanketed state. Isabel dismounted and walked along the bank. She bent to pick up a stone with her left hand and threw it into the stream, splintering the ice threatening to take hold.

She had explored here before, playing games with Julien when they were younger. Their youthful shouts still seemed to linger on the frigid air. If she squinted, she could see her brother's brown mop of hair as he crouched behind a tree trunk, ready to jump out and scare her. Tears blinded her as they slipped down her cheeks, blurring the memories. She angrily brushed them away.

Now was not the time for grief. Not with Normans in Ashdown. Now, she had to plan.

The Dumont lands were hers—to manage and, more importantly, to protect. And she needed to make sure they would stay that way. She also needed to ensure her people would survive the transition to Norman rule. She needed to know she had done all she could to prepare them and thereby honor her father's legacy.

With Alexandre and his band of Normans already enjoying her hospitality, she was at a loss as how to proceed. She took a deep breath, trying to steady the tumult she felt cascading through her. The sharp air burning in her lungs only provided a momentary distraction.

Her horse pranced fitfully beside her. She reached out to pat Hardwin's neck, but then she heard it too— men on horseback crashing through the underbrush.

Alexandre and a group of his men barreled toward her. Branches snapped, and snow swished in the wake of the galloping horses. She jammed her foot in the stirrup and hauled herself into the saddle. A sharp pain sheared across her body, daring her to cry out. She had reopened her wound, but if she stopped to check her shoulder, Alexandre would catch up to her.

She would not speak to him out here in the woods, surrounded by his men and not hers. She had seen the grim look on his face. He was definitely angry, but he needed to realize she was not some simpering, ignorant noblewoman who would demurely accept his authority. She was Lady Isabel Dumont, and would not stand to be ordered about by some brazen and bull-headed knight.

As it was, she had already made a fool of herself by collapsing in his presence. The reins dug into her palms. She had to show him she was no weak woman in need of his protection.

With the help of her superior mount and intimate knowledge of the forest, she led Alexandre and his men on a merry chase, through dormant thorn bushes and over fallen logs. She would have laughed every time one of their muffled curses floated within hearing if her shoulder did not pain her so much. She finally emerged from the woods and spurred her horse on. Hardwin kicked up clods of snow and easily outstripped Alexandre and his men.

In the bailey, she dismounted, spying Kendrick and Godric as they exited the stables.

"Isabel, my lady, you look well!" Kendrick exclaimed.

She clasped each of their hands in turn. "Where have you been?"

"Captain Thomas suggested we tend to the Welsh bodies and clear the site," Kendrick said. "He also thought it best we get out from underfoot of our Norman visitors."

"I am glad to see you feeling better, my lady," Godric cut in.

Isabel nodded. "I thank you. I am still—"

"They are still here?" Kendrick dropped his hand to the hilt of his sword. "I thought they would leave once they learned of your father's ties to Normandy."

Her chest tightened at the suspicion in his voice. She turned around. Alexandre and the rest of his men streamed through the gates.

The Norman dismounted and strode over to her. "Perhaps you forgot your promise, my lady." The Norman's icy stare did not miss Kendrick's defensive attitude or the protective stance he took in front of her.

"William is eager to renew his acquaintance with my father," she explained in English to Kendrick softly. "He sent these men here to escort him to London."

"And has your father returned?" Kendrick asked her without taking his eyes off Alexandre. Two more Normans now flanked the stormy-faced knight.

"No. The Normans will be staying here until he gets back. They have been..." she struggled for the right word, "well-mannered so far."

"So far..." Kendrick echoed hollowly as Alexandre turned his unbearable stare on her.

Isabel pushed past Kendrick and returned to her horse's side, head held high. Kendrick still had his hand on the hilt of his sword, and Godric was tense beside him. "Stand down," she said firmly. Kendrick's gaze flickered to her, and he reluctantly complied.

"My lady?" the Norman prompted. "I thought we had plans for today. And they did not include chasing you across the countryside." He came to a stop next to her.

Isabel busied herself with her saddlebags and the collection of medicinal herbs she had stored there for the ride. "Oh yes...that. I decided my horse needed the exercise."

Alexandre grabbed her shoulders and spun her around to face him. Her bundle of herbs scattered to the ground. He must have been too angry to see her wince in pain. Or the fact that Godric was barely able to keep Kendrick from attacking him.

The Norman held her in place as a stable boy hurried over to lead the horses away. The warmth of his hands sunk through her cloak. Her breath hitched. The sage-like smell of crushed yarrow leaves warred with the pungent odor of hyssop.

"I must insist you do not leave the castle grounds without my permission in the future," Alexandre said. "It is too dangerous for you to wander off without an escort. You could have been hurt!" By now he was shouting, his deep voice attracting more onlookers.

"I assure you I am perfectly safe on my own lands. Although, if you are concerned, you could return my weapons. And you, sir, are the only one who is hurting me." She looked meaningfully to his hand on her injured shoulder.

Alexandre immediately let go. "*Jesu!* I am sorry. Are you all right?"

Though ready to argue further, she remained silent as one of the servants gathered up the herbs and medicinal plants strewn across the ground. Alexandre watched her with concern. "I am fine," she said slowly once the servant had retreated.

"I forgot your injury in my concern for your welfare. A thousand pardons, my lady." He held out his arm. "We should get you inside so your shoulder can be tended."

She wanted to protest, but nearly all the castle inhabitants were watching their interaction now. A public quarrel would just make things worse. He had done it again—made her feel like a fool.

She hesitated in taking his arm just long enough to let the man know she was not happy about being led inside like a child. As they headed to the stairs, Matilde found them. Isabel instructed her to fetch more bandages and meet her in her room.

She felt the Norman's eyes on her as they walked to her chambers in silence. Alexandre waited for her to enter, and after a moment's pause, he came inside as well, hovering near the door. She removed her mantle and flung it on her bed. A small amount of blood had soaked through her dress.

She saw his grimace at the rust-colored stain and took pity on him. "It opened when I remounted in the woods. It was not your fault."

Alexandre looked at her for a moment, his ice blue eyes unreadable, before giving her a short nod. Matilde arrived moments later with two servants.

"It looks like you will be well tended, my lady. When you are through here, perhaps we can continue where we left off." It was not a request.

"Impossible, I am afraid. I have left the running of the household to Matilde for too long."

Alexandre studied her for a moment, silently challenging her. "*Très bien*. I look forward to seeing you at the evening meal." He gave her a slight bow and mercifully left the room.

# Chapter 6

Captain Thomas met Isabel as she reached the high table. "I see you have heeded some of my advice," he said as his gaze lingered on her gown.

For the meal, she had selected a soft green dress she trusted would remind all in attendance of her authority. The last time she had worn the kirtle trimmed with silk, she had successfully chased her latest suitor—all jowls and hair—away after tricking him into demonstrating his understanding of taxes in front of the other guests at the high table. The poor fool could not add or subtract. The guests' uneasy laughter soon had him fleeing the room.

Somehow, despite her dress or her cleverness, she did not think Alexandre would be chased away so easily.

Nevertheless, she was proud of her composure even though her hall was filled with strange men who wanted to take her away from her home. She did not want to greet William the Bastard, who had thrown her world into turmoil. As soon as William realized she was on her own, he would marry her off without a care to her father's wishes or her own. She could not let that happen.

She gave Captain Thomas a rueful smile. "If only the rest of my flaws were so easy to change as my clothes."

"Now, now. You are twisting my words."

"If I cannot tease you, then this meal will be most

tedious indeed." She took her place in the central seat
with Alexandre and Captain Thomas flanking her. The
rest of the men and women took their seats, and the
meal was served.

Captain Thomas shook his head as he surveyed
the room. "You placed all of Alexandre's men at the
lower tables, hmm? I did not realize you wanted to
command all of his attention."

Isabel grew hot, and it was not because of all the
bodies gathered in her father's hall. "I intended no such
thing! Indeed, I did it to make him uncomfortable since
he would have no one to talk to."

Captain Thomas chuckled. "My dear, you would
be wise to not provoke him so. You have clearly
captured his interest," he said with a brief glance at the
Norman looming beside her. "And he will expect your
attention over the course of the meal."

"Then you must simply keep me engaged in
conversation."

He sighed. "I fear I have spoiled you." But he
gamely talked to her about the training of the men and
other household activities that had occurred during her
illness.

When Matilde checked on the high table for the
third time, Isabel called the older woman to her side.
"Everyone is enjoying the meal. Please rest and find
someplace to enjoy it yourself," she said severely.
Matilde opened her mouth to protest but Isabel stopped
her and spoke in a softer tone, "Promise me."

"As you wish." Matilde gave a stiff curtsy before
she headed toward the lower tables.

"You should be kinder to her, my lady. You had
her so worried," Captain Thomas said after Matilde
left.

Before Isabel had a chance to respond to his
admonishments, Alexandre's shadow fell over her.

"What did you say to Matilde? She seemed upset," he said in French.

She had spoken sharply to Matilde out of concern, not anger. No doubt Alexandre misunderstood the exchange since he had no understanding of English. "I bid her to eat something. There are more than enough servants to administer the meal. She makes more work for herself than is required."

Isabel turned toward Captain Thomas, but Alexandre drew her back with a warm hand on her elbow. "I also wonder why you speak with Captain Thomas so long."

She bit down on her lip, reminding herself to remain civil. "He is my father's advisor. There is much to discuss." She thought she made it clear she was not interested in speaking with him. Captain Thomas's words came back to her. This was her fault since she made all his men sit elsewhere. She would not feel sorry for him. He could not expect her to be happy to have him as a guest.

"Why is he not with your father?"

"At the time, Captain Thomas was of better service here." Tired of Alexandre's probing questions, she tried to recapture Captain Thomas's attention, but he was suddenly in deep conversation with the man sitting next to him.

"Surely you would have been of better service here as well," Alexandre said, his voice impossibly close to her ear. Isabel stiffened. Captain Thomas saw her predicament and laughed. Alexandre leaned toward her once more. "What is so amusing?"

She faced him and was startled at how close he was. So close she could not concentrate on his face— just pieces of it. The small scar on his chin, his strong nose, his blue eyes... His gaze darkened, daring her to ignore him again.

She cleared her throat. "If you are so interested, why do you not ask him yourself?"

"You know very well I cannot."

"Indeed?" Isabel smiled very sweetly at him before turning to Captain Thomas and asking him in French, "Would you please tell this Norman oaf what it is you find so amusing?"

Captain Thomas looked from Isabel to the puzzled Alexandre. Isabel nodded for him to speak. "The lady does not like you," he said simply to the knight in serviceable French. "And I have no desire to be caught between the two of you, as she well knows."

Isabel tried to hide her amusement as the Norman processed Captain Thomas's words. Alexandre tightened his hold on his eating dagger and sudden tenseness squared his shoulders.

The knight sent her a sharp look but nonetheless feigned his good-natured reply. "That may be true, but she has the whole trip to London to know me." She nearly scoffed at his proprietary tone.

Captain Thomas laughed and said with a shrug, "As you say, lad. As you say," before he resumed his conversation with his neighbor.

People were finishing up with their meals. Isabel hardly touched her trencher, having long lost her appetite. She took a last sip of wine before she made her excuses. She was almost out of the hall, when she heard someone behind her. Alexandre, no doubt.

She refused to slow her pace or give any indication she knew he followed her. Their little trick had probably upset him. However, it had been a wise decision for Captain Thomas to command everyone to speak only English in her absence, and she refused to apologize for it.

She entered the hallway, readying herself for the coming argument. He would tell her how disappointed he was. She would explain how—

A hand grabbed her uninjured arm. Alexandre pulled her back and forced her against the wall. Her breath left her in a rush.

He put a calloused hand against her mouth and held her effortlessly immobile. Talking seemed like the last thing he wanted to do. He was angry. She saw the tightness in his jaw, the flash in his startling blue eyes. He wanted to hurt her, she realized, but he was too honorable to do so.

They stood there, scowling at one another, until a lute player began a cheerful tune in the main hall. Alexandre finally removed his hand from her mouth.

"Release me at once, you dog," she said without heat. She did not bother to struggle or scream in protest. She would not give him the satisfaction. Nor did she want to risk injuring her arm again.

"I would speak with you first, my lady. And calling me names will not distract me from getting answers." He cocked his head and looked at her for a long moment. "You know, you are cleverer than I originally thought."

"You will forgive me if I do not thank you for the compliment."

The arrogance of the man! She held herself as far away from him as she could, but still his taut, muscular body pressed into her. An inviting heat emanated from him. She tried to concentrate on the stone wall behind her and the way it dug into her body. It was no use.

All at once, the danger of Alexandre d'Évreux became astonishingly clear. How could such a hateful man have this effect on her?

\* \* \* \*

Lady Isabel looked down at his hands holding her in place before she met his gaze. "At least this time you have not hurt my injury," she said, not bothering to hide a sneer.

Alex felt a brief stab of guilt but pushed it aside. "A terrible accident, my lady. You already have my apologies." The girl frowned when he did not lessen his hold on her. So she would play games with him? He swallowed the blind anger rearing up inside him once more. He leaned into her face, holding her gaze. "You know I mean you no harm. Why can you not trust me? With all of your secrets?"

Isabel sniffed and twisted away from him. "What secrets? I have told you all you need to know."

"But not what I want to know. Why did you forbid your servants to speak with us?"

"I gave no such order."

Alex growled and squeezed her harder. "My patience grows thin, my lady."

She faced him this time, eyes dark with anger. "I most assuredly did not give that command. If you remember, I was not here to do so."

His grip on her lessened slightly. "Ah, yes. I still find it hard to believe you would willingly leave the safety of your home to fight the Welsh."

"I told you we were following up reports of raids," she said through clenched teeth.

"Yes, but why did you feel the need to be involved? Surely you could rely on your men to handle the situation."

Her mouth worked silently before she found her voice. "In my father's absence it falls to me to see to the safety of our lands. How could I stay behind and order my men into danger?"

"Because you are a woman, with no business being in battle."

She scowled. "Then you are a bigger fool than I thought. If I had not provided cover with my arrows, we might not have taken the day."

*Jesú!* What kind of woman had William promised him? One who would not cower at his greater strength and would boast of her exploits at the same time. He tried not to get lost in the self-righteous gleam in her eyes. "But even your efforts were not enough," he said, with a nod to her wounded arm. "That is how you received your injury, no?"

"I would not want to bore you with the details."

"Curse you, girl! Tell me what happened."

A quiet fury puckered her brow. "I cannot remember such things as I am only a simple girl."

"You are not," Alex said tightly.

"What is this, more praise? Indeed, sir, you overwhelm me."

He clapped a hand to his forehead. "Impossible woman! I wonder how you have not sent your father to the grave before now."

Isabel went completely rigid, her features stricken. Alex let go of her. What now?

She stood tall, anger mottling her lovely face. "How dare you! How dare you treat me thus! You come into my home and make demands. You stand here and expect me to tell you everything." She advanced toward him, and he found himself taking a step back. "There is nothing about you that would inspire me to share anything with you! If I am impossible, then you have been patronizing, arrogant and disrespectful."

With each word, she jabbed her index finger into his chest. He tensed at the wild and fearless look in her eyes.

"You talk of trust when you are but a stranger to me and to this land. You expect me to welcome you and your men with open arms, expect me to act like a foolish noblewoman. I may be a woman, but I am certainly not foolish! I—"

"My lady! What has happened?"

Likely drawn by their shouts, Captain Thomas entered the hallway. Alex simultaneously welcomed and cursed the interruption for he was dangerously close to taking Isabel over his knee and teaching her a lesson. Fists balled at her side, she continued to glare at him. He could not look away from her, from the way her chest heaved with each breath.

Isabel closed her mouth and fixed her angry stare on Captain Thomas once he reached them. They shared a few words in English. The old man's gaze flickered toward Alex, but he could not decipher the look. Isabel opened her mouth to argue some more with Captain Thomas but shut it as she looked back at Alex. Muttering to herself, she gave them a swift curtsy and strode away, her footsteps echoing off the slate floor.

Alex watched her until she disappeared. He took a deep breath and tried to ease the tension that had rushed through his body during their conversation. He was not usually so quick-tempered, but the girl fired his blood. And he did not like it.

"Sir, you must excuse Isabel. She is always in bad humor after an illness."

He turned his gaze on Captain Thomas. "I would thank you for your intervention, but I am disappointed I was not able to respond to her charges."

The older man shook his head. "I must apologize for her behavior. She is used to her independence, which is threatened by your presence here. She needs time to adjust to her new situation. I ask you to be understanding."

"Understanding? What that girl needs is a flogging." He pinched the bridge of his nose and took a deep breath as they returned to the main hall.

Alex gave Captain Thomas a pointed look. "When her father returns, he had better keep her in check, for I will not tolerate any more of her temper tantrums."

Captain Thomas cleared his throat. "Yes, well. You may find her father will not be of much help."

"What do you mean?"

Captain Thomas hastily looked away. "I mean only Lord Bernard has granted her a good deal of freedom growing up. She can do no wrong in his eyes."

Alex inwardly groaned. The girl was spoiled, too? William did not want to reward him—he wanted to punish him. He shook his head. "I have been meaning to ask why you are not with Lord Dumont. Surely he would want his trusted captain to accompany him into battle?"

The English knight looked embarrassed by the question. "I am afraid my age prevented me from accompanying my lord. The Welsh are not to be taken lightly, and Lord Dumont felt I would better serve him here defending the castle than by his side."

"I see."

"*Eh bien*," Captain Thomas said, eager to change the subject, "I will speak with Isabel tomorrow, after she has time to calm down. As she said, she is not without sense and can be made to see reason."

"How much did you hear?" Alex asked with a sidelong glance.

"Enough to know your handling of the situation also left much to be desired."

# Chapter 7

The first thing Isabel spied when she woke from sleep was Matilde's stern face. With a groan, Isabel sat up and rubbed her eyes. "Well? Out with it," she said when Matilde remained silent. "You are no doubt here to tell me I behaved childishly last night."

"At least you have sense enough this morning to recognize your foolishness," the woman replied.

"You do not know what you speak of."

Matilde did not cower at her harsh tone. "I know you insulted Alexandre, and he could not spare anyone a kind word for the rest of the evening."

A night of fitful sleep had done naught to quell her fury at the man or herself. "Then know he insulted me first."

"Such anger. I have never seen you so quick to temper. What is troubling you?"

Isabel opened her mouth to speak, then shut it. How could she possibly explain how tenuous her status was now with Father gone? How Alexandre's presence threatened any means she had to protect herself and her family's lands?

The older woman sat next to her and placed a comforting hand on her forearm. "My dear, you would be wise to mind yourself around Alexandre and his men—"

Isabel pulled away from her touch. "I know, I know. I must set the example for everyone else. But his attitude, Matilde. He has only to look at me and I feel my blood boil like a stewpot on the fire."

"What did he say to you?"

Isabel sighed. "It is not so much what he says but how he says it. He is suspicious of my involvement in the scouting party, he is concerned about my father, and I am certain he is looking for any reason to take control of Ashdown."

"You have good cause to be concerned for your future. We all do. That does not excuse your behavior last night," Matilde lectured. "You must apologize to him for your conduct."

Her stomach clenched at the thought. "Yes," Isabel said softly. Matilde patted her hand as though she assumed the matter settled. Isabel wished she could do the same, but recalled too well the way his body felt as he pressed her into the wall last night, the touch intimate despite the situation. She shuddered. Her reaction to Alexandre made him even more dangerous. Despite how much she disliked him, she had behaved abominably and would have to endure the consequences.

Matilde departed, and once Averill finished with her hair, Isabel left her rooms to attend Prime. Father Joseph's familiar voice leading the prayers was a relief after so much upheaval. Following the ceremony, she clung to her normal routine, answering the frantic questions of the household staff, approving the meals for the week and ensuring the household accounts were current.

The weak winter sun had reached its highest point in the sky when she finally remembered her promise to apologize to Alexandre. With her duties complete, she had no more excuses. She swept through the grounds and found the Norman outside, instructing his men in a drill.

Captain Thomas observed their routine and more

72

of her soldiers watched, some in awed curiosity, others sneering at the display. As soon as Captain Thomas saw Isabel, he hastened to her side, trying to head her off.

"Not now, Captain. I would speak with Alexandre." Captain Thomas had already conveyed his displeasure at her conduct in front of their guest. She paid no heed to his long-suffering sigh, but the way the chill air cut through her mantle was harder to ignore.

Alexandre must have heard her voice, for he turned around. "My lady, it is a pleasure." He smiled as he surveyed her, and she was not surprised to see it did not reach his eyes.

No matter. He would hear her whether he willed it or not. "I must apologize for my behavior last night," she said in a strong, insincere voice. "Nothing has gone right since my injury, and I have been ill-mannered because of it. If you have been arrogant, you probably have cause to be so." Some of his men snickered at the comment, but after a sharp glance from Alexandre, quieted. "If you have been disrespectful, it was probably done inadvertently."

"Isabel…" Captain Thomas warned.

She ignored him. It was past time she put Alexandre in his place. "I am not sorry, however, for calling you patronizing. You have treated me like a child when I am more capable of running and defending my home than you are." The Norman straightened at the charges, his face cut from stone. "You also forget I need not answer to you or your men. As William's errand-boy, your jurisdiction here is questionable at best, and I ask you to remember that in your conduct with the members of my household for the remainder of your stay here." She looked over his men before returning her attention to Alexandre. "Now, pray continue with your training exercises."

She turned on her heel, but the knight swiftly reached her side. "My lady, I ask for a chance to respond. I was denied the opportunity last night, and I have no desire to lose another."

Isabel sighed, her breath visible in the air. By now, the cold had crept past her clothing and she was already chilled through. She wished she had not been so eager to seek out the Norman. Facing him again, she crossed her arms to keep her body heat from escaping. She was surprised to find his countenance full of wry amusement. She expected annoyance, anger even. Not the hint of a boyish grin.

"If I have failed to treat you with the proper respect you deserve, I can only say the manner in which we were acquainted did not flatter either one of us." She had not forgotten the Norman's heated glances when she first woke from her illness. Isabel shifted her feet and prayed her cheeks did not redden at the memory. "By your leave," Alexandre continued, "I would ask we try to find some sort of accord in which we can work together."

"Agreed." Isabel walked toward the castle, her steps quick to melt the ice that had formed inside her.

Alexandre fell into step next to her. "My lady, how do you propose we proceed?"

She glanced sidelong at him, before staring ahead once more. Just looking at him made her stomach contort. "I suggest you accustom yourself to the fact I do not have to tell you any more than I deem necessary."

Alexandre shrugged off his mantle and placed it about her shoulders without asking, his hands lingering. His male scent enveloped her, clouding her ability to think clearly. She inwardly cursed. This man threatened more than her independence—he threatened her sanity. Yet her desire to rip off the cloak warred with the warmth thawing her body.

"Then, may I suggest you take care to ensure you recover fully from your illness and injury? I would also ask you acquaint me with the workings of your home so I can better understand it and aid you in whatever capacity you may require during our stay in Ashdown."

"*Très bien.*"

"Then we will start this afternoon, no?"

They reached the main hall. Isabel swiftly removed his cloak and handed it back to him. "Sadly, I must go over the week's meals with the kitchen staff today," Isabel said with what she hoped was an apologetic smile. She needed as much distance as possible from him while she developed a plan to turn the knights out of her home once and for all.

Alexandre pulled the mantle around himself. He smiled at her obvious desire to get away from him. "All pleasantries aside, you cannot hold me off forever, Isabel. You claimed I treated you like a child. Very well, I shall not dissemble anymore." His eyes burned like ice in the sunshine. She could not look away. "You think if you put me off long enough my men and I will pack up and leave you alone," he continued. "I can assure you that will not happen. I have an...interest in what goes on here."

Isabel cursed to herself, and the hold he had over her was broken. This man...how could he see into her mind, know what she planned? Alexandre was not going to leave her alone. He had too much honor and mayhap too much insight. The knight had already determined she had no intention of being cooperative. He was subtly warning her she was no match for him. She would prove him wrong. There was only one thing to do...

"What are you implying, sir?" Before he could respond, she continued, "Be ready after the church service at lauds on the morrow. I will not tolerate tardiness." Isabel swept into the castle as Alexandre chuckled softly behind her.

\* \* \* \*

The next morning Alex was waiting for her. He did not want to give her any excuse for not following through with their agreement, so he arrived to the hall early.

"My lady, you honor me," he said when she entered. She gave him a nod and was about to make her way past him, but Alex would not be dismissed like one of her servants. He held up a hand to stop her. "I want to return these to you," he said, producing the sword and seax he confiscated from her.

She looked at him in surprise before she snatched them out of his hands and unsheathed each blade to confirm they were hers. Always the warrior. She eyed the familiar scrollwork with relief and handled the smooth leather-wrapped grips of each weapon. "I am grateful to see my equipment returned to me," Isabel finally said as she deftly strapped both to her belt.

"*Certainement.* Such craftsmanship is meant to be used, not collecting dust somewhere."

Her head snapped up, an eyebrow arched in disgust. "Then you should have given them back sooner."

He grinned and moved to take her arm. "Perhaps." As he expected, she recoiled from his touch and pushed past him.

The battle of wills had begun. And a large part of him looked forward to it, he realized as he followed her outside. From those moments when he had first spoken with Isabel, he knew of her temper, despite her efforts to control it. Nor had he forgotten their quarrel the other night. At first he had been enraged by her outburst. No one—not even his foul-tempered father—

had ever dared to speak to him in such a manner. Still, Isabel's tirade gave him valuable insight into the woman he was to marry. She certainly did not like his methods of procuring information, and her fear for her future colored her thoughts and deeds.

He understood her sentiments up to a point, but she was not alone in this. Her father would soon return to help her shoulder such responsibility, and Alex was here in the meantime.

When they reached the stables, he was surprised to see her dismiss the stable boy and saddle the steed herself, her hands sure, moving swiftly over the straps. She behaved like no other woman of his acquaintance, noble or otherwise.

He had learned from Matilde she was not yet twenty. He had not expected to find such a woman, well-endowed with both beauty and lands, unattached. If she were in Normandy, she would have children clinging to her skirts by now. He did not pretend to understand how the English married off their daughters, but Matilde did say she had rejected every possible suitor over the years.

Was Isabel afraid marriage would steal away the freedom she so cherished? She wanted to be a man's equal, and was, he admitted, in many capacities. She would be a prize for any man, but her uncompromising attitude... Until she warmed to him, she must remain ignorant of William's intentions for her. It would be better to win her on merit. That way she would not feel manipulated when the truth was revealed.

He saw no other way to handle the situation.

They led the horses outside and mounted in silence. Isabel pulled up the hood of her cloak and spurred her horse forward, beyond the palisade walls and along a snow-covered road. One of her men-at-arms followed at a discreet distance. They held a moderate pace before she finally reined her horse to a stop.

"As you can see from here," she began, her face seemingly devoid of emotion, "my father's castle is but a few miles west of the village of Ashdown. The town of Gloucester is due south of here. A day's ride." He wondered what it cost her to hide her irritation with him.

The castle was well situated on a small hill with a good vantage in all directions. Even in the distance, Alex could make out the wooden palisade that enclosed the bailey and motte castle. "My lady, I confess I was surprised to find your father has begun renovating the castle with stone."

"Yes, we have begun with the walls of the hall and the motte itself. Next summer, we plan to reinforce the palisade with stone. Someday, my father hopes to move the living quarters into the tower."

"My father's castle is designed in much the same manner." He examined the castle in the distance once more. "Lord Dumont should be proud of what he has accomplished here. William was disappointed to find so few English lords built proper fortifications." He thanked God Dumont had already brought Norman architecture and sensibilities to Ashdown for it would reduce the burden on Alex to improve the holding in order to meet William's standards.

Isabel nodded in agreement. "Many English castles have been built on top of hillside forts and other sites dating back to the Romans. My father had different plans. He was convinced stone was necessary, given how close we are here to the Welsh border. It was also his idea to add a second story to the hall for our rooms and living spaces. An uncommon idea at the time."

"But the added space provides much comfort and

privacy."

"Indeed. I enjoy retiring to my solar every night. I am able to escape members of the household and our guests for a few hours. Especially the unwanted ones," she said with a sharp look at him.

He grinned at the barb. Eyes narrowing, she abruptly wheeled her mount and did not bother to see if he followed.

They spent the rest of the morning surveying the Dumont domain. While Alex had learned much about the holding from what he had been able to pry out of Matilde, it did not compare to the details and intimate knowledge Isabel was able to give him. She showed him the forest where her father's men hunted, the network of streams off the Severn River irrigating the fields and the leagues of snow-covered tenant farms that paid tribute to Lord Dumont. The holding impressed him, but only once the snow melted would he have a true picture of the land.

Isabel had at first been terse in her description, but she eventually warmed to her task. Pride imbued her voice as she explained what each field produced and the innovative projects her father had undertaken. Whatever questions Alex asked, she had a well-informed answer, and he was forced to conclude Captain Thomas was not the only one Lord Dumont had confided in.

At last they arrived in the village of Ashdown. Alex had not paid much attention to the village when he and his men first came through it, as he had been eager to meet with the Dumonts. This time, he listened as Isabel pointed out the blacksmith, the bakery, the watermill and the church. The few villagers who were out-of-doors eyed him warily but brightened upon seeing Isabel, and it seemed she knew all of them fairly well, judging by her ease in striking up conversations with them. The garbled, incomprehensible English words meant nothing to him, but it was obvious they respected her and were pleased with her interest in their lives.

Isabel stopped her horse outside the local inn. The ride had turned her cheeks dusky rose, and at some point, the hood of her cloak had been forced back. Strands of her rich brown hair floated about her face. Again he was struck by her beauty. Her temper would be a small price to pay for such a woman who could capture the hearts and loyalty of her people. If he could just win her over, it would make his presence in Ashdown all the easier.

She dismounted, and Alex let her lead the way into the inn. The staunch, gray-haired innkeeper smiled toothily at Isabel in welcome. Their familiar exchange showed him she was no stranger to alehouses. He could not decide if that bothered him as the old man disappeared to prepare them a luncheon.

At that time of day, they were the only guests in the inn. Isabel headed for a table closest to the fireplace. A wolfhound sprawled across the hearth. Just the thump of his tail and the crackling of the fire filled the room as they sat down on opposite sides. Isabel avoided looking at Alex, her gaze roving everywhere but at him. No doubt they would dine in silence if she had her way.

He cleared his throat. "I could not help but observe some of your men were...surprised to find Norman knights in Ashdown," he said, remembering the sting of Kendrick's blade against his neck.

She finally faced him. "I think we all were," she said. "After all, my father is no stranger to William."

"No indeed, but even so, I thought we would find your household a little more welcoming."

"You must remember, although my father is

proud of his Norman heritage, we are still English and are respectful of the traditions of my mother and her countrymen. The witan proclaimed Harold king, not William, and for many Englishmen, the council's decision is law despite pronouncements from Rome to the contrary." Alex opened his mouth to argue with her, but she raised her hand. "I am not trying to debate the legitimacy of William's claim, but you must be mindful the grisly accounts of the battle have spread through this country like wildfire. The reports have done nothing to recommend you or your people."

She folded her hands and looked down at the table. "And you must know many of us are still grieving," she said quietly.

"I understand." The hurt in her voice was almost tangible. Was she thinking about her brother? Alex sighed. "War is a hard thing. I learned that the first time I raised my sword in defense of my father's home in Évreux. I was barely sixteen. But at Hastings, I was surprised by the dishonorable actions of many of William's men. He was forced to hire mercenaries from France to round out his ranks, and their ungodly actions have sullied our presence in England."

Isabel raised her head, her eyes flinty in the dim room. "Not all the bloodshed can be laid at the feet of the mercenaries."

He shifted in his seat. "No. The bloodlust was strong on both sides. And when it grabs hold of a man..." He gathered his thoughts. "Be glad your father sought to protect you from it."

She turned away from him and warmed her hands in front of the fire. "Why are you a knight for William?" she asked over her shoulder. He could sense curiosity under her light tone. She sat back in her seat, waiting for an answer.

He would oblige her, as it was the first time she

took interest in him as a man. "I have two older brothers," he said. "I wanted much more than to sit in their shadow or dedicate myself to the church. Normandy is tearing itself apart with all the fighting between the baronies. I wanted the chance to start over."

Isabel nodded. "And how has such a life found you?"

"Very well, thankfully. I have accomplished much for myself, considering I am not yet twenty-eight. I am a respected member of William's army, and he knows he can depend on me for anything," he said with pride.

"And what happens now? Now the fighting is over..." She struggled to get the words out.

Alex looked away from her. "That depends..."

"Yes?"

"On a number of things." He watched her uncomprehending face, and for a moment wished he could tell her the truth to banish the uncertainty haunting her eyes.

The moment was broken as the innkeeper brought out a plate of cold ham, a block of cheese and a loaf of bread. After eating a few bites, Alex spoke again. "I want to thank you for showing me the area, my lady. It has been most enjoyable. However, I would ask in the future you do not venture out on your own, even if you plan on remaining on your family's lands. You may resent my interference or call me any variety of names, but my conscience will not allow me to let you ride unattended. Not when I or one of my men can prevent injury to you again."

The color in her cheeks darkened. She pushed aside her trencher. He steeled himself for another argument. Before Isabel could respond, the innkeeper bustled over with two mugs of small beer. Her eyes flashed, but she didn't stir until the innkeeper moved a discreet distance away.

"I wonder how long you have been waiting to recite your little speech, Alexandre," she said before taking a sip of beer.

He watched her lips close over the cup, the column of her throat working as she swallowed. He raised his mug to her in mock-salute. "For quite some time, I can assure you. And please, call me Alex," he said with what he hoped was one of his more disarming smiles.

"Alexandre, if you are available, I will tell you when I plan on leaving the castle grounds. Will that suffice?" she asked stiffly.

He chuckled. "But that leaves open the question of what will happen if I am unavailable for some reason."

Isabel took another sip and eyed him over the rim of her mug. "Then I shall exercise my own judgment."

"A mistake given your previous experience, no?"

She slammed her cup down. "And I think it is a mistake for you to pursue this matter."

Her hands balled into fists. Alex managed to grab her wrist and pulled her closer to him. "Then explain why you chose to leave the safety of your father's home that day. Why did you leave the other morn? And do not tell me your horse needed exercising. Give me the real reason why you behaved so recklessly, and I will consider it."

Isabel tried to tug her hand back. When he realized she was not going to relent, he let her go. She glared at him and kneaded her wrist. If he did not know any better, he would think she was pouting.

"Now, now. None of that. You do not want the innkeeper to think there is a problem, do you?" he whispered. He picked up his cup and took a long drink.

"You know I do not care what he or anyone else thinks," she whispered hoarsely.

"You are really quite lovely when you are furious. Perhaps I should anger you more often." He was taking a risk, but seeing her cheeks redden as confusion warred with her rage was well worth it.

"I have been wroth with you from the moment I met you!"

Alex laughed. He caught his breath and fixed his stare on her. Her body was tense, her hand on her belt as if she were debating whether to flee or fight. He rose and took her elbow to guide her to her feet. He ignored her brief struggle against him and put a more than sufficient sum of money on the table for the innkeeper.

A slight tremble ran through her as he led her to the door. "My lady," he leaned down, his lips hovering over the shell of her ear, "if I have angered you, think on how you have been."

Isabel shook him off and nearly sprinted to her horse's side.

He could not help but feel victorious as they rode to the castle in silence. He urged his horse to stay with hers. She had not bothered to look back once to see if he still followed. Stubborn girl.

He guessed Isabel agonized over their conversation by the dark look on her face. Good. If he could upset her with just a few words, what would more direct methods yield? Repressing a grin, Alex guided his horse as close to hers as possible when the palisade walls were in sight. His heavy thigh pressed against hers as the horses moved closer together, the leather of their saddles squeaking at the contact.

"My lady, there is no need to brood. I promise I will not tease you anymore today."

"And what of tomorrow?" she asked suspiciously.

Alex smiled and said only, "I look forward to it."

# Chapter 8

At that moment, Alex decided she was worth whatever grief she gave him. After all, she could not help but lose her hostility against him eventually, and the rewards of having her grew each day he knew her. William said Alex would not be disappointed with his choice. And Alex certainly had misgivings, but he could not deny his attraction to the girl. She would not be a model wife but would bring things to their marriage that would be impossible for another woman.

If only her eyes would not cloud over every time she caught sight of him.

When they rode into the courtyard, Captain Thomas was waiting for them, Hugh standing grim-faced beside the older knight. What now?

Isabel dropped to the ground. "What has happened?"

"More Welshmen have been sighted, my lady," Captain Thomas replied in French.

Alex dismounted and exchanged a glance with Hugh, who silently confirmed the old man's words. "How many?"

"A dozen, we think," Captain Thomas said. "From the northwest, like before."

Isabel idly patted her horse's neck. "Reinforcements." She sounded disappointed but resigned.

"I believe so, my lady."

She blinked and looked once more at Captain

Thomas. "Then we will have to be more convincing
this time."

Alex turned to her. "What do you mean 'we'?"

Isabel flinched but otherwise acted as if she had
not heard him. "Captain, have the men make ready."

"The preparations are already underway."

"Good. I will change and join you in a moment."

Before she took two steps, Alex's hand clamped
down on her upper arm. "I think not. You are in no
condition to leave the safety of the castle."

Isabel whirled and faced him. "If you recall, I left
the safety of the castle today."

"Ah yes, but you were under my protection then."

Isabel's head reared back like an incensed filly. "I
have no need of your protection!"

"That may be," he said with a dip of his head.
"But you will allow my men to help yours in this
matter. Our orders are to assist your family while we
are here."

At his nod, Hugh left to gather the men.

Alex returned his attention to Isabel. "And you
will do us the favor and stay behind so you do not
become a distraction when we fight the Welsh."

"A distraction? How dare you!"

His mouth thinned. "Your injury has not fully
healed. You would just be a liability."

"You know nothing. This is not your fight."

Alex laughed. "Nor is it yours, my lady," he said.
The emphasis curled her lip and brought angry color to
her cheeks. "Let your father's men do their duty, and I
will do mine."

By now, the men had gathered in the courtyard,
English and Norman side by side. Alex looked them
over and smiled when he saw Captain Thomas had
donned his mail and was already astride a fine mount.
"*Bon.* Captain Thomas will be responsible for

communicating my orders to the English soldiers." The old man would be an asset against a Welsh foe Alex had only heard rumors of.

His gaze then landed on Kendrick. As much as he respected Captain Thomas, his trust did not extend to his young protégé, who still eyed him with hatred. Alex would not fight alongside a man like that. "You will stay behind and ensure the safety of Lady Isabel." The lad spat on the ground but dismounted nonetheless, and before Captain Thomas had a chance to translate. No surprise, that.

Isabel tugged on the sleeve of his overtunic. "You are making a mistake. I need to be there!"

Alex rounded on her. Her desperation was almost palpable, but she had no place on the battlefield, no matter how much she wished otherwise. "My lady, if you do not willingly stay behind, I will clap you in irons and chain you to your bed."

Her mouth parted. It was a bluff, but she did not know that. Her gaze darted to Captain Thomas, and a whole conversation passed between them in silence.

Finally, she gave him a sharp nod and stepped away from him. She faced her men and said something in English. A lusty cheer went up.

His fellow Normans looked at each other uneasily. The cheer was eerily similar to the battle cries that had propelled the English army against them at Hastings. He shook the thought away as Hugh brought his mail and helped him slip it over his head.

He remounted and directed his horse so he once more faced Isabel, the boy Kendrick standing a few feet behind her. "What's this, no words of encouragement for me and my men?"

Her frame still trembled with fury. She would forgive him this. Eventually.

"I hope the Welsh flay you alive."

Alex laughed. "I look forward to disappointing you."

\* \* \* \*

Kendrick followed Isabel into the castle. He did not say anything, but she knew the same fury twisting its way through her body wound through his. Servants scuttled away as she approached the main hall. She stood in front of the fire pit, holding her hands near the flames. She had not felt the chill earlier, but now it seemed to imbue everything.

Kendrick cleared his throat. "Your father would not have let you go either, if he were here."

Isabel snorted. "And I suppose you and Captain Thomas would have made similar arguments."

"Yes. Arguments you would have ignored."

"Precisely." She sighed. "I know he is William's envoy, but Alexandre..." She trailed off, at a loss to explain how infuriating he was.

"He is a devil, and a highhanded one at that."

Isabel looked at him sharply. "Still, I suppose we must not provoke him."

Kendrick scoffed. "And you have done such a good job of that." He shook his head. "Even if we wanted to fight them, it would be a fool's venture."

The bitterness in his voice surprised her. "I scarce knew you felt so strongly about this. For a moment I thought I was talking to my brother, Julien."

He looked at her. "Do not mistake me. Your father is a good man. But William's soldiers... You heard the reports as well as I."

"I know." Pevensey had been ransacked as soon as the Normans reached the English coast, Dover nearly burned to the ground, not to mention, the towns and villages the Norman army plowed through on their march to London. "But despite their faults, I think Alexandre and his comrades are honorable. I do not

89

think William would have knowingly sent untrustworthy men here," she said slowly, uncomfortable with the need to defend their Norman visitors.

Anger tightening his mouth, Kendrick turned away.

"God's truth." She placed a hand on his arm and tugged him back to face her. "Despite our misunderstandings."

Kendrick eyed her carefully. "What do you think your father will do when he comes?"

Isabel blinked and turned back to the fire. "I know not."

Her father would have pledged his loyalty to William, she had no doubt. However, as to Alexandre's dealings with members of the Dumont household, she did not know how her father would have handled the situation. Not for the first time, she wished she had his guidance.

Kendrick shifted his feet beside her. "I hope he will put Alexandre in his place. He has taken too much of an interest in you."

"What do you mean?" She hoped the question kindled Kendrick's dislike of the Norman and distracted him from asking any more uncomfortable questions about her father.

"I heard him speaking with Matilde about you. He wanted to know why you had not married. What your mother was like."

Isabel clenched her jaw. "Matilde should know when to hold her tongue. I will speak to her."

Kendrick gave a short chuckle devoid of humor. "Alexandre is quite the charmer, I guess."

"I do not understand why he would care about such things."

"Do you not? He is not just here to escort your

family to London. He is too interested in you and in Ashdown, for that matter."

She waved him off. "I am sure he is only trying to discover new ways to annoy me."

"Isabel, I am serious. I think he wants to win your affections."

"Ridiculous. I cannot stand the man," she said loftily.

"Surely you are not blind to the way he looks at you."

She frowned at the unfamiliar intensity of his words. "You cannot mean it. Even if Alexandre is interested, he is naught more than William's messenger. As a thane's daughter, I could do much better." She shook her head. "No, I'm certain William has already lined up a man of equal station to marry me when I reach London."

"Are you certain that will happen?" He took a step toward her. "Are you certain that is what you want?"

"Surely not!" Anger and helplessness at her situation rose, suffocating in its intensity. "But I must comply with whatever William asks of me. Ashdown will suffer if I do not."

Kendrick opened his mouth to argue, but she waved him off. She could not bear to discuss her future any longer. Nor could she idly stand by when she could be doing something to protect her people. While she still had the chance.

"Where are you going?" he asked.

She turned back to him and smiled. "I cannot fight the Welsh in this," she said, pointing to her dress, "now can I?"

* * * *

Convincing Kendrick was easy enough. Finding the trail the soldiers had taken was child's play, as it was clearly marked in the lingering snow. They made good time and came across the men waiting in a small clearing as the mid-afternoon sun beat down.

At her signal, she and Kendrick dismounted. Now that she was here, there was no going back, but she found herself wanting to delay her inevitable confrontation with Alexandre. From behind a tree, she peered into the clearing. Most of the men had dismounted to rest their horses before the fighting, and they were now making last minute adjustments to their armor or polishing their weapons. Cuthbert and one of the Normans had gone missing, probably to scout out the location of the Welsh forces to the northwest.

When she turned back, Kendrick was surprisingly close, his eyes on her, not the men in the clearing. He had been abnormally quiet during the ride, and now a surprisingly severe look marred his face.

"What is wrong?"

Kendrick grabbed her hand and pulled her close. "Isabel, you know the men would protect you, even if you went against William's wishes. Or Alexandre's."

This again? Did he not understand her position? She gave him a sad smile. "I am grateful for their loyalty, but it is too much to ask of them."

"The offer still stands. None of us want you to suffer."

"I am sorry, Kendrick, but it is too late. For all of us." The England they knew was changing, and they could do naught to stop it.

He shook his head. "I refuse to believe it. Could you not join a convent and gain sanctuary?"

"Not now, not with Alexandre here."

She had contemplated flinging herself upon the mercy of the church, hoping she would be allowed to join a convent and thereby save her respectability and her lands as much as possible. The church would own the land but she might be able to retain the management of it. Yet, something held her back. She still clung to the small hope William could be reasoned with, he would see the qualities her father had cultivated in her, and he would understand her need to choose her future.

She swiped a hand over her forehead. "This is not something I can run away from."

"What if you were already married? Surely that would prevent William from giving you to another."

"And who would that be? You know very well how many suitors I have chased away."

Instead of agreeing with her, Kendrick stood straighter, his gaze never leaving her face. "I could do it. I could protect you. Then when your father comes—"

"No, Kendrick. It would not be fair to you."

"Why not? I would gladly do that and more for you."

Isabel realized how close he stood, saw the genuine fear and love shining in his eyes. How had she not known? How could she have been so blind of his love for her?

She blinked. "Kendrick..."

"Foolish girl!" The deep timbre of Alexandre's voice snapped Isabel out of the staring match with Kendrick. She turned to find Captain Thomas and Alexandre standing not three feet away. She pulled her hands out of Kendrick's grasp and took a step back from all three men.

The Norman stalked toward her, his face a stony mask. "Explain yourself."

\* \* \* \*

Isabel rested her hand on the pommel of her sword and did not flinch when she met Alex's gaze. Her hair was pulled back into a tight braid beneath the hood of her cloak. She had slung a quiver of arrows and an ornate yew bow over her shoulder. Much like the first time he set eyes on her, she wore a padded tunic over her dress. She had come to fight.

"I am needed here," she said in clipped tones.

How dare she! She had disregarded his orders and now flaunted her bad behavior in front of the men— hers and his. Alex would not stand for any more of her impertinence. Even if it meant hauling her over his shoulder and dragging her back to the castle.

Alex took a step after her. Captain Thomas whipped out a hand and held him back. "Alexandre, a word."

She sauntered past him and joined a knot of her men, many of whom smiled in welcome as if this was all great fun. Kendrick followed, a dark look on his face, leading both their mounts.

Alex growled but stayed put. "I should have chained her up."

Captain Thomas inclined his head and did not disagree. "You must understand. Isabel feels her responsibilities most acutely."

Alex watched her across the clearing as she joked with her men, keeping their morale high even in the face of battle. He met Captain Thomas's questioning face. "They would do anything for her."

Captain Thomas looked at Isabel, who was laughing at a comment one of the soldiers made, and then turned to Alex. "Yes, but would not all of us?"

"Yet it seems Kendrick in particular has fallen for her charms." The boy stayed close to her, reverence and desperation at war on his face whenever he looked at her.

Captain Thomas raised his graying eyebrows. "You see much. Isabel herself does not know the lad is in love with her. But Isabel can be blind to what is in front of her, wouldn't you say?"

Alex did not like the intelligence in the old man's gaze. He only shook his head. "She is unlike any woman I have ever met."

"That I do not doubt," Captain Thomas said with a chuckle. "But given how close we are to the Welsh border, it is good she is able to defend herself. She has more heart than some of my men."

Despite not knowing the Englishman well, the rebuke in his words was clear. Alex opened his mouth to reply, but closed it at the sound of someone crashing through the brush.

Jerome and a young English scout burst through the trees. "They're coming."

\* \* \* \*

Isabel lined up another shot and let go before she allowed herself to exhale. The arrow buried itself into the back of a Welshman trading blows with Godric.

The Welsh had stumbled into the clearing, stunned to find so many armored soldiers saddled and ready for them. The fiends often relied on surprise to fuel their attacks, but it would not work this time.

Their leader gave up a cry, and the Welshmen ripped their swords from their scabbards and charged. They scattered when they hit the line of English and Norman soldiers like waves against a rocky coast. Alexandre ordered the men forward, and the battle began.

Isabel knew her shoulder could not handle wielding a sword and fighting on horseback, so she stayed back with her bow and her arrows, taking shots when she could. Kendrick stayed as close to her as he dared, protecting her from any Welsh fighters who managed to break through the line of men on horseback. They had learned their lesson from the previous skirmish.

Alexandre suddenly reined his horse to a stop beside her. He had been fighting on the other side of the clearing only moments ago, before she lost sight of him in the chaos.

The weight of his gaze settled over her as she lined up another target. Easy now. She released the arrow and could not quite hold back the quirk of her lips when it hit a Welshman's shoulder. An eye for an eye.

Alexandre grunted. "Perhaps you are not so helpless after all."

She bared her teeth at him. "Be glad I have not turned my sights on you."

He laughed, a full and throaty sound, at odds with the groans and shouts of the other men. "Oh, I am. But that does not mean I am pleased to have you here."

She reached for another arrow. "I am just doing my duty."

A Welshman bellowed and launched himself toward them. He must have broken through the line. Kendrick was too far away to help, locked in battle with another opponent.

Isabel cursed and scrambled to nock her arrow. Before she raised her bow, Alexandre's mount squealed as his heels dug into the animal's flanks. The beast reared in front of her, protecting her from the brunt of the Welshman's charge. Alexandre swung his sword down, breaking through bone, as the animal returned to all fours.

Her heart lurched against her chest as she sucked in air. So close...

Alexandre looked down at her through his nose guard, his eyes dark with an emotion she could not identify. "Be safe. I still have words for you." He spurred his horse into a group of Welshmen, his sword an arc of fire in the afternoon light.

She wrenched her attention away from the man and readied another arrow, then let it fly. It glanced off a Welshman's chest plate and distracted him long enough one of Alexandre's men struck him down once and for all. The Norman gave her a nod in thanks before moving on to the next opponent.

By now her breath echoed harshly in her ears, and handling her bow had left her fingers numb. Many Welsh had fallen. Their leader called for a retreat, but most of the survivors were struck down before they managed to turn back the way they had come. Such a difference from the first battle.

Captain Thomas instructed Alexandre to call off his men. The few Welshmen who remained were not worth chasing down. They would slink back across the border and lick their wounds, telling tales of the battle. Tales that would make them think twice before venturing into the Dumont lands again.

Yet it was not a complete victory. Isabel hurried to two of her men curled up on the ground. She crushed some yarrow leaves she had stowed in her saddlebags and bandaged the sword wounds the best she could—enough for them to travel back to the castle to receive more skilled care. Alexandre and Captain Thomas discussed the disposal of the bodies while Martin and Godric gathered up discarded blades and arrows. One of Alexandre's men clutched his upper arm, a nasty gash from a broad sword bleeding through his fingers. She dressed his wound and ensured the rest of the soldiers' bruises and busted knuckles could wait until they returned to the castle.

When she could do no more, she mounted and slowly rotated her arm. She had put more stress on her injury than she expected, but at least it had not reopened again.

Alexandre rode toward her with a serious look, so

different from his mirth before. A wave of unease
flowed through her when he stopped beside her.

He turned to address the other men. "I will escort
Lady Isabel back to the castle. Return as soon as you
have finished here." Before Isabel could protest, he had
seized Hardwin's reins and led them away at a gallop.

Cursing, she clung to the pommel of her saddle
for balance as Alexandre dragged them through the
woods. She pitched forward to avoid the sweep of
branches on either side and pressed her face into her
horse's neck. What did the man hope to accomplish?
She finally managed to snatch the reins back from him,
but not before they were well away from the others.

She pulled her horse to an abrupt stop. "I did not
realize you liked to be so dramatic. But if you ever
perform such a stunt like that in front of my men again,
I will kill you."

She dismounted and inspected Hardwin for
scrapes from the trail. What a careless, unthinking man.

He only laughed. "My lady, you are the one who
likes to make a spectacle. You are the one so fond of
disobeying orders. I think it is time someone put you in
your place," he said in a serious tone. He dismounted
and strapped his helmet to his saddle.

"I thought we would return to the castle." She
threw a look over her shoulder. He took a position right
behind her.

"We will, but there are things we need to discuss
first."

She finished running her hands down each of the
horse's legs and then straightened. "I have nothing to
say to you."

"But I would say some things to you, Isabel. You
disobeyed me. I cannot ignore that."

She spun toward him. "I told you I would not
send my men to fight a foe I am unwilling to face

myself."

"And I told you I would face the Welsh in your stead. You may not have a care for your safety, but you are my responsibility until I take you to London." He loomed over her. "I have thought on the best way to rein in your recklessness." His mouth firmed into a hard line. "Somehow I doubt a flogging will make you respect me."

She shied away from him. The dark look in his eyes was back. "Alexandre…"

"Call me Alex." Her eyes locked on his mouth as he leaned toward her. His words drifted across her lips. "*Non*, I think there is just one solution."

Her breath halted in her chest. "I think it is time we return." She tried to push past him but he would not move out of her way.

He took hold of her arms and held her still. A muscle worked in his jaw. "That would be prudent." She stared up at him, transfixed by the way his mouth shaped the words. "But I have not known you to be prudent."

Before she could think to protest, he bent down and claimed her lips with his. Isabel went rigid, too surprised to respond. Then he pulled away, an unknown look glittering in his eyes. He fingered the hair that had fallen out of her braid.

She should say something to stop what was going on, to stop the confusion coiled up inside her. The words of refusal formed on her lips, but he just watched her, as if he were trying to tell her something with just a look. He moved his warm hand to her face, caressing her cheek. She trembled.

The scent of man and cold snow clouded her mind. A good maiden would slap Alexandre for such boldness, but she could not muster the willpower to push him away. She could not pretend she did not want this.

She let her words fall away.

Alexandre lowered his head and warmed her lips with another kiss. He cupped her face, angling it against his just right. Moving his other hand to her waist, he pulled her hard against him as she reached up and twined her fingers in his long, thick hair. Overwhelmed by the sensations coursing through her, she clung to him. She gave herself up fully, and trailed her hands down, fisting them in the folds of his cloak.

With a groan, he kissed her lips apart. As he slipped his tongue into her mouth, more heat charged through her body. She was lost in his taste, so different from hers, but desired it—him—all the same.

He abruptly broke away from her, and pressed his face into her neck, his nose cold against her skin. His ragged breaths floated between them as he moved back and stared down at her. He smoothed her hair away from her face. The dark, piercing look in his eyes made her guts churn. The tenderness was still there, but the want was more visible.

She was not a naive little girl. She knew what a man wanted from a woman. He leaned toward her again, but this time she managed to pull away.

She remounted with forced calm. Kendrick had been right about Alexandre, and the thought brought a fresh rush of guilt. She took a few deep breaths to quell the unease that had immediately taken the place of the warmth she felt in Alexandre's arms moments before. Of all the things that could happen, this was the worst. How could she let him kiss her? Why had she given in? She wanted to think this did not change anything but could not convince herself.

Alexandre got back on his horse but his eyes were still on her. The hunter in him was back, his dark hair tousled, his eyes sparked with hunger, his lips surprisingly red. She touched her own and found them swollen.

"My lady…"

She hated the fact she was trembling. "It is already as if it did not happen." Her life was complicated enough without this added predicament.

"But Isabel, it does not have to be—"

"I will not debate this with you."

# Chapter 9

Her horse lurched to the side of the trail, then righted himself. He lurched again, favoring his right hind leg. Isabel dismounted and ran her hand down his leg. No hot spots.

"What is it?" Alexandre called out.

"Something is wrong with his leg." She picked up the hoof. The iron horseshoe seemed sound enough. She felt underneath, along the calloused pad at the base of the hoof, and dislodged a sharp stone. The muscles in Hardwin's hindquarters bunched, then went still as she let go.

"A stone." Isabel's hands fisted at her sides. "No doubt because of your carelessness earlier." She wanted to hit him. It was his fault, this…everything.

Alexandre gave Hardwin a long look. "He seems fine to me now."

That was true enough, but she well knew how a minor injury could turn into something far worse. "I will not risk lameness by riding him the rest of the way."

"Surely it is not that serious."

She nearly stamped her foot. "I said I will not risk it."

He looked like he would argue with her but shook his head. "Very well. My mount can carry both of us."

Oh yes, he would like that. Having her cling to him all the way back to the castle. She pushed her hair out of her face. "I will walk."

"I cannot leave you out here alone. Look at the sky. More snow, I warrant." She followed Alexandre's gaze and frowned at the sight of the setting sun almost overtaken by gray clouds. He drew his horse closer to her. "I doubt we will make it back to the castle before it hits."

"That matters not to me, but if the weather conditions are not to your liking, you are welcome to ride ahead."

His shoulders drew back. "I am at your service." He dropped to the ground.

"That will not be necessary." She took her horse's reins and tugged him along, telling herself it did not matter if Hardwin was not favoring his leg anymore. "We will be fine on our own."

Alexandre chuckled, the sound echoing forlornly in the empty woods, and followed her. "That may be, but you are still my responsibility." He looked around. "Is there a tenant nearby we can shelter with?"

"*Non.* But even if there were, I would not have you bully them into offering us hospitality. I refuse to subject my people to the likes of you."

She thought she saw a flash of disappointment in his eyes but must have imagined it, as his arrogant features hardened once more. "Then what do you suggest, my lady?" A sharpness that was not there before edged his tone.

She looked to the sky for strength and led her horse onward.

"Where are we going?" Alexandre called after her.

She did not bother to answer, knowing he had no choice but to follow.

After pushing their way down an overgrown trail, they emerged onto the road connecting Ashdown to Hereford to the north. She pulled her cloak closer to her frame. "Stay alert. The roads can be *dangereux*."

His answering grunt was lost as the wind picked up, bringing with it a chill that cut through her cloak.

The road was a dirt track, more mud than snow, barely wide enough for a team of four horses to travel unhindered. They trudged along in the muck for a long while before it began to sleet. Just when she was about to lose hope, she saw the old tree stump marking the little side trail she had been looking for.

They led the horses off the road and into the shadow of forest. It took longer than she liked to get her bearings in the gloom. She stopped once, wondering if she had blundered off the trail. It had been years since she had had reason to be here. After a frantic moment, she resumed walking, Alexandre following silently.

She was grateful he made no comment at her indecision. He was probably exhausted. He still wore chain mail from the battle. The heavy metal links would wear down even the sturdiest of frames after so long. Her father always claimed mail was the worst part about warfare.

Her foot finally struck stone. "We are here."

Alexandre looked where she pointed—at a small crevice in a wall of stone too small and shallow to be considered a cave. But the overhang was enough to provide them cover from the sleet now streaming down.

Alexandre looped the reins of the horses on a low hanging tree branch, and grabbed their saddlebags. Isabel sat and shifted back until she fitted her spine against the cold rock.

"How did you learn of this place?" The tinkle of metal links echoed off the stone as Alexandre struggled out of his mail.

She closed her eyes to ease the pressure building

there. She had been seven, young and foolish and full of grief in the wake of her mother's passing. "My father said something careless when I was younger, so I ran away. It grew dark, and I found this place to pass the night."

"Headstrong, even as a child, no?" Alexandre settled down next to her, placing his mail on the opposite side so it would not rust further. He rummaged around in his bag and pulled out flint and tender. "I will start a fire."

Isabel tugged him back and then folded her hands in her lap. "*Non*. We are still too close to the road. We do not want to attract attention."

"But you must be freezing." He rested a heavy hand on her shoulder. Tendrils of warmth sank through the wool of her cloak. "Come now. You are shivering."

"Pray do not trouble yourself with me." She pulled away from his touch.

He crossed his arms and leaned back. "No fire. I suppose it is too much to ask for something to eat on a night such as this."

"Perhaps not." Isabel pulled her saddlebag close and fished around inside. "Ah." She pulled out a stale loaf of bread and wedge of hard cheese. She had had no way of knowing how long they would battle with the Welsh, and had packed provisions just in case.

Alexandre watched her carefully as she used her seax to slice the bread and cheese. She moved to sheath it, but he caught her wrist and peered down at the dull glint of the knife. "An English blade, if I recall. Why do you wear it?"

She tugged her hand from his grasp and slid the seax into her sheath. "It was passed down through my mother's family."

"Same with these?" Alexandre reached out and fingered the golden brooches on her shoulders. "Most of Harold's housecarls wore similar gold bands and bracelets at Hastings."

She looked down at his hand and counted her breaths until it fell away. "Yes."

"You are very proud of your English background."

She could not tell if there was implicit censure in the comment or not. She sniffed. "I try to honor the heritage of both my father and my mother."

Alexandre watched her with a thoughtful expression. "I was told your lady mother was an Englishwoman of some standing."

"Yes," she said through gritted teeth. The Norman was surprisingly well-informed. Matilde's doing, no doubt. "She was a distant cousin of Earl Godwin. When King Edward brought his Norman entourage to England, my father met my mother, Alvina of Wessex, at court. After they married, he was able to stay in England even though many of Edward's Norman advisors were exiled."

He nodded and took the bread and cheese she proffered. "And Lord Dumont has made a name for himself here with his cavalry training to help defend the border against the Welsh."

"Yes. Decades of bloodshed have done naught to quell the bitterness between Wales and England, and raids are all too common—even when Gruffydd ruled. But thanks to my father's efforts, and that of FitzOsbern in Hereford, the local thanes have learned to repel them."

"I must say I was impressed with your father's men today."

"They have been well trained." She swallowed, her throat working hard to gulp down the dry bread. "I thank you for the assistance you provided. It was a victory we should all be proud of."

He waved away her thanks. "It was the right thing to do." He was quiet a moment. "I meant to ask what you and Kendrick were discussing so intently earlier. For a moment, I thought you were fighting about something."

So he had seen their conversation. She took a deep breath, and nearly choked as the cold swarmed into her lungs. "It was an old argument," she lied. "Do not concern yourself." With everything that had happened, she barely had a chance to think on Kendrick's offer, surprising as it was.

She found Alexandre staring at her thoughtfully. "I hope I have not caused you trouble. I do not think Kendrick likes me very much."

"Not at all," she said sincerely. "But he is just protective of me."

Alexandre nodded and ate the rest of his bread and cheese, chewing slowly. Finished, he cleared his throat. "Your father still owns land in Normandy?"

"A small holding in Lisieux. He visits every few years but usually leaves it in the hands of his castellan." She turned to him, desperate for a change in topic. "And what of your father?" she asked. "You said he had nothing for you in Normandy."

"Yes. He is a small lording pledged to the Count of Évreux. He already has two sons who would gladly take over for him. A third son is just a nuisance." There was old bitterness there. For a moment she felt badly for him. Norman inheritance laws were far more restrictive than English ones.

"Would you go back if you could?"

"Would your father?"

She shook her head. Although he remained true to his Norman roots, her father had become attached to English soil. In that respect, she was glad he had passed on so he would not have to choose between the land he had grown to love and the land he hailed from.

Alexandre exhaled. She could not tell what emotion was behind it. "I am in England for as long as I can serve William. My future is here, for better or worse."

He stretched out beside her. Leather scraped against rock and his cloak slapped against stone as he settled. She tensed, remembering the unexpected press of his body against hers. Only the outline of him was visible in the darkness, but his silent presence nearly dwarfed her under the overhang.

He brought his shoulder and leg to a rest against her, and she nearly jumped. She did not dare shift away, though, given the cold that had crept underneath her clothes.

"Come now, you should rest," he said as if nothing improper had occurred. "You have had a full day, riding across your father's lands, slaying Welshmen and dealing with me."

She laughed, one short, unexpected note, soon lost in the fall of the sleet. "Yes, your presence has certainly been exhausting, Alexandre."

"Alex," he said sharply.

"Alex."

"*Bon*. Now close your eyes."

She hesitated. How could she relax, let alone sleep, with the devil himself beside her? She gripped her seax.

He leaned down, his mouth hovering over her ear, and she froze. "I will take the first watch. You have nothing to fear."

\* \* \* \*

She woke, curled into the side of Alexandre, his arm cradling her shoulders. How... She lay there in a stupor. Her back and sides were cold but the front of her was warm where she pressed up against the

Norman. Had he taken any liberties once she had fallen asleep? Or worse, had she sought out his warmth as she slept, like a moth seeking flame?

It mattered not. She only knew she did not want him to wake and find her there, wrapped around him like...like some harlot. She straightened and eased away from his slumbering form. When he did not stir, her heartbeat slowed its pace.

The sun barely hovered above the horizon. She walked a fair distance from their camp to relieve herself. Still unbalanced, she did not want to face Alexandre just yet, so she saw to the horses, which both eyed her balefully. "We will be home soon, I promise," she said, giving them a pat. Alexandre's mount, a black charger with powerful hindquarters, snorted and stamped his feet at her touch. Temperamental and bred to fight, just like his master.

When she returned, Alexandre was nowhere to be seen. She took a few tentative steps down the trail they traveled the night before. The wind stirred, bringing with it sharp voices. Had he met someone on the road? Had Captain Thomas sent someone after them when they did not return?

She could not make out the words. Wrapping her cloak around her, she crept closer to the voices drifting from the road.

Through the trees, she spied a merchant's wagon—old Dalston, from the look of it. He always made a point to stop in Ashdown a few times a year, hawking his wares and spinning tales of his travels. Two men, rawboned and savage looking, spoke with the merchant. The morning sun glinted off sword blades too finely wrought to be theirs. No doubt the ruffians had snatched them from hapless travelers they had targeted in the past.

One of the men, scarred by pox, glanced at the

trees. Isabel dropped to her knees. She could still hear Dalston bargaining with the thieves for safe passage. "Spare my horses and the wagon, and you'll have your choice of my goods."

Laughter tinged with cruelty was the response. She slipped her sword out of its scabbard. The thieves did not seem moved by Dalston's offer. She tightened her hold on the grip and eased into a crouch.

She was jerked back before she could do anything. A hand snaked around her mouth. Someone else's breath ghosted across her neck. "Easy, *ma petite.*" Alexandre hunched behind her. He slowly removed his hand from her lips. "There are two more of them waiting down the road."

She glanced back at him. "Oh." He was close, the blue of his eyes startlingly clear. All thought left her.

His mouth quirked. "I took the liberty of scouting out the area since you said the roads were *dangereux.*"

She blinked and remembered herself. "Now do you believe me?"

"I never doubted you." He pointed to the wagon with his head. "We should think carefully how to proceed."

"But we must help—"

His gaze flicked toward the road. "Quiet!" He grabbed her and forced her onto the ground. His body pressed against hers shamefully. She felt every breath, his chest expanding and contracting against hers like a blacksmith's bellows, throwing off so much heat she hardly felt the frozen ground digging into her.

The pressure eased as Alexandre lifted himself off her to peer through the trees. She barely heard the men haggling over the sound of her racing heartbeat. "I never said I would not help." He sounded insulted. "Come." Alexandre pulled her to her feet and led her through the trees, moving more silently than she could have thought possible for a man his size.

He stopped, and she almost ran into him. She grabbed his woolen cloak to steady herself. The weave felt smooth against her fingers, and was nearly as fine as hers.

"There." He pointed through the trees. Two more men sat on a fallen log set along the road, their sickly mounts cropping the dormant brambles that grew alongside the muddy track. Rather poor lookouts.

Alexandre beckoned her to follow him.

When he was almost directly behind them, he raised the pommel of his sword and slammed it down on the first man's head. He pitched forward, unconscious. Before the other man could get his wits about him, Alexandre punched him in the face, and he slumped to the ground alongside his companion.

Isabel found rope attached to one of the men's saddles—long enough to stretch between two trees bordering the road to fell any rider who would pass through. Alexandre grunted in approval at her find and trussed the men up.

She wrung her hands. "Hurry. I do not want Dalston to get hurt."

Instead of ducking back through the forest, they trotted down the road. Isabel wiped her palms on her dress and kept her sword in front of her.

A shout rent the air. Alexandre sped forward without a backward glance. The man certainly moved when he wished to. Isabel hitched up her skirt and ran after him.

The thieves, no longer interested in negotiating, dragged Dalston from his seat on the wagon. One of the fiends leveled a knife at his back, while the scarred one rifled through his wares.

Alexandre slashed at the thief holding the knife. The man screamed and grabbed his arm, now streaked with blood. The knife thudded to the ground.

Wide-eyed, Dalston pulled away. He collapsed near the tree line, clasping his chest. The old man should have known better than to travel without guards.

The scarred man at the wagon fumbled for his blade as Alexandre approached and managed to hold off the knight's first sweep of his sword.

Then the man lunged at Alexandre, the sword striking only air.

Alexandre chuckled and flinched toward his opponent. The man gave a cry and scrambled back from the Norman until he was pressed against the side of the wagon.

Isabel had taken two steps toward Dalston, when the other thief reached for his sword despite his damaged wrist, his eyes on Alexandre's back as he traded blows with his scarred partner.

She pointed her blade at the man's neck. "Drop your sword."

The man looked at her out of the corner of his eye and spat. She pressed the tip of her blade into his skin, making him wince. "Now."

The sword clattered to the ground, and he held up his hands.

Alexandre disarmed his opponent and knocked his head into the side of the wagon. He collapsed to the ground in a heap.

Alexandre turned to her, looking inordinately proud of himself.

She forced her gaze away from his eyes, which were merry with victory, and turned to the merchant. "Dalston, you old fool, tell me you have rope."

\* \* \* \*

Isabel dashed out instructions for dealing with the bound thieves and turned her horse over to the blacksmith within moments of their return to the castle.

Alex stood back and watched her work, a flurry of orders and vigor.

Captain Thomas, Hugh and Jerome had been waiting for them. "My lady, I did not know what to think when you did not return," the old man said once he was able to get a word in.

Isabel's cheeks reddened. "As you can see, we are no worse for our travels."

Alex could feel the inquisitive gazes his men gave him. Jerome, especially, eyed him with a smirk on his lips. "She feared her horse injured so we walked."

"Walked?" Hugh asked in a startled voice. He turned to Alex. "Why did you not ride together on your mount?"

Isabel stiffened. "I did not want to inconvenience Alexandre."

Hugh snorted. "It would be no inconvenience. He's supposed to be your—"

"Escort," Alex cut in. "And as such, it was Lady Isabel's decision how we traveled," he said, giving Hugh a warning look.

Isabel rested her gaze on Hugh for a long moment before she darted a look around the courtyard, worrying her lip with her teeth. "Yes, well, if you will excuse me." She did not look at Alex once before she headed indoors.

Alex watched Isabel's trim figure disappear before turning to Captain Thomas.

"Thank you for keeping Isabel safe," the old knight said, his face always the benign mask of civility. "That horse was a gift from her father. She would never let any harm come to it."

"So I have learned."

Captain Thomas excused himself, and Alex let Hugh and Jerome lead him to the training ground where the rest of his men waited. "To be honest, Alex,

I do not know how you can be so casual about your good fortune," Jerome said as they walked.

"Good fortune?"

"Yes, in Lady Isabel."

"How can you say that? She has been a shrew since we arrived," Alex said even as he thought back to the way her unkempt hair had shone in the morning sun filtering down through the trees. He had feigned sleep when she woke, curious to see how she would react when she found herself tucked against his side. As much as he wanted to explore her mouth again, self-preservation told him not to push her too far much too soon.

"I am sure she will come around. You have always enjoyed a challenge. And Lady Isabel seems to have captured your attention," Jerome said playfully.

"But do you think you can trust her?" Hugh asked.

Alex turned to Hugh. "I want to. She has been cooperative up to a point, but I do think she is keeping something from us."

"I am not surprised. Her father may be Norman but she has been raised in this barbaric land."

Alex gave his shield bearer a sharp glance. "She is no barbarian. She is just confused and needs time to adjust to her new circumstances. But my first concern must be her father. Do you think it strange he has not returned home yet?"

Hugh shrugged. "Perhaps. The weather could have worsened, or he may have taken ill. Any number of things could have happened."

"Indeed. I am just impatient to have this business over with."

Jerome laughed. "Well, who would not if the prize was Lady Isabel?"

# Chapter 10

Isabel crouched before the wooden trunk set along the wall of her room. Dresses and blankets spilled out over the edge like candle wax. Where was it? Ignoring the way her thighs burned in protest, she rifled through the chest until her hand reached the bottom. Her fingers finally closed over a linen-wrapped piece of vellum. She pulled it out and sat on the bed, tucking her legs underneath her. She pushed aside the fabric, exposing her mother's will, delicate as an eggshell.

She read over the familiar words, her gaze tracing the curve of her mother's hand where she had signed at the bottom of the document. The words were as she remembered. Her mother's personal effects were hers, the land her father's until his death. He could cede up to half of the holding but the rest was to remain in the family to be split between Julien and herself. There were no stipulations on her marital status that would affect her inheritance, so she probably could donate the lands to the church and cloister herself in a nunnery, if she had more time to put such a scheme into place. Not now, though, with the Normans underfoot. And part of her was frustrated she would not be able to marry on her terms.

When her father and brother had pestered her about marriage, parading eligible men through Ashdown and sending her to court for one miserable summer, Isabel had been happy to point out

Englishwomen could not be forced to marry, thanks to laws dating back to Alfred's time. She did not need to say her mother would have supported her decision. Her father had relented after that, and things continued as they always had, with Isabel managing her father's household.

She had never realized how much her parents cared for each other until her mother died and her father was forced to go on alone. In the wake of her passing, he had done all he could to be respectful of her memory and the English traditions she believed in. Something Isabel was grateful for since Englishwomen had more freedom than Norman customs allowed. She thanked God her father had not been so close-minded as his countrymen, but she also knew she would not be in such a delicate position now if she had heeded his wishes to marry.

Her thoughts rushed to Kendrick and his proposal. He must have harbored feelings for her since they were playmates. Only the dramatic upheaval caused by the Norman presence in England gave him the opportunity to voice what would have otherwise been forbidden to say. Her father had his limits—he would never sanction a union between his daughter and a landless soldier, even if she wished it.

Kendrick had always been a close friend. There may have been a time growing up when she might have fancied the Englishman, but she was certain her feelings for him now were nothing more than sisterly affection. Nevertheless, Isabel momentarily indulged herself, wondering what life would be like with Kendrick at her side. She tried to imagine him kissing her, his kind, familiar face filled with passion, but it suddenly contorted into the dark planes of Alexandre's, the hunger in his icy eyes still sharp in her memory. She ran a shaky hand over her brow.

When she and Alexandre returned to the castle, she had locked herself in her rooms. She told Matilde her head ached, which was not completely untrue, and Matilde had promised she would not be disturbed so she could rest. Matilde was as good as her word and Isabel had plenty of solitude to think about what happened yesterday as the afternoon wore on.

Was it as disastrous as it seemed, for Alexandre to kiss her? She did not realize such a simple act produced such a rush of...feeling. Yet, if the man could irritate her before such intimacies, how much more chaos would he be able to inflict on her afterward, now armed with the knowledge he affected her?

What she really wanted to know was what prompted Alexandre's actions. At least she knew Kendrick's feelings were honest and pure, but the Norman was different. She had sensed his interest in her before, but had wanted to think it only his concern for carrying out his orders. After what happened, she could no longer believe that to be true. Was he simply a man acting on instinct or had he felt the same need, the same desires, she had?

Isabel reminded herself he was a soldier of fortune, seeking to better his lot by fighting for William. By his admission, he was only to be her escort. What if he wanted the Dumont lands for himself? Mayhap he saw her only as a conqueror's prize. She shook her head. Unacceptable.

With a groan, she rewrapped her mother's will and repacked her trunk. When she finally left the sanctuary of her rooms, she sought out Matilde. She was overseeing the cleaning of the main hall. Two servants scrubbed the tables, a bucket of water between them.

"Matilde, I would speak with you if you have a moment."

She greeted Isabel with a smile. "Certainly, my dear. How is your head?" She reached Isabel's side and squeezed her hands.

"Oh, it is much better. Some rest soothed the pain," Isabel lied.

"I can hardly speak with you these days."

"I know. All my time is taken up by Alexandre."

"He is just doing what he feels is right."

"Of that I am not so sure." She eyed Matilde. "I heard he has taken quite an interest in my past."

"Yes, he has been most curious about you. He wanted to know if you took after your mother."

She frowned. "He did? What did you tell him?"

"I told him you are just as spirited and beautiful." Matilde continued, "Alexandre also wanted to know if you had many suitors and I told him—"

Isabel raised her hand, silencing the woman. She did not want to hear the details Matilde unwittingly had passed on to Alexandre, as it would only increase her anger. "Matilde, if he asks you any more questions like that, please let me know."

Matilde grew concerned. "Was I wrong to tell him about your mother?"

Isabel sighed. She could not fault Matilde for answering the Norman's questions. "No. But we need only to be courteous. He does not need to know everything about me. He may be able to force me to go to London, but he should respect my privacy."

Isabel looked around the room and froze. "Enough of that. He is coming over here." Alexandre had just come in from the bailey. His gaze immediately sought out Isabel, and he strode toward them.

Isabel winked at Matilde and raised her voice, pretending not to see Alexandre advancing. "That simply will not do," she berated her in French. "We must go back and clean all of the tapestries."

"All of them? Uh, yes, my lady."

"I shall come with you this time, to make sure it is done properly."

Matilde nodded in feigned shame, finally catching on to Isabel's scheme.

Alexandre cleared his throat. "Pardon, but I would ask how you are recovering, Lady Isabel. Better, I hope?"

Isabel did not have to pretend to be startled. Her body was drawn as tightly as a bowstring, and the rumble of his voice beside her was enough to jangle her calm. "Alexandre, I did not see you there. Yes, I have recovered. And how has the afternoon found you?" she asked, unwilling to look him in the eyes.

He stood much too close to her. "*Très bien*, thank you, my lady. I would like it very much if you would walk with me before supper. Perhaps the fresh air—"

"I am afraid I must decline the offer," she said more harshly than she had intended. She saw the humor in his eyes. He knew she did not want to be near him. Curse the man! In a more controlled voice she said, "I have just been informed of a most pressing household matter I must take care of."

"These household matters do seem to require much of your attention." Alexandre's gaze was a challenge, but she decided she did not care.

"If you will excuse us?"

"If I must. I look forward to seeing you tonight," he said with a short bow.

Isabel inclined her head and led Matilde out of the main hall. Once they were well away from him, Isabel heaved a sigh of relief and sank against the wall of the corridor. "Well, that got rid of him for a few more hours."

"He is doing you a great courtesy, giving you all this attention."

Isabel did not appreciate the reproach in Matilde's voice. "Is that what you think? No, he only wants to keep me under his watchful eye. He wants me too afraid to pass beyond the castle walls."

"But my dear, in truth, he has been most understanding."

"Understanding? How can you say such a thing? He understands naught. About the castle, about the way things are run, about..."

"You?" The old woman chuckled. "Yes, my dear, he understands you too well."

Isabel froze. "Then he should know better than to follow me around like a dog. He is driving me mad. Asking questions... All the time, questions! I simply cannot put up with him anymore."

"If you will only go with him to London and get this whole business over with—"

"Go to London? No!"

Matilde's mouth flapped open. "But you must..."

"Matilde, do you not see? Once I am in London, William will marry me off to one of his men. I am to have no choice in the matter, and certainly no future," Isabel said.

"You always knew you would marry someday. Women, much younger than you, get married all the time."

"My father gave me the gift of choice, so I could marry for love. And now that he is gone..."

"My dear, my dear," Matilde said soothingly as she gave Isabel a hug. "This William, mayhap he will surprise you. You are worrying yourself unnecessarily. And your father will put it all to rights when he returns, that I'm sure of."

Isabel pulled away from her and shook her head. "That is just it, Matilde." The concern in the older woman's face twisted her gut. She could not lie to her any longer. "He is not coming home."

"Nay, my lady, you are just upset. You will see."

"No, Matilde. How I wish that were the truth. Julien sent a messenger here with the tidings. Father died of a fever after being injured in the fight at Stamford Bridge."

Isabel held Matilde's hands as the old woman's eyes closed in pain and watched as Matilde waged a war with her emotions and won. "Your father," she said roughly, "was a good man, and he will see to you from heaven. Everything will turn out for the best. You have to trust in that."

Isabel forced herself to smile, a strange sensation. "Mayhap you are right. But you cannot blame me for putting it off for as long as possible, can you?"

"Certainly not. But Alexandre will have to be told eventually, and, if he finds out for himself, he will be furious."

"I do not care."

"I am not so sure…"

"What do you mean?"

"Nothing, nothing. Just the way the pair of you have been sparring… I thought…"

"Thought what?" Isabel prompted, not liking where Matilde's thoughts were likely taking her.

"I simply think you care more than you say."

"Do not be ridiculous. He is everything I hate in a man. Pompous, arrogant, insufferable."

"As you say."

\* \* \* \*

"Going out, my lady?"

Alexandre's voice accosted her as soon as she entered the main hall the next morning.

She wanted to ignore him, but courtesy demanded she acknowledge the knight. Even when her heartbeat thrummed in her chest as his gaze skirted over her figure before it came to rest on her face.

She had to remind herself he could be a powerful ally, especially now when she could not count on her father. Nor had she forgotten how he and his men contributed to their victory against the Welsh. When she went to William to confront him about her future, mayhap Alexandre would vouch for her and profess his confidence in her capabilities. It was possible, she supposed, but only that. Alexandre was still a man, and, further, William was his liege lord. She could never compete with that.

Isabel walked over to the Norman, his eyes still trained on her. "As you see." The stable master had told her Hardwin could be ridden again. She had dressed with greater care than usual, selecting a simply cut riding gown made of deep blue lamb's wool. Over it, she wore a fur-lined mantle, with her mother's brooches on each shoulder.

"Then I should be happy to accompany you."

She waved him off. "Please, do not trouble yourself. Captain Thomas has already agreed to join me."

"May I ask then what is the purpose of your trip?" As always, his words were polite, but she heard the unyielding steel in his voice. If she did not supply a satisfactory answer, he would no doubt prevent her from leaving.

"We will be inviting my father's tenants, the townspeople and the neighboring thanes to the castle in three day's time for a feast." She had already gone over her meal ideas with the kitchen staff and informed Matilde and the other servants of the decorations she wanted for the hall. Seeing his surprise, she continued, "The winter months are hard for some people, and our stores can support them for at least one night."

"Why not wait until Christmastide?"

"We usually hold a large celebration for Epiphany but have smaller gatherings for Christmas. Besides," she looked away from his warm gaze, her fingers plucking at her mantle, "morale is low among our people, with their king dead. They need fellowship at this time." She decided she would also announce Lord Dumont's death at the gathering. It was time for her people to know, and past time for her to finalize her future.

She hated to admit it, but she could no longer postpone meeting with her new king. Alexandre and his men grew more impatient as each day passed with no tidings of her father. The longer she delayed, the more she risked reprisals from William. And she well knew the Welsh would not be scared away for long. The sooner things were settled, the better.

Isabel relaxed when Alexandre finally nodded. "That is very generous of you. Are you sure I cannot be of service to you or Captain Thomas?"

She shook her head. "Most of our people would be uncomfortable around Normans at this time. I am sure you understand."

"You are worried my presence would kindle their fears."

"Yes."

Alexandre nodded again. Isabel thought she saw a flash of regret pass over his face, but before she could be certain, a servant announced a messenger. She was taken aback to see the messenger address Alexandre.

"I come with news from William."

Alexandre turned to her. "I must attend to this."

"Certainly," she said, doing her best to pretend the dismissal meant nothing to her. What was so important about William's message that she must be excluded? Unease coiled in her stomach like a snake. She wanted to stay and hear his response, but she needed to make preparations.

She strode out of the hall to meet Captain Thomas, determined to put Alexandre out of her mind.

They rode through town, visited the freemen's farms and even sought out the remote charcoal burners' huts along the edges of the Dumont lands. Everything seemed so ordinary, despite Norman control over England. Her people were busy with their daily chores. Even though they would soon have a new king, meals still needed preparing, livestock needed care and firewood needed collecting. There were still squabbles over chickens, cattle and the occasional counterfeit silver penny, and news of a feast was a welcome distraction from not only the invasion but the dullness of the everyday.

Many were scared, but their apprehension visibly diminished when they saw Isabel on her horse and heard her assurances. As long as Isabel feigned normalcy, she knew her people would do the same. What would happen when they learned of her father's death? Would they accept her authority over them?

They respected her, that much she knew, but did they trust her enough to see them through this time?

\* \* \* \*

"My lady, I would speak with you." Alex entered the solar, the private room over the hall Isabel often retreated to at the end of the day. He pulled the door shut behind him without bothering to wait for her response. She would hear him, regardless of whether she wished it.

"What is it?" Isabel looked up from the accounts she had been reviewing by candlelight.

And for much too long, based on the redness rimming her eyes. She had been pushing herself too hard of late, and it showed. He had no desire to add to her troubles, but circumstances would not allow otherwise.

"The messenger today brought some news of interest to you," he told her.

She looked down at the papers on the table. "When will you be leaving us?"

He gritted his teeth. "When my lady is willing to accompany me." Already, Alex's temper wakened at her careless tone, but he could not afford to engage her in another verbal sparring session. He cleared his throat. "I took the liberty of contacting London to inquire after your brother, to be certain."

Isabel finally gave him her full attention. "And?"

Alex squared his shoulders and kept his gaze on hers. "I am sorry, my lady, but as we suspected, he is dead."

Isabel rose, her face the color of ash, but managed to maintain her composure. "And the body?"

Alex shifted his feet. "Reports say he fell in battle." Anything of value on her brother's person would have been scavenged before the army moved on. He and other fallen soldiers might have been buried unshriven in mass graves, if they were lucky enough, but there was no way to be certain.

She nodded with great effort. "I see. Thank you, sir, for bringing this to my attention. You will excuse me?" she said as she walked past him. Her hand trembled as she reached for the door.

"*Non*, Isabel, you are not to be left alone."

She spun and faced him. "Tell me not what I can and cannot do."

Hurt throbbed in her voice, and he wanted to dispel it. As he took in the remote expression on her face, the strict way she held herself, he knew she would reject any of his attempts. But he had to try.

Alex strode to the door, blocking her exit. "I can and I will. You have carried too many burdens for anyone, let alone a woman."

"Why will you not leave me alone?" she demanded.

"You are suffering, Isabel, and I cannot bear to see it." He fell silent.

"I must go." She tried to push past him, but he remained immobile. The first tear slid down her cheek. She stared off at some point over his right shoulder as if it were the most fascinating thing in the world.

"Isabel, please." He grabbed her wrists and held them. The sleek muscles in her forearms corded under his palms as she clenched her hands into fists.

"I do not want your pity."

"I do not pity you, Isabel, but I do understand."

"Get away from me." She tried to step back from him.

"*Non*. You are so strong, so capable. But no one can be strong all the time. Nor does anyone expect you to be. Look at me." He shook her until she looked up at him. "I am not going anywhere. You need this, whether you know it or not."

"All I know is I have put up with your nonsense for far too long." Her voice quavered, then steadily grew stronger. "You have countered my every command, disregarded my every wish. I will not tolerate any more interference. Release me or I will—"

"What, Isabel? What will you do?" He did not let go of her hands, and she finally stopped pulling away. "As much as you have tried to hide it, I have seen your fear, seen your grief. Trust me. Let me help you." He released her.

She paced around the room with increasing agitation. "Trust you? How can you ask me to trust you when you have invaded every aspect of my life? Is my privacy yours to conquer in addition to my authority?"

"*Non*, it is not like—"

"What do you gain by turning my household against me?" she said without pausing. "I have seen the way they look at you. It is not fair! I have devoted my life to serving my people and earning their respect, and you suddenly appear and destroy everything. Just because you are a man does not mean—"

"Yes it does," he cut her off, reminding himself not to lose his temper. "This is the world we live in. You are a woman and despite all your admirable skills and learning, a man, however inferior, will command greater authority. You will have to accustom yourself to such a life, my lady, for I doubt you will remain unmarried for much longer."

Her eyes widened. "That is not your concern! And I will not have you speak of such things again, you hateful man!"

Under different circumstances, he might have laughed. "You do not hate me." He knew all too well how much easier it was to be angry with him than acknowledge the hurt of her brother's death. Or anything else, for that matter.

"Yes, I do! I hate the way you are always watching every move I make. I hate the way you can always make me angry. I hate the way you make me feel…" More tears slipped down her cheeks.

He came up behind her and put his hands on her shoulders. He resisted the urge to pull her closer. "Isabel, I know you are suffering. Captain Thomas told me how close you and your brother were."

"Curse you!" Isabel spun toward him. "You know nothing, despite your attempts to learn all there is to know about me and my family! Why am I so important to you?"

Alex froze. Dare he tell her William's plans? After a moment's hesitation, he dismissed the idea. She was still fresh with sorrow for her brother and not yet comfortable with him. It would be unfair to press the subject. She needed more time, but he found it increasingly difficult to keep the truth from her.

Isabel's mouth hardened. She dropped her right hand to the hilt of her seax, and pointed the other to the door. "Leave me. I will not tell you again."

He could disarm her eventually, he was sure of it, but he had well learned some battles were not worth the fight. He tipped his head toward her. "As you wish, my lady."

# Chapter 11

As Isabel struggled to alertness, she prayed the events of the previous evening were naught but a dream.

Matilde stirred in a chair beside her. "My lady, Alexandre said you might have need of me when you woke."

Isabel grimaced. He must have asked Matilde to watch over her. Despite her anger at his continuing interference in her affairs, his thoughtfulness still touched her.

She looked at Matilde and noted her unease. "What did he tell you?"

"Only that you were not feeling well. He said I should be here when you wake up."

"I see." Isabel raised her fingertips to her eyes. Still swollen. Perhaps a cold soak would help. She slowly sat up.

"My dear, what is wrong?"

Isabel sighed. "Julien is dead. Alexandre only told me of it last night." She closed her eyes at Matilde's gasp. "It is not a surprise, but..." Even though she could see no other outcome for her brother, she was still heart-sore to learn of his fate. "We must make preparations. For both Julien and my father. I will make the announcement at the feast."

"Yes, my lady." Unshed tears filled Matilde's voice. "Is there aught I can do for you?"

"Nay. I thank you, Matilde."

Matilde clasped Isabel's hand in a warm, firm grip. "I am here if you have need of me."

"I know."

Matilde nodded and left the room.

Isabel willed herself to get dressed. That Alexandre had seen her tears... A fresh, hot wave of embarrassment rushed through her. She had wept for her brother, but unknown to the knight, also cried for her father. She had ignored the pain of losing him as much as possible, but last night she reached her breaking point.

Now, she wanted nothing more than to sink into bed and sleep away her memories, her responsibilities, as well as everything to do with Alexandre.

Most of the men had finished eating, and only a few faces were scattered around the room when she reached the main hall. Including Alexandre's. Upon seeing her, he bounded out of his seat and strode over. Isabel felt a tinge of humiliation wash over her as he took her hands and peered into her face. How she wished she had the strength to pretend nothing was altered between them after last night.

"My lady, I confess I did not expect to see you so soon. How are you feeling?"

She forced herself to return the gaze, trying hard to keep him from seeing more than she wished. "Better than of late." She tugged her hands out of his warm grip and glanced around the room. "I am looking for Matilde."

"I believe she is assisting the cooks."

"Yes, I should go help her," she said, hoping he would realize she wanted to be left alone. She began to move away.

"My lady, allow me to suggest an alternative." His voice called her back.

She stopped and inclined her head, waiting for

him to speak.

"Ride out with me. Give yourself time to recover."

Isabel arched an eyebrow. "Do I not look recovered?" She faced him, waiting for his appraisal. She loathed the way her body trembled as his stare moved over her with deliberate slowness.

"To some, but not to those who know you."

"And I suppose you think you know me?" She scoffed, but even she could hear how feeble it sounded.

He gave her a small smile. "I at least know how much you enjoy riding your horse."

A moment of indecision passed over her as her responsibilities warred with her sensibilities. Alexandre took her hesitation for an answer and drew her outside. He steered her toward the stables before she could protest. "It is a glorious day, is it not?"

Isabel surveyed the crisp blue sky with its smattering of clouds the texture of unspun sheep's wool. The sun shone brightly and tempered the gusty wind.

Alexandre led her into the stables. Their mounts stood waiting, already saddled. Isabel stiffened and looked askance at him. He had planned this ahead of time. Her fingers curled at her sides. How dare he presume she would comply with any of his suggestions?

She took a step back, poised to return to the hall, but Hardwin whinnied, drawing her gaze. Spoiled creature, she thought fondly as she patted his neck. She would ride for Hardwin's sake, not Alexandre's. Without a look at the meddling knight, she mounted and urged her horse out of the stables.

She let Hardwin have his head, and they wandered for a long while. She hardly cared Alexandre and his steed accompanied them. Her heart and mind were so full of feeling, she was only barely aware of what surrounded her.

They reached the apex of a small hill looking out across the muddy fields, her father's fortress in the distance. Isabel reined her horse to a stop. Both she and Alexandre stared out across the countryside, still dotted with melting swaths of snow, in a strangely companionable silence.

Isabel let out a soft sigh before turning to Alexandre. "I must apologize for my behavior last night. The report...upset me. I would ask you not make mention of the incident to anyone."

"You have my word, but you should not feel shamed by what happened."

"But I do, as it is just another weapon you can wield against me," she muttered to herself.

"I beg your pardon?"

Guilt pricked her, for she was being unfair. "What I should say is, you have my thanks. For sending out inquiries and for sending Matilde to me." The words felt woolly on her tongue, but they needed to be said.

"There is no need to thank me. I only hope you do not resent my interference."

A wry laugh escaped her. "Resent your interference? There is naught I can do to stop it."

He frowned. "Do I take it then my lady finally accepts my presence?"

Isabel looked away. "Only until we reach London." It would not be long now. After the feast, there would be nothing to keep her here.

"I do not think you realize how important it is for us to get along."

"What more do you want from me?"

"I want you to trust me. I am your friend in all this, and I could be more if you would let me."

Isabel flinched at his words, and heat crept up her

cheeks.

He ran a hand through his hair and sighed. "I do not want to fight anymore."

"What makes you think I do?"

"Need I list the examples?"

"*Non.* And I do trust you. I trust you are a determined, honorable man. And for that, I respect you."

"Yet you are still afraid of me."

Isabel squared her shoulders. "I am not afraid."

"Yes, you are. You feel threatened by me. You are scared I could release all the emotion you keep locked up inside."

"*Non!*"

"Yes. This is where all our hostility begins and ends. You are scared of losing control."

"I do not have to listen to this." She tugged at the reins and directed her horse away from him.

"You cannot ignore me. I will not let you." He commanded his temperamental mount to stay with hers.

She glared at him, at the determined set of his face. "Is that so?"

She brought her open palm down hard on the hindquarters of Alexandre's horse. Unused to such treatment outside of battle, the animal reared up, its front hooves flailing in the air. While Alexandre struggled to regain control, Isabel spurred her mount down the trail the way they had come.

\* \* \* \*

Her heart kicked against her chest as Alexandre's horse thundered past her hiding place. She needed to get herself under control before she returned to the castle.

The way he had looked at her was too similar to the last time they were alone. The kiss they shared after fighting the Welsh. She shuddered, remembering the way he had touched her, his hands warm, and the undeniable heat in his eyes. She was afraid. Afraid of what she felt. Afraid that Alex felt it, too.

Not Alex, but Alexandre, she scolded herself. To call him Alex was to concede the way she felt about him. It signaled she was softening toward him—something that could not happen. Yet she feared she was losing command, not just of her household but of herself—to him.

The day grew late, and she was chilled through. Certain Alexandre had not doubled back in his search for her, she urged Hardwin home.

In the quiet of the stables, she sent the stable boy away and removed her horse's saddle and blankets and proceeded to groom him. She almost dropped the comb when the stall door shut with a soft snap.

Alexandre. She should have known he would not be so easily discouraged.

"How did you know I—"

"You dismissed the stable boy. You always do."

A shiver stole through her. He had been watching her more carefully than she had realized.

He fell silent and picked up a comb to help her. Every so often, their hands brushed against one another as they worked over the horse, sending a frisson of awareness through Isabel each time. She forced herself to look Alexandre in the face, but he avoided her gaze and concentrated on the strokes of the comb.

Confusion welled up inside her. This man... Her hands stilled and fell to her sides. Alexandre came to a stop, watching her as he set the combs aside.

Hardwin tossed his mane in annoyance as Alexandre stepped around the horse and moved closer to Isabel, his blue eyes smoldering with an intensity that was not quite anger. She had never seen him look that way before. Apprehension slithered through her body. She involuntarily stepped back from him and found herself flat against the wooden panels of the stall.

"Thank you for your help, Alexandre. Now if you will excuse me…" She inwardly cursed the quaver in her voice.

"No, Isabel." He continued to stare at her, his look asking questions she did not understand. "I am not going to let you go so easily. Not yet."

She cast her gaze to the straw-strewn dirt floor. "I did not think you would."

He closed the gap between them. "I would never hurt you, Isabel. You do realize that?"

"I would not let you."

"Then why are you afraid?"

She stared up at him, not knowing what to say.

He placed his hands on the wall behind her and leaned in. "I wonder what you would do," he whispered in her ear, "if I did this?" He moved his lips over her forehead with feather-light pressure.

"Please stop." She braced herself against the wooden boards. Rough splinters dug into her palms.

"Or this?" He brushed his lips over her closed eyelids.

"*Non.*"

He paused, his lips hovering over her earlobe. "Why not, Isabel?"

"Because…" She hated how easily he could make her tremble.

"Tell me."

Isabel glared at him. "Because I do not want you to touch me."

"Liar," Alex scoffed, the earlier tenderness no match for his self-confidence.

Before she could think better of it, she struck him

across the face. Hard. He caught her hand in a viselike grip. Isabel willed herself not to cry out in pain. The slap echoed through the stables as they stared at one another, the only other sound the soft whicker of horses.

She slipped her other hand to her seax, but Alex anticipated her. He grabbed her arm and forced her against the stall once more. Alex's outraged gaze bored into hers. Isabel could do nothing but stare back, surprised by her loss of control, surprised by her desire.

In the next instant, Alex pressed his brutal lips to hers. The full impact of the kiss broke upon her and made her forget her protests. Then she kissed back. Alex groaned and gathered her up in his arms, pressed her against his long body. Wildfire spread down her limbs. He forced her mouth open, his lips hot and demanding against hers, allowing him better access.

Isabel shivered as Alex stroked the inside of her mouth with his tongue. She clung to his shoulders. He slid his hands down her back and explored her hips, his touch consuming her senses. She arched into him, enjoying the hardness of his body against hers.

The strange feelings Alex evoked overwhelmed her ability to think. She was certain of only one thing. She wanted more.

Too soon, Alex pulled back and set her away from him with his hands on her waist. "Do you still deny it, my lady?" he asked in a ragged voice. He watched her with hooded eyes as she tried to catch her breath. Her hair had tumbled down to her shoulders, thanks to his errant hands. Her face was hot with shame even though she gasped with newly awakened passion.

"*Non*," she whispered. She desperately tried to ignore the way his features relaxed in triumph.

"*Bon*." He pulled her close again, a predatory gleam in his eyes.

"But this cannot continue." Isabel squirmed out of his grasp and held up her hands, palms facing out. She took a deep breath, trying to dismiss the way her body ached for his touch. "Since you have more experience in these matters, I would ask that you refrain from demonstrating your affection for me as it has become apparent I am unable to deny you."

"I cannot pretend there is nothing between us," he said, a hint of danger in his voice.

"And what am I supposed to believe when I see a mere sword-for-hire attempting to seduce a thane's daughter?"

Alex's handsome face tightened with fury. "It is not like that, Isabel."

"Why should I believe you?"

"Because I am much more to you and to William than a borrowed sword, and you know it." He reached out to her.

"Do not touch me. I ask you to recall your own words. My family and I are to reach London unharmed. I ask you to remember your promise." Her voice grew stronger. "I appeal to your sense of honor."

"Curse you, Isabel Dumont!" He slammed his fist into the side of the stall. Hardwin snorted in surprise. Alex flexed his hand and took a steadying breath. "You may come to regret what you have said today once we reach London, my lady. I will not touch you for now, Isabel, but I will not leave you alone."

# Chapter 12

The evening meal was not going well.

With the household ban on speaking French now lifted, Isabel witnessed an uneasy truce gradually developing between her men and Alexandre's. However a handful of the older servants and men-at-arms remained particularly standoffish.

Kendrick, too, had not warmed to their Norman visitors. He was more withdrawn than usual, and it pained Isabel to think their interrupted conversation the other day the cause. She had been unable to speak with him privately since. Should she pretend he had not asked for her hand, that she was still ignorant of the love he felt for her? It might make things easier for both of them.

Then there was Alexandre's young and cocksure shield bearer. His constant scowl made his dislike of being around so many Englishmen clear, but from what she could tell, he did not hesitate to follow any of Alexandre's orders. For everyone else, the language difference between the Normans and her own men was a source of constant amusement. Laughter often floated toward her from the lower trenchers.

Perhaps most alarming was the friendship of sorts that had formed seemingly overnight between Alexandre and Captain Thomas. They chatted about the training of men, discussed military strategies and laughed over remembered conquests. The only positive aspect about the situation was they spent the majority of meals talking to one another, allowing Isabel a brief reprieve from the Norman's attentions. Plenty of time for her to reflect on all the ways Alexandre had encroached upon her life.

Time to be angered by her inability to stop it.

The food made no impact on her as she mentally reviewed the day's events to determine what still needed to be done for the feast in two day's time. Isabel left the hall as soon as she could politely excuse herself from the evening meal. For once, Alexandre gave her little argument.

Her thoughts weighed heavily as she moved past the diners and into the hallway. Soon she would be able to relax in her quarters. Her steps quickened.

"Isabel, a moment."

She froze as Kendrick's words cut through the darkened hall. She clutched her chest and willed her heart to slow to a normal pace. "You startled me."

He emerged from the shadows. "Forgive me." He must have been waiting for her to appear. "I would speak with you." His golden brows were drawn tight over his eyes.

"Certainly," she said, doing her best to regain her composure.

They walked in silence and stepped out into the bailey together. The chilly dark stole her breath after the warmth of the hall. The strikes of the blacksmith's hammer echoed around them. She hoped Kendrick would be quick, as she had no desire to linger out-of-doors.

Kendrick turned toward her. "I will be leaving Ashdown."

Isabel's breath left her in a rush. "What? But why?"

"I cannot stay here any longer." He gestured toward the hall. "Not while they are here."

"Have Alexandre and his men offended you in some way? Or is their Norman blood the problem?" She hoped such prejudice beneath him. After all, she was half-Norman herself.

He shook his head. "Nay, it is not what they have done, only what they stand for." He looked up at the night sky and then back at her, anger and something else simmering in his otherwise mild brown eyes. "I wish they had never come. They will ruin our land and our customs."

"Come now, I agree our guests have been bothersome, but they have not been aggressive, and they have respected our traditions. We should be thankful. Others have not been treated so fairly. My father—"

"Is not coming home," he finished for her.

She blinked back her surprise. "What do you mean?"

"He should have returned home by now."

She shook her head. "The weather could have worsened, or—"

"Do not lie to me, Isabel. How long have you known?"

She closed her eyes at his accusing tone. Her fingers ached, clenched at her sides.

"The tidings the messenger brought the other day." Kendrick said. "Were they tidings your father was dead?"

She finally opened her eyes. "Yes. Julien sent word of my father's death and his intentions to join Harold in fighting the Normans. That day the safety of our lands became my responsibility."

"So you ordered the scouting party."

"Yes, what little good that did." Her thoughts flew to Edgar, who had fallen in the first skirmish with the Welsh.

"When will you tell the others?"

Isabel sighed, her breath visible on the cold air. "Soon. I will make the announcement at the feast. It will matter not what Alexandre does then. I will make my excuses to William, and he will marry me off to one of his men. I can only hope I will be able to help our people adjust to a new Norman lord."

Kendrick gave her a tight nod. "And I will not stand by and watch you sacrifice yourself for such a life."

"I have no choice—" The flash of pain in his eyes had her cursing to herself. She had been so preoccupied with Alexandre's presence, she had unintentionally hurt Kendrick in the process. She held out her hands. "Kendrick, you must understand. I cherish your feelings for me, but I cannot return them. I cannot afford to be selfish. There is too much at stake."

"I know. Which is why I must go."

"Do not be foolish. My father's name will not protect you if you leave. Our Norman visitors have been understanding so far, but you know others will only see you as a conquered Englishman."

"It is better than staying here and watching you destroy yourself and your family's legacy out of a misplaced sense of duty."

The words were a slap to the face. "Kendrick..."

"My mind is firm. I will leave tonight." He glanced over his shoulder to ensure they were still alone. The next thing she knew, he pulled her into a hug, his beard pressing against her cheek. "Make sure Captain Thomas understands why I had to go. Be safe."

He released her and vanished into the stables. In moments, he reappeared, mounted. Isabel realized he had already prepared his things and had only come to tell her of his decision. She would not have been able to persuade him to stay. He gave her a short wave before he passed through the gates and into the night.

Isabel shivered, but she did nothing to warm herself as she watched him fade into the night. Gone, like so many others.

\* \* \* \*

Alex battled back his dislike of the young Kendrick as the man-at-arms directed his mount away from the Dumont castle. He would say good riddance, if not for the forlorn look on Isabel's face as she stood there, huddled in her cloak. Lovelorn or merely surprised? His fists clenched. He would learn the truth of her regard, once and for all.

"You will grow ill if you stay out here much longer." Alex came up behind her as the main gate swung shut.

Isabel gasped and whirled toward him. "Alexandre."

He peered into her face. "Where do your thoughts go?"

She stared up at him, mouth agape. His gaze fell to her lips as he waited for her to answer. She bristled and crossed her arms. "I was only thinking on how much I enjoy my solitude."

Alex frowned. Solitude? "Then what of your father's soldiers? You did not seem to mind Kendrick's company." The young man had been much too familiar with her.

Isabel gritted her teeth. "So now I cannot speak with my men without your permission?"

"*Non*, that is not what I meant," he said as gently as he could. "But I would know what he said to you. You are trembling."

Isabel shook her head. "Nothing you need to concern yourself with. I am merely cold."

Alex bit back his irritation and gestured to the gate. "I assume he is leaving. I saw your tender goodbyes. I do not understand why you think you should hide such things from me. I am here to help, as you well know."

Isabel scoffed. "Help? Is that what you call it?" She groaned and raised a hand to her temples. "You are right. He could not stay here any longer."

"And why is that?" He was pushing her, but he had to know.

She looked away. "It is personal."

"I may not know your language, but I know Kendrick did not leave here with your blessing."

"He did not," she said with a soft sigh. "I cannot protect him past these walls."

Alex followed her gaze to the gates before returning his attention to her. "He is man enough to protect himself," he said dismissively.

She shook her head. "He does not understand the position I am in. I thought because he accepted me and my father, he understood the reasons I must tolerate your presence here, why I must acknowledge William as my king."

"Then it is better he move on."

"You do not understand."

"I understand that he is in love with you," Alex bit out, ignoring her surprised gasp. "I understand that he hates me and my men for being here in Ashdown, for being here in England. And he hates that he is helpless to stop it. Do you deny it, Isabel?"

He said her name with a hint of possessiveness. Her face reddened. He stood close to her, very close. He could touch her if he wanted, feel her warmth and softness once again. He had been true to his word and not made any more advances toward her, but denying his attraction to her was a sore trial. Especially when he was certain she felt it too. If Kendrick was the reason she kept refusing him...

*143*

Alex took another step toward her. "Did he swear to protect you? Did he ask you to run away with him?"

"It was not like that."

Alex glared at her. "Tell me, do you return his feelings?" he said, his voice tight with frustration.

Her head snapped back toward him. "*Non.* He is dear to me like a brother, but nothing more."

He straightened his hunched shoulders. Her swift denial, the confusion in her eyes, set his mind at ease. The boy had Isabel's affection, nothing more. So why was she still so resistant to him?

Alex stared down at her, and her breath caught. He could affect her with just a look. Something primal stirred inside him. He would make her acknowledge the pull between them. "You are trying very hard, are you not? To ignore it?"

"What are you talking about?"

Her feigned ignorance did not fool him. "The way you look at me when you think I am not looking, the way you try to act as though I do not affect you, the way—"

Her cheeks darkened. "Enough! I told you never to speak to me of such things."

"*Non,* my lady, you did not. You said not to touch you, and I am not touching you, yet."

Though he was sorely tempted. He advanced upon her. A few scant inches separated them. He flexed his fingers, wanting nothing more but to crush her against him and silence her objections with more kisses. Isabel stepped back until she found herself against the outer wall of the hall. Still afraid. He did not want that.

He leaned in and gazed down at her. "Isabel," he said softly, "I cannot pretend I feel nothing for you."

He reached out a hand to touch her cheek, but dropped it to his side when she flinched.

She breathed deeply and drew herself up to full height, facing him head on. "I will not be drawn into another discussion about this, sir. There can be nothing between us, and I would suggest you accustom yourself to the idea."

She slipped past him.

"Isabel..." he called after her.

She turned, her face cloaked in shadow. "You of all people should know what awaits me in London," she said slowly, taking care with each word. "Do not make the situation any more difficult."

He straightened as her meaning washed over him. She was not denying her attraction to him. She only refused to see where it led, when, as far as she knew, William would marry her off to another.

Admirable. And infuriating. The truth clamored to be told, but something held Alex back. Perhaps it was the dark look on her face, her forbidding tone. Or perhaps it was that selfish part of him that still wanted to see if he could win her for himself. No decrees, no mandates. Just a man and a woman, stripped of both duty and obligation.

He had to hope she would still be his as he watched her retreat inside the castle.

\* \* \* \*

Matilde worked the spinning wheel while Isabel bent over her embroidery, berating herself whenever she made a mistake. Sewing was not a favorite task of hers, but she did enjoy the peacefulness it brought her.

"So this is where you have been hiding," Alexandre said as he entered the solar.

Startled, Isabel stabbed her forefinger with the needle. She cursed and sucked on the injured digit as she glared up at him.

He stepped past her and stood near Matilde. "One of the serving girls from the kitchen needs assistance with some household matter, Matilde. I told her I would let you know."

"You are so kind for telling me, sir." She smiled at him and bobbed a curtsy.

Before leaving the room, Matilde gave Isabel a significant look she ignored by busying herself with her needlepoint. She highly doubted Matilde was needed in the kitchen or that any of the servants would dare approach Alexandre for such a trifle. They were too well trained. Matilde was blind when it came to the Norman knight, as if the man—

Oh no. With a frown, she eyed her work. She had missed her mark and needed to redo the stitch.

"My lady, such domesticity. I am surprised to not see you deficient in womanly tasks."

Isabel trembled at his teasing tone. "I have learned all the tasks necessary for the caring of this castle."

"As well as the unnecessary ones for a woman of your quality," he said. He held up his hand and counted off his fingers. "You read, you write. Matilde told me how your mother insisted you and your brother be educated. But then you also are skilled in horsemanship and weaponry. You handle all the household accounts, and I've heard from the cooks that the meat pies come out better after you've been in the kitchen. And now I see you embroider as well."

"Then let me be clear: I have learned all the tasks I deem necessary." His exuberance made her uncomfortable. Was he mocking her or was he actually surprised by her abilities?

"I must say I am impressed by the range of your interests," he said, not unkindly.

She frowned at him. "At least I serve my own."

He watched her for a moment, no doubt waiting for her to elaborate. She avoided his gaze and continued to stitch with careful attention.

He sighed and took another step toward her. "I suppose my lady thinks I am only serving William's interests by being here, no? Let me assure you by serving under his orders, I am achieving my own aims." He paused for a moment, as if gathering his thoughts. "I assume you are responsible for all of the beautiful tapestries gracing the hall and my chambers?"

She shook her head, but did not bother to look up. "*Non*, they are by my mother's hand. My work is but a mere shadow of hers."

"I heard from Matilde about your mother. It must have been difficult growing up without her."

Isabel bristled. "That was a long time ago." Her mother died in childbirth when she was seven. It still hurt to remember her warm smile, to imagine the confidences they could have shared now that she was older. Thinking about it, however, would not bring her back.

"Even so," he continued, "to be such a young girl when it happened... My mother passed away only a few years ago, and I still miss her."

"I am sorry for your loss," she managed to say before returning her attention to her work. She did not want to appear unfeeling but she had no desire to dredge up any more painful memories.

Alexandre watched her embroider in silence for another long moment before he spoke again. "I must apologize for my conduct last night."

The topic was an improvement, but not by much. Isabel strove to keep her eyes on her work. "It is already forgotten."

"For being such an intelligent woman, you enjoy forgetting a great many things."

She scowled and twisted away from him in an attempt to continue her sewing.

He leaned over her shoulder. "But what if I do not want to forget?" he whispered in her ear.

Isabel remained silent, willing herself to make one stitch at a time. And another. And another.

Alexandre sat beside her. "Why have you not yet married?" he asked, sounding genuinely curious.

She glanced up at him, uncertain what had prompted his question. "I have not met a man I could fully commit myself to," she said slowly.

"Surely your father could have found such a man."

"My father wanted me...wants me to marry a man of my choosing. Englishwomen can decide whether to accept a man's troth, and I had intended to do the same. With my father's blessing. But that was before Hastings..." Isabel's throat was suddenly dry and she could feel the telltale pressure behind her eyes.

"He must love you very much."

Isabel turned back to her sewing, but he was not put off.

"Have there been men who asked for your hand?"

"Yes," she answered in a huff. She was growing tired of such personal questions. The knight was determined, knowingly or not, to bring up every aspect of her life she strove so hard to ignore.

"And how did you find them?"

"Lacking."

Alexandre let out a short bark of laugher. "Are you so sure you could ever find a man you deem worthy?"

Isabel cleared her throat. "Sir, I must beg you to let me continue my work in peace."

"You know what I think? I believe it is not the men you find so distasteful but the idea of marriage itself."

"You are being ridiculous."

"No, no, my lady. I am only being honest. What are you waiting for? Is it riches you crave? More land?"

Isabel jumped to her feet. Her sewing fell forgotten to the floor. "I care for nothing but the freedom to love who I want!" She glowered at him and calmed herself. "I had hoped we could move on and be civil to one another but you are determined to be ill-mannered." She shook her head. "Now what was so important you had to invent more work for Matilde?"

He straightened at her charge. "I would ask if you would like to accompany me into the village this afternoon, but it seems you are already quite busy here."

"Yes." She tried to swallow her irritation at his interruption for such a trifle. "With all the people who will be in attendance tomorrow night, there is too much to be done to warrant a merry jaunt into the village."

He chuckled, a rich sound. "Merry jaunt, indeed. No, I just thought it would be best to get out from underfoot as your servants scurry about. I saw Captain Thomas earlier, and he could barely spare me a kind word."

"Do you ever deserve one?"

"Not everyone shares your high opinion of me," he said in a mild tone.

Isabel gave him a stern look. "You know very well what I think of you."

"Think? I have no idea what you think. I only know what you feel," he teased her.

"You mean annoyance, revulsion and loathing?" She tried to ignore the fact she was all alone with the confounding man. He was still able to unnerve her without even trying.

"*Non*. In fact, I believe it to be quite the opposite." She gave him a warning look, and grinning, he moved toward the door. "But I think we should speak no more on this subject in order to preserve the peace between us."

"That would be most intelligent of you. I had almost given up hope you could be reasonable."

\* \* \* \*

Isabel held up the linen table runner, turning it this way and that in the candlelight. She might not have her mother's mastery, but her handiwork was competent enough and would serve them well at the feast.

Indistinct shouts filtered into the room. She could not make out the words, but their urgency troubled her. She set aside her sewing and rushed down the stairs, the echoing cries growing louder with each step.

"A fire's broken out in one of the buildings in the village," a passing servant told her.

"Oh no!"

Fires were a too frequent hazard in the wooden houses and outbuildings of the town. That had been one of the reasons her father had insisted on reinforcing the Dumont castle and battlements with stone. The villagers did not have the same option, what with stonework still rare and even more expensive. Given the cold weather and the approaching feast, there were more people than usual staying in the village. With the overcrowding, she should have been prepared for something like this. She could only hope no one had been hurt.

She commanded one of the stable boys to saddle her horse since speed was of utmost importance. As soon as her mount was ready, she flew out the gates and down the road toward the village of Ashdown. Thick, black smoke stifled the sky. Thankfully, a steady breeze carried the worst of the smoke away to the east. Isabel entered the town and picked her way carefully along the streets to avoid villagers, who ran about in a panic.

Ahead, Alexandre's men and a few of hers were positioned on different sides of a small dwelling. Flames climbed up the exterior walls. Alexandre strode among the men shouting out commands in French. He had them organized with buckets of snow and water from the nearby stream, and their efforts soon reduced the blaze to a few stubborn flames. Once she was close enough, Isabel alighted from her horse and ran to Alexandre's side. "What happened?" She scanned the charred building, looking for anything the Normans might have overlooked.

Alexandre barely spared her a glance, too intent on the actions of his men. "From what I could understand, a group of children started a fire on the road too close to the house. Do not trouble yourself. The fire is almost out."

"Was anyone hurt? Anyone still inside?"

"We got the family out in time, and Hugh is tending one of the injured over there," he said with a touch of defensiveness. He pointed to a space well away from the blaze.

Isabel could see Hugh setting the broken arm of a young man who must have fallen in the confusion. A nearby knot of villagers uneasily watched the men heave a few more buckets of snow and water. Others helped by smothering the lingering flames with blankets and furs.

A few wisps of smoke were the only reminder the blaze. Isabel straightened her shoulders as relief coursed through her.

She took Alexandre's arm and made him face her. "Sir, I thank you. Thank you for responding so rapidly to the needs of my people."

Alexandre smiled faintly. "It was nothing, my

lady."

"Please give my thanks to your men. It is well deserved." Isabel looked at him closely for the first time. "You are burned." He had discarded his cloak, and part of his sleeve was singed, leaving behind patches of raw and blistered skin. Small cuts marked his hands. She took one in hers. "What is this?" Her gaze raked over his knuckles, which bled freely.

"Merely a trifle, Isabel." He snatched back his hand. "One of the cross beams fell on me when I was bringing out the old man."

Concern choked her as she imagined the ordeal. "You are a better man than I thought. Be sure Matilde treats you and the men for burns when you return to the castle."

Before he could respond, Isabel left to find the family who had so recently become homeless. After encouraging the cooper, his wife and their two children to stay at the castle until their home was repaired, Isabel trudged back to her mount. By now, charred rubble was the only evidence of fire. Alexandre's men had dispersed and the villagers returned to their work.

She sighed. What would have happened if Alexandre had not been there? Her thoughts flew to her future husband. Would William select a man who would be able to protect her people as successfully as Alexandre? She did not think so. She was terrified her betrothed would be uncaring or incompetent.

She was surprised to find Alex was neither.

# Chapter 13

Clad in her best dress and her mother's brooches, Isabel stepped toward the high table. A hush fell over the crowd of knights, thanes, soldiers and villagers who had assembled in the main hall. She came to a stop in front of her seat and looked out across the room, at the sea of people waiting for her to speak. Deep-seated terror lurched about in her stomach. She could only guess what her people's reaction would be. She had reviewed this moment over and over again in her mind but knew it was not going to be any easier in actuality.

"Well met, friends, neighbors, comrades. We meet at a curious time, where the mettle of the English will be tested by a new era under a new king. You have heard about William of Normandy's success at Hastings and the death of King Harold." As she spoke, Captain Thomas translated her speech to Alexandre, Hugh and Jerome standing nearby. "The Normans now rule this land, and we must accept that. We must trust our new rulers will see us through this time of sorrow to one of prosperity. And I believe that is possible, if we look to the future.

"I know there has been much sorrow. The passing of loved ones and the conquering of our country has had a profound impact on us all. And I am afraid I must bring you more sad tidings. Lord Bernard Dumont of Ashdown, thane to the king, and his son and heir, Julien, are dead." Isabel waited as alarm spread through the people, their surprised murmurs echoing throughout the hall.

Out of the corner of her eye, Isabel saw the look of astonishment on Alexandre's face, his hand suddenly clenching the hilt of the sword at his side. She forced herself to ignore him. "My father, Lord Dumont, died following the battle at Stamford Bridge. And I just learned from a recent report my brother Julien fell at Hastings.

"Because of this sad turn of events, it now falls to me to go to London and swear my allegiance to William. My escort will be Alexandre d'Évreux and his men, who have been heretofore our honored guests." Isabel gestured to the fuming knight before she looked back to her people. "While in London, I will most likely be asked to take some Norman lord as a husband."

A current of dismay traveled through the room.

Isabel shook her head and raised a hand for silence. "I do not wish this, but I also know it will be the way of things. When I return, we will have a new lord, but I beg you to remember you shall still have me as your mistress, and I hope that will give you some small comfort," she said in subdued tones.

"In the meantime," she resumed in a bolder voice, "we shall remain hopeful. Tonight we feast together." She raised her cup before her and waited as the others around her picked up theirs in salute. "Let us enjoy the food before us as we honor the past, and let us drink to our future."

Cheers, gradually building in volume, rose through the crowd. Isabel sank into her seat. Everyone was soon in his or her place, and the first platters of food were brought out.

"Excellent speech, my lady," Captain Thomas said to her in French, deliberately including their Norman guests.

She searched the faces below. "I cannot tell how upset they are."

"I am sure they are more than willing to be distracted from their sorrow by the feast," Alexandre said, sitting on the opposite side of Isabel. "But I keep forgetting how distracting my lady can be."

Isabel sighed. "I know how upset you are to learn of my father in this way, but—"

"I doubt that very much, Isabel," Alexandre interrupted. "How long have you known about your father?"

"I will not discuss this matter with you if you cannot behave in a reasonable manner. I will cause my people no further unease by publicly quarreling with you," she said.

Alexandre stabbed his eating dagger into the cut of roast duck lying on the platter before him. "How long, my lady?" he said, struggling to moderate the tone of his voice.

"My brother sent word the morning you arrived in Ashdown."

"You knew the entire time," he said.

"Yes." Isabel stared defiantly into his still-angry countenance. "I kept it a secret to ensure my people would be safe. I did not want the Normans to forget my father's lineage if and when they sought him out."

"That, my lady, is the only thing preventing me from clapping you in irons this moment."

"Alexandre, what could I have done otherwise?"

"You should have cooperated with me from the outset."

"I beg your pardon, but I had no reason to trust you. You are conquerors, and despite my bloodlines and connections, I could not be sure you would treat me honorably."

"I told you from the very beginning I would treat

you well. I am hurt you did not take my words to heart."

She wanted to throttle him for such arrogance. She had no way of knowing he would be true to his words. How could he not see that? "These are uncertain times, and you cannot fault me for being overly cautious," she said in clipped tones.

He studied her, his dark brows drawn down into a line over his eyes. "*Non*, I cannot fault you for that," he said after a moment. "But I must ask why you waited so long to tell me."

She sighed again. She could no longer put off the truth. "I wanted to ensure my people were prepared. I knew the moment I told you about my father, you would drag me off to London. I needed more time before I accepted whatever future William will no doubt plan for me."

He shook his head. "Isabel, that still does not explain—"

"I would speak of this no more, sir. You know," she said, allowing her resignation to imbue her voice. "You now know everything. Let that be enough. There is nothing to stop you from taking me to London. And we can leave tomorrow if you wish. I promise I will give you no more trouble."

"My lady, that is hardly a comfort. How do you expect me to trust anything you say?"

"Because I give you my word."

"What if that is not enough?" he demanded.

"Sir, I have other guests I must attend to." Isabel rose, stung by his unwillingness to believe her. She sought to visit with her father's vassals sitting further down the table, but Alexandre stayed her with a hand on her arm. His grip was firm but not painful.

"My lady, this discussion is not over."

Isabel inclined her head as she shook him off.

"Another time then."

\* \* \* \*

Alex watched her as she moved away. He resisted the impulse to look at his men for guidance. He knew they would be shaken and distrustful.

He was not surprised Lord Dumont was dead. In fact, at this point he would have been even more surprised if Dumont were still alive. It had been too long since anyone could account for him in this war-torn country. Alex had dreaded telling Isabel his suspicions, especially so soon after the report of her brother's death arrived. But for her to hide the truth from him? He had thought he had everything under control. He had assumed Isabel, despite her resistance, was beginning to see him more as an ally. That she still did not trust him was a blow to his pride. He had not anticipated the possibility of her lying to him—whatever her motivations. His attraction to the girl had blinded him from seeing the situation for what it was. And her ability to make him disregard his duties shook him to the core.

Captain Thomas scraped his chair closer to Alex's, interrupting his thoughts. "Alexandre, I am sorry if the announcement came as a surprise to you."

Alex smiled ruefully, as Hugh snorted in disbelief beside him. Alex gave his shield bearer a warning look before turning his attention to Captain Thomas. "I take it you were informed about the situation before tonight?"

Captain Thomas nodded. "Yes, I was there when Isabel received the news. I do not deny she should have told you sooner, but she had her own reasons for doing what she did."

"*Certainement.* And they included treating me like a fool."

"I am sure my lady did not intend that. As you

have probably realized, my lady felt threatened by you and your men's presence here. Without her father and brother for guidance and support, it was natural for her to be defensive. By withholding her father's death, Isabel thought she was rectifying the balance of power between you."

"There was no need. She could have confided in me at any time. She was in no danger."

"She did not know that and thought she was acting in her best interests," the older knight explained. "I believe you are taking this too personally."

"I hear what you are saying, Captain Thomas, but you cannot tell me she did not enjoy the prospect of getting the better of me."

Captain Thomas shook his head. "You misjudge her. She has been through a great deal and feels her responsibility to her people and her land most desperately."

"She makes too much of those responsibilities. I would have gladly shared in her troubles and helped her in her duties."

"You know nothing of the woman you have come to marry, do you?" Captain Thomas's tone held a touch of condemnation.

He sucked in his breath and felt Jerome start beside him. Alex recovered and cleared his throat. "You are very shrewd to have seen so much."

Captain Thomas waved him off. "I am not blind to the way you look at her. Nor am I blind to your intentions. You are hoping William will promise her to you after all this, are you not?"

Alex contemplated Captain Thomas for a moment, his fingers tightening over his eating dagger. Had Lord Dumont been alive, there would still be the matter of asking and granting, but now, with no one recognized under Norman law in a position to speak on

Isabel's behalf, it fell to the king to decide her fate.

And William had already made his intentions clear.

Alex felt Hugh's gaze on him and ignored it. "William would grant Isabel to me for my services."

"And is there a reason why you have chosen to keep my lady ignorant of this development?" Captain Thomas asked mildly.

Alex dropped the dagger onto the table with a clatter. "I did not think Isabel would be receptive to any match, based on what William told me. So I vowed to charm her myself. By doing that, I hoped she would not be so angry when the truth was made known."

Captain Thomas laughed, and Alex was hard-pressed to keep from hitting the man. "What is so funny?"

"Isabel will be furious, no matter how charming you have been. And I do not doubt you have been very charming. You must understand Isabel is not like other—"

"I have become well aware of that," Alex snapped. "But I thought I would be able to make a more favorable impression this way than if she had known the truth from the beginning. Can you honestly tell me she would have given me the chance if she felt forced into the situation?"

Captain Thomas was quiet for a moment. "*Non*, I cannot tell you that. Do not think I do not respect you for trying to win her over this way. I mean only to prepare you if all does not go well."

Alex ran a hand through his hair in agitation. "I know it is a risky gambit, but I do not want to repeat the mistakes of my parents. I cannot ignore William's offer of marriage despite my misgivings. I respect Isabel and I know we could have a strong future together if she is willing." He sighed and looked back at Captain Thomas. "What else can I do? You see how she reacts to me."

"Yes, I do, and that is the one thing in your favor."

"What do you mean?"

Captain Thomas took a breath and spread his hands apart. "Isabel is indeed affected by you. Most men of her acquaintance have been uninteresting and easily dismissible. You, sir, are neither, and as much as the two of you disagree, you would complement each other very well."

Alex nodded. "I know, but whenever I try and get her to realize it, she pulls away. I cannot reach her."

"Telling her what to think and feel is a grave mistake, and, despite your intentions, I have no doubt that is how she has interpreted your actions. She needs time to adjust to her feelings for you, and if you try to force her, she will fight you all the more."

"I do not have the time. She will know the truth in but a few days. And I do not want to kill the potential between us."

Captain Thomas shrugged. "You must let things develop naturally. Isabel will still be angry, but the less she feels manipulated, the better it will be for you."

The older knight moved to get up, but Alex stopped him. "I appreciate your counsel in this. I would ask you continue to remain silent on this matter. I have no desire to inform Isabel of the situation until it becomes necessary. I must still harbor the hope she will come around."

Captain Thomas nodded. "Be gentle with her. I cannot give you any promises, but I know Isabel is not blind to your quality. She is an intelligent woman, and I have every confidence she will see what you have to offer is much more than what some other untried, untested soldier from William's army will bring to her and this land."

The older knight walked away, and Alex turned to Hugh and Jerome. Hugh's face was nearly purple in the attempts of holding his tongue while Alex spoke with Captain Thomas. "Out with it," Alex said bleakly.

Hugh tried to look offended but failed. "There is certainly more to the old man than I thought."

Alex grimaced. "Too much, I expect."

"Do you think he approves?"

"I know not. If he truly opposed the match, I do not think he would be so encouraging."

"That was encouraging?" Jerome asked doubtfully. "What will you do?"

Alex sighed. "I do not know."

"You do not regret accepting William's offer, do you?" Hugh asked.

"*Non*, I just did not expect to wage another war so soon after Hastings."

Jerome looked up from his wine cup. "You mean with Lady Isabel?"

"Yes. I have bullied her too much. I suppose reparations are in order."

Hugh grinned. "I bet I know just what kind of reparations you'll give her, too."

Alex gave a short laugh, "*Non*, seduction will not win this for me."

"That may be, but at least you'll get a taste of heaven before hell breaks loose," Jerome said with a wink.

Alex shook his head. "Enough of this for tonight."

He surveyed the room. Many apprehensive faces had been replaced by smiling ones, faces both merry and increasingly flushed with drink. His gaze rested on Isabel, speaking with one of the guests across the room. As he watched her, he realized how tense and drawn she was. He felt his conscience snag and tried to ignore it. After a moment, she glanced up but quickly turned away as if embarrassed at being caught looking at him. He cursed to himself, knowing he was the cause of her discomfort.

He turned to Hugh and Jerome, and their smirking faces told him neither was ignorant of where his attention had wandered. "We should be celebrating along with everyone else," Alex said with forced joviality.

They refilled their wine goblets and clinked their cups together in a mock-toast.

"To heaven," Jerome said, grinning at Alex's unease.

Alex gave him a sharp look. "To hell, more likely."

\* \* \* \*

As the evening wore on, Isabel grew increasingly concerned at the prospect of dealing with more of Alexandre's accusations. He had not taken his eyes off her all night. At least that was how it felt from across the room as she spoke with her father's well-favored thanes and vassals and gave them assurances she did not believe.

Although she was exhausted, she refused to retire to her quarters. Not yet. It was still early. And she did not relish the idea of being found alone by Alexandre. He was probably all too eager to castigate her for her behavior...again. She tried to remind herself of the reasons why she felt her deception was necessary, but she forgot them all as she recalled his angry countenance.

The vassals and villagers had taken the news hard, but they clung to the opportunity to enjoy their time together now when there may not be another chance to do so in the future. Tonight, flagons of wine and barrels of ale flowed freely. Lute and fife filled the hall, and soon people joined in, clapping their hands and stepping in unison as they went through the dances. Everyone was so merry, it was hard for her to remain unaffected. She had even taken a turn around the room with Captain Thomas. Her happiness was bittersweet, though, as her thoughts lingered on her father and brother. And part of her wondered if some of Kendrick's resentment and anger would have been soothed had he been willing to stay and enjoy the feast. She chased those thoughts away and refilled her wine cup as the musicians prepared for another song.

Out of the corner of her eye, she could see servants and guests edging away. No one but Alexandre would be given such wide berth. She should have known she would not be able to escape him this night.

She turned around slowly, keenly aware of how many pairs of eyes were on them. She hoped the formal setting would prevent him from starting another argument, even as she prepared herself for more unpleasantness. When she was finally brave enough to meet his eyes, he surprised her. Gone was his earlier anger. All she could see in his face now was entreaty.

"My lady, would you give me the honor?"

Isabel could not, in courtesy, refuse. She nodded her assent. Alexandre set her cup aside and took her elbow, led her to a group of eager pairs.

The song started but Isabel did not hear it. All her attention was concentrated on her dance with Alexandre. At least he did not attempt to talk to her. Her mind already clouded with drink, she would have given away his effect on her through a stumbled reply. She feared there was not much doubt he already knew...

While dancing in circles, her body brushed up

against his. She was entirely too aware of the intensity in his eyes and his hands, gentle on her as they went through the steps. Heat rioted through her. Her senses rang with warning as she felt her resolve slip away.

The music finished. Isabel curtseyed as Alexandre bowed, his blue eyes unwavering.

One of the men, well into his cups, raised his glass for a toast, and the hall echoed with cheers. The spectacle momentarily stole Alexandre's attention away from her, and Isabel seized the opportunity to escape. In her confused state, she did not want to spend a moment longer in his disturbing company lest she make a fool of herself. She darted through the crowd.

Away from the revelry. Away from him.

She slipped up the stairs and went into the solar, shutting the door behind her with sincere relief. She lit a lone candle and looked about, suddenly at a loss as to what to do. She had nothing to hold over Alexandre anymore. She had no more secrets. No more lies to keep him at bay.

The door opened. Isabel spun around. Alexandre stood on the threshold, his unmistakable form outlined by the torch illuminating the hall behind him.

"Why have you left the festivities?" he asked.

Isabel tried to still her heartbeat, which galloped in her chest at his bold interruption. She struggled to find her voice. "I wanted to be alone."

"I did nothing to offend you, I hope."

"No," she said with a wry smile. "Not this time."

"I am relieved." Alexandre shut the door behind him. "I am sorry I lost my temper earlier. I should have offered you my condolences."

Isabel did not know what to say as he walked over to her. She was grateful he had not sought her out to renew their argument, but that did not explain his presence.

"I should also tell you how beautiful you look tonight, Isabel."

She tried to ignore the way her body softened at his compliment. She looked away, thankful for the darkness.

He came to a stop just as the flickering candlelight fell on him, the planes and hollows of his face standing out in sharp relief.

"Why are you here?" she asked.

"You should not be alone. You are dwelling on the past, no doubt. You should be thinking about your future and what our trip to London will bring."

"And what kind of future do I have?" she asked, not bothering to hide her bitterness.

He moved closer. Melting beeswax scented the air, his warm breath caressed her cheek and her heartbeat filled her ears—a rapid drumbeat that drowned out the lingering swells of the lute from the hall.

"We can find out together," he whispered.

She shook her head. "You know that is impossible."

"Isabel, please…. What holds you back?"

"Everything." Isabel held up her hands in exasperation. "All that I am."

"Not all."

Isabel gaped at him, too surprised to think of a rebuke.

"And it does not trouble you we may never get the opportunity again?" Alex asked.

"You cannot pursue me," she replied flatly. Her future was already set.

"Why not? Does someone else have your heart?"

She refused to meet his eyes. "*Non.*"

"Then that is all I need to know."

Something between them shifted. She did not

know what caused it, only that it was something she did not know how to stop. "But—"

"Isabel," he cut her off, "I cannot be convinced otherwise."

"You can only offer me passion, and that is not good enough." Even if I could consider you, she finished to herself.

"You are wrong, my lady. I have much more to offer."

"I believe you not." She wondered if she could move past him even as her body trembled under his gaze.

"Then let me show you," he said with a predatory growl.

He pulled her into his arms despite her lackluster protest and kissed her tenderly. The rush of feeling left her lightheaded, and she clung to him for balance, enjoying the way she felt in his arms in spite of herself.

He pulled back and watched her face. She looked up at him, trying to shake the fog from her mind. "Your promise..." she murmured.

Alex tensed under her hands. "I curse the day I made it! What we have between us is not going to go away."

He swooped down and seized her mouth. Isabel could not contain her ardent response as he drew his arms around her shoulders and crushed her to him. She swept her hands over his torso, hungry for the feel of him through the soft folds of his tunic. Alex found her waist and sought out her curves. She barely held back a moan as he kissed down her throat, his breath harsh against her ears. Quivering, she arched her neck against his warm mouth helplessly.

She wanted more of him. Curling her hands around his head, she directed his lips back to hers. He groaned and knocked aside her headrail as he dug his hands into her hair, renewing the kiss.

Alex maneuvered her against the wall and pressed his hips against hers, nudging her legs apart to accommodate him. A frisson of feminine awareness flooded her. She was well outside the realm of her experience, but she was in no condition to protest. She enjoyed every sensation far too much to think about the danger of their spiraling passion. Or the consequences...

Suddenly Alex was everywhere at once. Isabel gasped in surprise as he cupped her breast. An intense wave of passion gripped her. Wherever Alex touched, there was fire. The flames licked along her skin, charged up her limbs and enveloped her chest.

He consumed her, his ministrations growing increasingly urgent. He tugged down the neckline of her gown, revealing her soft breasts to his moist, hot mouth. Nothing had prepared her for the magnitude of the sensations he elicited as he suckled the taut peak of each breast. She writhed in his arms and could only urge his mouth up to hers.

The door banged open, revealing Alex's comrade Jerome. Blinded by the sudden infusion of light from the torch the Norman brandished, Isabel let out a soft cry and disentangled herself from Alex. She hastily slipped into the shadows and straightened her clothing.

"What is it?" Alex demanded as he stepped in front of Isabel.

"Two of the men have started brawling over one of the serving wenches." Jerome eyed Isabel and then looked at Alex. "It's grown too wild."

"I will be there in a moment," Alex said, slightly out of breath.

Jerome bowed and backed from the room, but not before he gave Alex a knowing look.

Alex turned to Isabel and caressed her cheek. She

gave into his touch for one brief moment before willing herself to move away. What would have happened if Jerome had not interrupted them? She shuddered. Too much.

She retrieved her headrail from where it had floated to the floor. Her fingers knotted around the lacy material. "Alex, we cannot—"

He reared back, his mouth an angry twist of lips. She fell quiet, unable to meet his eyes. "One day soon we will not be interrupted," he told her.

He strode to the door, and left her hoping he was right.

# Chapter 14

On the second day of their journey, a slow, soaking rain found them. Only the slight jingle of the harnesses, the creaking of saddles and the sound of the horses plodding through the snowmelt interrupted the silence. Isabel shifted uncomfortably in the saddle, trying to keep her legs from falling asleep.

They were certainly a grim little group. Some of the men's wits were still addled from the ale they enjoyed at the public house the night before, and the rain did naught to raise their spirits. All but two of Alexandre's men traveled with them to London, the others were tasked with monitoring the Dumont household in their absence.

Alex permitted Captain Thomas and Isabel's servant, Averill, to accompany them. She did not feel quite so alone with them at her side. Averill was probably more miserable than the others, being unused to riding horseback for long periods of time. The poor girl clung to one of the packhorses carrying extra supplies and provisions for camping. Isabel hoped they would come across another inn for the evening. The prospect of sleeping on the ground in the rain only deepened her foul mood.

Alex trusted her enough to travel with him to London as a free woman, without shackling her hands or keeping her horse on a lead. She also had possession of her sword and seax, which gave her some measure of relief. Nevertheless, she deliberately kept her distance from the man. Their encounter the night of the feast had left her raw and she could not quell her unease around him. He thankfully respected her need for solitude. It gave her plenty of time to think, an opportunity she simultaneously welcomed and cursed.

On the one hand, her trepidation would soon be at an end. It took a full four days to reach London from Ashdown on horseback, and once she met with William, all would be decided. Her only purpose would be to ensure her people did not suffer at the hands of her new Norman husband. There could be nothing more to her life. Her happiness would only be contingent on the health and prosperity of her people.

Perhaps if she had let her father arrange for her happiness well before now... No. She had not been ready then, no more than she was presently. And even if she had married some English lord, he would have been called to fight for Harold and stripped of his lands if he had managed to survive Hastings. If he had died, she would have been forced to remarry so her dower lands—her family's lands—would have gone to a Norman. The same situation she faced now.

She flicked the reins, thinking back on yesterday morning. Matilde had been tearful when they made their goodbyes. The elderly woman even offered to travel with them to provide Isabel support. Isabel knew the trip would be too much for her, but she was still touched by the gesture.

Instead, Isabel merely had shaken her head at Matilde's protests, given the older woman a hug. "I need you here."

Matilde had squeezed her hands in reply. "Be happy."

Isabel had not been able to hide a grimace at those words as she had straightened and turned to mount her horse, and the same expression marred her face now.

What would make her happy at this point? She did not know. Too much had changed, and Isabel doubted she could be the shining example her people needed right now. She locked away her bitterness and pain with the rest of the grief the past few weeks had brought her.

Despite her heavy thoughts, it was too easy to slip back into the madness that always consumed her in Alexandre's arms. When her morose musings became too much, she found herself remembering his words, his caresses, his kisses... She was embarrassed by her response to his continual assault on her senses, but she still craved so much more.

She recognized she could come to love him, and the thought added to her despair. He must know it too. It explained why he refused to leave her alone even though he, of all people, would know what William planned for unwed English heiresses. However, the promise they had together could be nothing more, since she would be the sacrificial lamb for one of William's knights. And she would not complicate matters by realizing the potential of one lover while being legally bound to another.

They rounded a bend in the road bordered by forest. The mud stretched on in front of them, no public house in sight. Isabel tried not to let her disappointment show. After an already long day of riding, she was eager for a break. Every time she moved, moisture seeped past her traveling cloak and further chilled her.

Alex steered his horse closer to hers so they were side by side. He held the reins in his left hand while with the right, he idly tapped the pommel of his sword. Still plagued by her treacherous thoughts, she did not want to acknowledge him. She kept her eyes straight ahead and willed Alex to move on, but he stayed with her, his silence disconcerting as the rain fell around them. Like her clothing, things between them were saturated, but with conflicting emotions, need and duty. Surely he felt it. She was growing tired of their games. It was past time for plain speaking.

An irritated growl escaped her, and she tightened her hands on the reins. "Please say whatever you have mind to," she snapped. She finally turned to him, surprised to find he was not even looking at her.

He raised his hand for silence, momentary annoyance flashing across his face. "Quiet," he whispered as he scoured the woods lining the road.

Isabel bristled at his dismissal. "Why—"

An arrow passed by her face with an unmistakable whoosh and became wedged in a nearby tree.

"Get down!" Alex grabbed her shoulder and forced her closer to Hardwin's neck so she would present a smaller target.

Alex's men urged their horses into a tight formation with a precise combination of commands using both their reins and the pressure of their legs to direct the animals. They circled around Isabel and Alex's mounts, holding their kite-shaped shields in from of them.

The men swiveled their heads, trying to locate the threat. Isabel's heartbeat drummed in her ears. Was there just one archer or more men hiding in the trees looming over either side of the road? Rain rolled down the men's helmets, dripping onto their chins and into the neck of their hauberks.

Alex drew his sword from his scabbard, and the rest of the men followed his example. He ordered two of the men to scout out the woods on either side of the road. Before they could dismount, more arrows whistled through the air, bouncing off the knights' armor. Isabel, without mail, did not welcome the thought of having another arrow lodged in her body.

And so soon.

Their attackers broke from the trees and came at them on foot, brandishing swords. Had Alex somehow known of the threat? Was that why he took up position by her?

Averill screamed. The knights on the perimeter spurred their horses forward. Alex commanded Hugh to protect Isabel and her servant, then his mount surged into the fray. Captain Thomas also stayed behind as the rest of the Normans engaged their attackers.

The arrows lessened. There was no question their attackers were English, given their clothes and shouts. Two men wielded axes while the rest relied on swords. She knew Alex and his men could not afford to be lenient on their attackers, but English retaliation against their conquerors was to be expected. She only hoped to avoid fighting against her father's soldiers and vassals.

"Do you recognize any of them?" she asked Captain Thomas in French.

"No, my lady."

"Very well." His words confirmed her assessment of the situation. She straightened and readied her blade, waiting uneasily for the moment she would need to act.

Averill whimpered, her knuckles white where she clutched the reins.

"It will be all right. Just mind Captain Thomas," Isabel said to her.

"I thought we got rid of these English fiends at Hastings," Hugh said beside her. She gave him a sharp look, but now was not the time for an argument.

"Probably what's left of Harold's forces," Captain Thomas allowed.

"Rebels, then?" Hugh asked.

Captain Thomas nodded and adjusted his shield.

The English were surprisingly nimble against the

mounted Norman knights. The road was only so wide, which made it difficult for Alex and his men to wheel their mounts around to attack.

Captain Thomas's muttered curse tore Isabel's gaze from the spectacle. She shifted in her seat to see what had caught his attention along the road behind them. More men poured out of the woods to surround them. "Stay here," she said to Averill.

"My lady, wait—"

Captain Thomas's words were lost as she urged her horse forward to engage the closest rebel. Dressed as a foot soldier, he wore a simple leather tunic that provided scant protection. He had no shield and only a rude blade to defend himself, but that did not stop him from meeting her first strike.

He pulled back to take another swing at her. She saw the blow coming and blocked it, knocking the man off-balance. Her sword plunged into his shoulder. He screamed, his eyes impossibly wide, as she wrenched it back. A threat no longer. She tried to tell herself she had no choice but to defend herself against her countrymen.

Hugh caught up to her and kicked his horse into a gallop, scattering the other renegades. Captain Thomas matched blows with an axe-wielding rebel. Isabel cringed each time the blade struck Thomas's shield with a sickening metallic clank.

She braved a glance over her shoulder. Alex and his men had largely dispatched the initial wave of attackers. Some rebels had fallen back to the woods while the rest were strewn around the road, their tunics stained with blood, rainwater and mud.

She whirled around. Hugh was now too far away for comfort, grappling with three Englishmen. Captain Thomas still traded blows with his opponent but seemed to be holding his own. Isabel urged her mount closer to Alex's shield bearer.

A particularly cruel blow to his arm nearly knocked Hugh from his seat. With a yell, she launched an attack on the nearest man. He pivoted away from Hugh to defend himself. The impact rattled up to her shoulder as she slammed her blade against his. Her old injury smarted, and she stifled a groan.

Hugh's sudden cry wrenched her attention away from her opponent. She watched helplessly as an Englishman hauled Hugh out of his saddle. Her breath left her in a rush. Just like poor Edgar had been dragged off his horse when the Welsh had attacked her and her men. She had not been able to help the unfortunate Englishman, but she vowed in that moment to protect Hugh.

She tightened her hand around her sword.

\* \* \* \*

After a brutal kick to the head, the last rebel sank to the ground, but Alex was not ready to celebrate. He urged his mount around and sought out Isabel. His stomach clenched at the sight of his hapless shield bearer unhorsed and in no position to protect her. Alex cursed. The fiends had tried to trap them on both fronts.

He dug his heels into his horse's sides.

Before he could render aid, Isabel was there, commanding her mount to rear in an impressive show of horsemanship. The animal's flailing hooves caught Hugh's attacker in the shoulder. The man dropped like a sack of flour, rolling away to avoid the horse as it came down on all fours. Heedless of the fallen Englishman, Isabel slid out of her saddle and rushed to Hugh's side.

The handful of remaining rebels fled into the woods after seeing Alex and the rest of his men advancing. Isabel examined Hugh's injuries while

Jerome dismounted to inspect the bodies. Another man collected the arrows strewn about the road.

Alex resisted the urge to dismount and crush Isabel in his arms. He already knew she would not appreciate the display of affection. Since the night of the feast, she had done an admirable job pretending he did not exist, but he knew she was simply struggling with her attraction to him and what it meant. He did not like keeping his distance, but would allow it for now. She would be his soon enough.

He forced his attention to more pressing matters. "Any survivors?" Alex asked, pushing off his helmet. The rain cooled his heated face.

Jerome dropped his hand from the last body and rose to his feet. He faced Alex and shook his head.

Alex nodded grimly, disappointed they would not be getting any answers. He turned to Hugh. "Get up," he said, ignoring Isabel's reproving glance.

Jerome returned to his mount. "What did they want?"

"I know not." Alex gave the trees bordering them a long look. The niggling sensation they were being followed had struck him after midday, but the evidence confirming his suspicions had come too late.

"One of the men shouted for them to fall back, and after that, they scattered into the woods," Captain Thomas reported.

"Do you think there are more of them?" Hugh slowly raised himself into the saddle.

"I do not care to find out," Alex said, still on edge. "Come. We must find an inn before it grows dark," he said with a last look at the bodies.

"If I remember, Aylesbury is but a few miles from here. And there should be an inn," Captain Thomas offered.

"Good." Alex nodded to the rest of the men, and

they readied their mounts.

They traveled at a brisker pace than before despite their exhaustion. No one wanted to risk another confrontation along the road. Only a few men suffered injuries in the battle, and those were minor enough to tend once they reached the relative safety of the public house.

Alex directed his mount back to Isabel's side, his mind still full of the image of her commanding her horse to rear. He glanced sidelong at her. The knuckles on her right hand bled freely. "You are hurt."

She looked down at her hand with a start. "Oh, it must have happened earlier."

He frowned. Hugh should have protected her.

"It does not bother me," she added carefully.

He nodded. "You did well."

It was inadequate praise—she had been magnificent—but he would never forgive himself if something happened to her. Even though she would be infuriated at his protectiveness, he would not apologize for his concern for her or his duty.

Alternating between a trot and a canter so they would not overly tax the horses, they soon reached Aylesbury. As Captain Thomas promised, the village had a public house. The knight negotiated their stay while Jerome oversaw the stabling of the horses in the inn's outbuildings.

"Hugh, a word," Alex called out as the others drifted inside. Once everyone else was out of earshot, he faced Hugh. "What happened back there?" he demanded

Hugh grunted. "Their numbers overwhelmed me."

Alex quirked a brow. That much was obvious. "I told you to protect Isabel, not get yourself killed."

"I am fine."

"Only because she came to your aid."

"I would have done without her interference," he said even as he covered the wound snaking up his forearm. A wound that would have been worse if Isabel had not been there.

"Then you would be dead." Alex shook his head. "You are too practiced a fighter to make mistakes like this. Let it not happen again. Isabel's well-being is too important."

Hugh eyed the muddy road. "I don't understand how you can say that after the other night. She lied to us—to you—about everything!" He finally raised his head, his eyes burning indignantly.

"Of that I am well aware."

"And you still plan to marry her, despite her treachery?"

"You know as well as I do why she felt the need to hide the truth about her father."

"Yes, but you are the only one who believes her. You are too busy lusting after the girl to see her for what she is."

He froze, anger and incredulity flaring through him. He glared at Hugh for a long moment, battling back his urge to hit him. Although the shield bearer glowered, he would not meet Alex's eyes. Hugh knew he had gone too far.

Alex took a deep breath. "You forget William has ordered us to escort Isabel and her father to London. He will be the one to decide if she deserves punishment for her actions," Alex said with a calmness he did not feel. "But for now, she is our responsibility and you will respect her, do you understand?"

He waited for Hugh's nod before he brushed past him and entered the inn.

* * * *

"Be still," Isabel said as she inspected Hugh's

forearm.

The shield bearer groaned in annoyance as Isabel dabbed at the deep cut running from wrist to elbow with a moist rag. The fool thought he did not need tending, but Isabel was not about to let a minor injury fester because of carelessness. Joining them at the table, Alex's men passed around tankards of ale while they waited for the innkeeper to serve them supper.

"I think you should have Captain Thomas ask whether there have been any incidents lately. Perhaps the hosteller can offer us some clues as to what happened today," Jerome said with a glance around the room.

"Perhaps," Alex allowed.

"It will be a waste of time," Hugh cut in. "I doubt he knows anything, and even if he does, why would he share it with us? These English dogs are all the same— full of lies and cowardice."

Isabel's head snapped up at Hugh's comments. "Who are you to make such judgments?" Hugh ignored her outburst while the other men struggled to keep their expressions neutral. She shook her head in disgust. "The English people have every right to be terrified after hearing how the Normans have savaged the countryside en route to London. And you wonder why they have not dealt honestly with you?" With each word her voice had grown in volume, punctuated by her hands furiously wrapping Hugh's arm.

He winced as she drew the bandage tight. "Leave off, woman." Hugh jerked his arm out of her hands.

"Not until I knock some sense into that Norman head of yours!"

"Enough." Edged with anger, Alex's deep voice ended their conversation. "It cannot hurt to ask," he ground out, his eyes on Hugh's mutinous face. "Lady Isabel is right. The English have no reason to trust us.

We must remember we have only conquered these people, not convinced them to respect us. We need to set an example for others to follow."

Isabel was relieved to see the men nodding at Alex's words. She knew he was their leader by rank, but at that moment, he also had showed leadership that did not rely on how well one could wield a sword or control a charger. He commanded with intelligence, tempered by a strong sense of honor. If more Normans were like Alex, perhaps the transition to Norman rule would go smoothly. She only hoped William would find such a man for her.

With one last glance at the belligerent man, Isabel got up and moved to the other side of the table. Sitting next to Captain Thomas on the bench, she busied herself with inspecting his shoulder.

The door to the inn slammed open. The candles on the table flickered at the sudden gust of air. Another group of Normans made their way to the fire to warm themselves. The leader, his armor of finer quality than that of his men, eyed Alex's table with interest. After alerting the innkeeper of their presence, he strode over to them.

"A relief to find a fellow countryman in this barbaric place. I am Captain Radolf."

Alex inclined his head. "Alexandre d'Évreux."

"Well met."

"And you. We are on our way to London to meet with William." Alex introduced the other knights. "We have had a tiring journey from Gloucestershire."

"It is not just weariness that plagues your men." The captain indicated Hugh's bandaged arm.

"*Non*," Alex said quickly. "A group of Englishmen attacked us on the road today."

"God's truth? We have been sent here to capture a band of rebels spotted in this area. William fears the remnants of Harold's forces will rise up against us. And we aim to stop them."

"That sounds like what we encountered today. Most were dressed like poor soldiers, armed with swords and axes."

"Yes, they have been targeting the Norman forces stationed in this area. No doubt they saw your group as another opportunity." The captain glanced along the table. His gaze rested on Isabel briefly before he returned his attention to Alex. "Any deaths?"

"Thankfully, no. Although I cannot say the same for the English," Alex said with a small grin.

Radolf's face brightened. "You saved us the trouble then. How far from here were you attacked?"

"Tomorrow, if you travel west a few miles, you will come across the spot. We did not want to risk caring for the bodies in case they came back with reinforcements."

"I am grateful to you." Radolf turned, spied one of the serving wenches and whistled for her attention. He pointed to himself then at Alex's table. "We will be dining together," he barked in French, gesturing with his hands. The girl eventually nodded in understanding, and soon enough served the table a simple stew.

Alex's men had spent too much time in English company in Ashdown and welcomed the chance to socialize with some of their people. After dining, Alex and Captain Thomas spoke with the Norman captain at a table nestled into the corner of the room, learning about the events that had transpired since Alex set out for Ashdown.

Isabel was left alone with the rest of the men as Averill, quite undone by the day's events, had already retired to the room they would share. Naturally, the conversation veered to the conquest and the battle with the rebels. Drink soon increased the men's boasting.

Why must male gatherings be so bloodthirsty? Did they not have enough of warfare? She still could not rid herself of the image of the young rebel's eyes, frozen open like a gutted fish, as her sword ran him through. She shivered.

She glanced around the room but did not feel it would be appropriate to draw the agitated servant girls into conversation. They were too busy fending off the men's increasingly intoxicated advances.

She slipped away from the table and made her way outside. The rain had finally stopped. The temperature had dropped considerably, but the chill was refreshing after the oppressive heat of the fireplace inside. She drew her cloak tighter and stared out at the darkness eddying around the edges of the torchlight. She could still hear the shouts of men from indoors. Their voices echoed eerily in the forlorn darkness.

She was not surprised when she felt Alex slip an arm around her shoulders and fold her into his warm embrace. He must have noted her absence and come looking for her. He bent down to see her face.

"You have been through a difficult time," he said softly.

An understatement, to be sure. Isabel nodded, struggling to keep her composure. She found herself watching the way his breath condensed around their faces, a warm caress on a cold night.

With Alex there beside her, it was hard to hold herself back. In the battle, she had raised her sword against her people. And to hear the Normans boast of their victory... She hated the circumstances that made her nothing more than a traitor to the English people.

"I am sorry I could not do more to protect you," Alex said.

"*Non*, that is not..." As she watched him, in one heart-stopping moment, she realized the magnitude of what she was going to lose by William's decision, and it went beyond her people, her lands, her home...

Alex pulled her closer, and Isabel arched her neck, eager for his kiss. Without thinking, she wrapped her arms around him, giving Alex better access to her willing mouth. It would have to be the last one, the one to last her the rest of her life.

Before the sensations completely carried her away, she pulled back, gasping and shaking her head, ashamed for giving into her needs, however fleetingly.

"Do not tell me *non*," he pleaded. He still held her close, his face pressed into her hair.

"I must. We cannot do this... I cannot do this." She tried to increase the distance between them.

"Why not?" he demanded. "Why do you keep holding back?"

He spoke sharply, and she replied with equal heat, "Because I have to!" She continued more quietly, "William is going to marry me off to one of his knights, and this," she said, gesturing helplessly to him, "this will only get in the way."

Alex shook his head and tried to interrupt, but she forestalled him. "I must do what is best for my people, and my feelings for you would be a distraction."

"Isabel, it does not have to be like that."

"You do not understand," she said. "William will decide—"

Alex straightened, his face set. "William has already decided," he said grimly. "You do not need to deny your feelings anymore because I am more than entitled to them."

"What do you mean?"

"William has already given you to me."

# Chapter 15

Alex's voice was a death sentence.

"Given you? He has already decided...as if I were a brood mare and not a person? And you knew about this?" With every successive word, Isabel's fury grew. Despite her feelings for Alex, this was not the way she wanted to be with him.

Alex raised his hands. "Isabel, let me explain."

"This is my future. I had every right to know!" Her voice almost broke. "How could you keep this from me?" She dug her hands into her skirt, gripping the fabric roughly so she would not give in to the urge to hit him.

"Because you would have never given me a chance!"

His accusing tone destroyed any remorse she may have had. "You do not know that," Isabel challenged, squaring her shoulders as she would against any other opponent.

He bent down so he could peer into her face. "Yes, I do. You would have done all in your power to push me away. And as it was, you very nearly did. I wanted the chance to win you on my own terms before you felt forced into the situation." He looked out into the night, a muscle in his jaw working. "I know it is commonplace for arranged marriages, but I saw first-hand the bitterness and grief such unions caused. I did not want that for us." He swung back around, facing her head on. "I wanted to give us a fighting chance."

She stepped back. Away from him. Away from the yearning in his eyes.

"So that is why you would not leave me alone," she said, evaluating every past encounter with Alex in a new light. Anger and uncertainty bolted up her spine. Every word he uttered now smacked of deception. Was it all a ruse? Was naught real to him?

"That is the problem, Isabel. You only know how to be alone. You pushed me away, just like you push away everyone else."

She shook her head. Surely she was imagining the wistfulness in his voice. "That is not true."

"Yes, it is." He stepped toward her, a hand span separating them. "Your father and brother are gone. You are too Norman for your own people and too English for your conquerors. But you are not alone in all this. Not anymore."

She scoffed. "Because of you?"

"Yes, because of me. You are bound to me whether you like it or not. Together we can help your people adapt to Norman rule."

"I do not need your help."

"Yes, you do! Would you rather have another of William's knights take command and potentially destroy everything you and your father created in Ashdown? I have seen how much you care. I have seen your people through your eyes, seen their quality. Do you think another man will give them that chance? Do you think another man will respect your counsel? I am more than prepared to give you my protection, my name and my respect. Accept my troth and let me help you. If you will allow yourself, you will see how much we will give to each other."

"You only want me to give you my lands, a conqueror's decree." He would not fool her again.

"God's truth, Isabel, I will admit I set sail with

William to better my lot. You can hardly blame me for taking the only chance available to me," Alex said, the hurt clear in his voice. "And yes, William promised you to me as a reward for my services in the campaign, but you must look beyond that." He reached out to her and put his hands on her shoulders. "Because you are more to me than a reward. You are just as much a new beginning for me as I am for you."

Isabel tried to pull away. He could not touch her. Not now, not with all this between them, but he held her fast.

"No, look at me. Listen." Alex's voice pleaded with her. "We complement each other perfectly. How can you be so blind to it, to us?"

She forced herself to blink, to sever whatever hold his eyes had over her. "I beg your pardon for being so blinded by your lies." Isabel finally succeeded in shaking him off. She crossed her arms, scowling at Alex in the darkness.

He shook his head. "Do not profess your innocence in all this, my dear. You lied to me countless times. And your mistruths have higher penalties associated with them. A less understanding man could interpret them as treason." He gave her a considering look. "You should thank me for being so forgiving."

"I lied to protect my people. You lied to protect yourself. The difference is clear."

"We both know you were the one who needed more time to come to terms with what happened," he said, his voice heavy with condemnation. "You needed the reprieve. The interests of your people were only a handy justification."

Isabel almost choked on her rage. "How dare you say that!"

"I dare because I am right. How many more excuses are you going to levy at me, Isabel? You and I already know that deep down you are relieved." He reached out again and cupped her cheek. The touch bruised her heart. "Relieved that it will be me and not some brute or lackwit."

He spoke the truth, but Isabel's realization of it threatened her already tenuous control of the situation. "I hardly see the difference."

"I will show you what the difference is," he growled, moving closer to her.

She pulled back, sensing his intentions. "Do not touch me."

"Isabel, we belong to each other."

She continued to back away, shaking her head, resolve stiffening her frame. "Not yet. Not if I can put a stop to it."

"If you would calm down, you will realize what an opportunity this is." He took another step toward her.

"Do not," Isabel said in a steely voice. Her hand hovered over the hilt of her seax. "I have killed men less deserving than you."

Alex stared at her in outrage but nonetheless heeded her. "Come now, you must see reason."

"Do not tempt me, Alex."

He eyed her sword arm warily. "You know I would not hurt you…"

Isabel's resolve slipped. "How can I be sure?" she cried. "You have hidden your true reason for coming into my life. You once asked for my trust, and now you have completely lost it. As far as I know, you are the devil himself," she said, her voice hardening. "And I vow to keep you away from me and my people."

"Nonsense. Nothing has changed. I am still the man you know."

"*Non*, you are not."

Alex shook his head in protest. "Enough of this or

I will—"

"Or you will what? Kiss me against my will? Rape me to prove your claim?"

Alex stood, aghast, for one long moment. "How could you even suggest such a thing? What we have between us is—"

"There is nothing between us."

Alex held up his hand for silence, his voice heavy with repressed fury. "I have heard enough, my lady. I will not waste any more of my efforts trying to convince you a match between us would be ideal. That is for you and William to discuss. My feelings toward you, my intentions, have always been honorable. I have come to care too much for you for them to be otherwise." He pointed to the inn, hardly looking at her. "You must get some rest. We have two more days of hard riding ahead of us."

"Alex..." she whispered, but she had no idea what she would say.

He turned away from her to look into the night. "Just go."

\* \* \* \*

Isabel had long been awake before Captain Thomas's soft rap interrupted the morning stillness. A night of fitful sleep failed to soothe her fury at Alex's deception. The rope-slung mattress was no better than a night on the hard ground. Once she heard the servants moving about, she dismissed Averill and dressed in her traveling clothes. The only armor she had to face the day, and Alexandre.

She bid Captain Thomas enter. He eyed her clothes and her packed saddlebags, which rested beside her on the bed, but made no comment. "The men will be ready soon."

"Very well." She rose to her feet and shook the skirt of her riding dress into place.

Captain Thomas nodded and moved to leave, but Isabel forestalled him.

"I would speak to you, Captain Thomas, if you have the time."

"Certainly, my lady." He searched her face and shut the door behind him. "What is troubling you?"

Isabel took a deep breath and started to slowly pace across the wooden floorboards. "I am to be married."

"I know. We have already assumed as much."

"It is to be William's choice," Isabel continued.

"Yes, I am afraid that will no doubt be the case," he said, his gaze wary as he tracked her around the room.

"I had hoped he would be reasonable and allow me some input, but it is too late."

"Why do you say that?" he asked. "You have not even met with him yet."

She stopped and whirled toward Captain Thomas. "Because Alexandre has already informed me of William's decision—him." The disgust in her voice left no doubt as to which him she referred to but the old knight made no reply and only raised an eyebrow.

"I could barely stand his impudence when he told me," she said. "Of all the men to choose, William picked Alexandre."

"Are you more upset William has made a decision or that he decided on Alexandre?"

Isabel sputtered for a moment, taken aback by the question. "But are you not surprised?" she asked.

Captain Thomas chuckled. "Surprised? Not at all. Indeed, my dear, I am surprised you did not see such a possibility yourself."

"How did you know?"

"It became obvious to me when Alexandre not only tolerated your appalling behavior but provoked you at every opportunity. I assumed your..." he trailed off, searching for the right word, "...passionate nature intrigued him."

Heat suffused her face. She scowled at Captain Thomas. "Why did you not inform me of your suspicions?"

"My lady, why did you not form your own?"

His words stung her in their clarity. She started to answer and then shut her mouth with a teeth-rattling click. Originally, she had interpreted Alex's interest in her as one of the hazards of being a woman alone among battle-weary men. Then she had felt his interest in her was spurred on by the challenge she posed to his manly pride. Alex had made his feelings toward her known, but she had not considered him a feasible choice for a suitor. However, just when she thought his regard for her went deeper, she had learned he only wanted to win her favor so she would blindly agree to marry him when William proposed the match.

She shook her head, pacing the room in agitation once more. She had not expected Alex to be her betrothed. She was worthy of men well above an escort's station, but Alex had shown on countless occasions the extent of his merit, and William needed to reward such men for their competence, honor and loyalty. But why did it have to be her? Her father had told her stories of how fickle William could be, and she should have been prepared for such a surprise.

She dragged her thoughts back to Captain Thomas, wanting to protest her ignorance, but he was already speaking, oblivious to her preoccupation. "The signs were there, Isabel, but you would not see them. You wanted to pretend William would treat you like your father did and let you do whatever you willed. Knowing all the difficulties you have faced these weeks, I thought it cruel to disabuse you of such notions. Forgive me for not saying something sooner."

Did Captain Thomas think she was not strong enough for the truth? Isabel shook her head in disbelief. "Did you not think I should be prepared for this turn of events? That after all the upheaval, the chance to have my future's uncertainty made certain would not bring some small comfort to my life?"

Captain Thomas raised his hands. "Isabel, would it have made a difference if you knew now or a week ago? Answer me truthfully, girl."

She held his gaze for a moment, then looked away. "No, I suppose not. But Alexandre, of all people." She pushed a stray lock of hair away from her face. "I have been such a fool."

"Now, now. It is not so bad."

"It is. He deceived me, lied about his intentions. And I was none the wiser. How could I ever trust a man like that, let alone marry him and grant him reign over my people?"

"I cannot speak as to why Alexandre misrepresented the truth of things between you. That is something you will need to ask him yourself, but I am certain you can learn to trust him, Isabel. Just as he will have to learn how to behave with you."

"He would do well to learn to leave me alone." As she spoke the words, Alex's words the night before echoed in her head. Alone. She was utterly alone, was she not? No family, an uncertain future. Both English and Norman, and neither at the same time.

"That will not happen and you well know it." Captain Thomas watched her for a moment, letting the silence fill the space between them. He shook his head. "I do not understand where all this hostility is coming from, my dear. I have seen the way you two interact. Despite your anger at how Alexandre handled the situation, some part of you must know your true feelings for him."

"You are mistaken." She put all her anger at Captain Thomas and his well-intentioned and entirely too truthful words into her voice.

"I am not, my dear. And it is high time you sort out your feelings on the subject before your audience with William. He will not be so tolerant with your meager excuses."

Isabel glared at him, but he just gazed unapologetically back. He finally cleared his throat and headed to the door. "I will check on the horses," he threw over his shoulder.

She gritted her teeth as the door slammed shut behind the knight. Isabel knew she should not be fighting with Captain Thomas when her real complaint was with Alexandre. However, the knowledge did nothing to soothe her ire. As she picked up her saddlebags, a wave of helplessness threatened to engulf her, but she fought it. She still had her meeting with William to contend with, and she would not see her people punished for her behavior.

With newfound resolve, she donned her traveling cloak and made her way to the stables.

* * * *

When they reached the outskirts of London, the late afternoon sun smoldered behind low clouds. Just as Alex warned, it had been two exhausting days in the saddle. Alex had set a grueling pace that pushed the limits of the horses' abilities. Even Isabel, an experienced horsewoman, was sore and tired from their journey. Though she soon forgot about her mild aches as they made their way toward William's quarters in London.

Seeing the condition of the town put uncomfortable pressure on her chest. Whole rows of buildings, shops and houses alike, were burned to the ground, the rubble in turn sheltering every creature of the town. Injured and sickly people crowded the streets. Norman soldiers patrolled the area, too often picking fights with the English townsfolk.

The crowds, the smells, the cacophony overwhelmed her senses. She looked forward to the chance to get off the streets and away from the soldiers who sneered at her English garb but appraised her figure. The displaced English people milling the streets either begged her for coin or cursed at her for joining with the Normans. All too aware of the attention Isabel received, Alex ordered the men to flank her and Averill, but every so often, some nimble fellow would break through their ranks to beg, barter or blaspheme.

An acquaintance of Alexandre's—another of William's knights—happened upon them and joined their party as they carried on to the motte and bailey style castle William had hastily erected as soon as he had claimed London. He told Alex the cramped conditions at the castle had forced many of William's men to take rooms at common houses. Getting an appointment with William was also problematic. He spent much of his time handling various disputes with the London townspeople or meeting with the obsequious English nobility who continued to funnel into the city to pay homage. All of William's men, now that the fighting was over, expected to learn whether their rewards comprised of lands, riches or titles.

As Isabel listened to the men talk, she realized she had not been the only one who wanted to know her future. All of the Norman soldiers had placed their hopes in William's hands as well. That was true power, to control the destinies of so many.

When they reached the bailey, a servant directed Isabel and Averill away from the men and horses to the room Alex managed to procure. Alex must have been more important to William than she had been led to believe if he was granted rooms in the castle. Even if some parts of it were still under construction. It certainly was not on her account. Despite her father's friendship with William, he would be foolish to treat her differently than the rest of the conquered.

Before long, a servant brought her a small basin of hot water and some fresh linens. Another pleasant surprise. It felt good to clean away the smell of horse and the dirt of the road. She donned one of her simpler gowns and smoothed her cloak into place.

As she ran a hand over her mother's brooches, fear lanced through her. All of William's men would be converging in the great hall for supper. Dare she join them? Would she, English-born but Norman-blooded, be welcomed to walk among the men who had shaped the fate of her country? She quailed at the idea. Her bravado with Alex was just that, and Isabel was afraid it would not stand up to an entire room of Norman men, let alone the very presence of William.

Alex knocked on her door once and then walked in. Isabel clutched a hand to her chest and urged her heartbeat to slow when she realized who her guest was. Averill hovered in the corner of the room, her attempts at unpacking halted.

Being with Alex again brought back too many memories. Before Isabel could address him, he spoke. "My lady, I would escort you to the evening meal."

Hesitating for only an instant, Isabel nodded. "I will be but a moment." She walked toward her bed and reached for her seax and sword, which she had not yet had the chance to don.

"You will not need those." Alex's voice interrupted her actions. "I do not want you to attract any more attention than necessary."

"I understand." Suppressing a frown, Isabel let

her hand linger on the hilt of her sword briefly before following him into the hall. She felt naked and vulnerable without her weapons, and her proximity to Alex only intensified her apprehension. She wanted to pretend she did not need him to navigate William's inner circle, but she could not afford to ignore him, not when the stakes were so high.

After a moment, he cleared his throat. "I hope your room is suitable."

"Yes. It is." It seemed an inadequate, even ungracious answer, but she let the silence between them fall.

"I am sharing a room with some of the other knights down the hall from you if you have need of me."

"And Captain Thomas and the others?" Isabel asked.

"They were forced to find lodgings in town. I had a hard enough time securing our rooms."

"I see."

They came to a short flight of stairs, and after they descended, Isabel recognized the raucous laughter and shouts for more meat and ale—unmistakable sounds of a feast already in progress.

Alex placed her hand on his arm, and she let him. He watched her for a moment. "Isabel, there is nothing to be afraid of."

She wanted to deny it. She faced him, a tart reply at the ready, but then thought better of it. "You are not the one walking into the lion's den."

Alex chuckled softly. "No one will bother you. Not if you are with me," he said with a wink. He stopped, his face suddenly serious. He turned Isabel toward him, his hands heavy on her shoulders. "It would be wise to stay by my side or with my men while we are in London. I do not want you to have any difficulties with the soldiers."

The intensity of his gaze fooled her into thinking he would kiss here right there and then. She knew she should say something, push him away... She should do any number of things to let him know he had no hold over her. Not after he had lied to her.

Before Isabel could react, Alex took her arm again and they walked into the hall together. She breathed a sigh of relief when she realized William was not in attendance. They wound their way around the many tables filled with reveling Normans. There were only a few women who were not servants scattered around the hall, probably sisters and daughters of English nobles seeking clemency. Cringing at all the attention she was getting, Isabel realized she was no better.

Alex finally led her to one of the upper tables where Hugh waited for them. Isabel was surprised at how glad she was to see Alex's taciturn shield bearer. He was a veritable prince among the drunken unknowns who filled the room.

Hugh and Alex sat on either side of her, a comforting buffer between her and the rest of the main hall. She ate her meal in relative peace and let conversation wash over her. She learned where Hugh, Captain Thomas and the rest of the men were staying. Alex also told her and Hugh his meeting with William would be in four days' time. In the interim, Alex would have to attend various meetings and councils.

Four days. An eternity. The sooner she met with the new king, the sooner they could return to Ashdown. What if the Welsh attacked again while she was stuck in London? But she was the one who had delayed the journey, was she not? If anything happened in Ashdown while they were away, the blame would lie with her.

As the meal continued, Isabel watched the people around the room, all unmistakably Norman, unmistakably male. She watched them eat, laugh and drink. A few gazes lingered on her but most attendees were indifferent to her scrutiny. She could not help but compare the other Normans to Alex. Even in a room full of men, she was still aware of him and his every action. He sat so close to her, the heat of his body sank through the fabric of her dress to her skin. But he never touched her except when they both reached for the wine cup they shared at the same time. Seeing her start, he pulled back and let her drink first.

Even though it was difficult to make sense of the man who would soon be her husband, she could not deny Alex's quality. His was the first face she turned to when she entered a room. His voice stood out even when he was among other boisterous men. His image remained ingrained in her mind whenever she closed her eyes.

He had invaded her life in so many ways.

At one point Alex must have felt her eyes on him. He leaned toward her. "Is something wrong?"

She hastily looked away from him. "I do not think so."

# Chapter 16

"Oh, my lady, look at this one." Averill held out a bolt of silk just as fine as the last four she had pointed to.

It mattered not Norman soldiers patrolled the streets, the girl was making the most of her first visit to London. She gaped with childlike wonder at the street vendors and merchants, where ready coin, not country of origin, was the only currency.

"Yes, yes. Very nice." Isabel craned her neck to see where the men had gotten to in the crowd. She spotted Captain Thomas's gray head and the downturn of Hugh's mouth a few stalls ahead. "Come along," she said to Averill. She pretended not to see the girl's pout reflected on the silk merchant's face as she pushed forward through the crush of bodies.

The smell of freshly baked bread warred with tallow and smoke. Always smoke.

"Need you a good luck potion, miss?"

"Fresh meat pies. Piping hot."

"Old Mildred's remedies will cure all that ails you."

Isabel ignored the shouts and kept moving. Ahead, Captain Thomas conversed with another Englishman while Hugh stood off to the side, tapping his foot.

Alex let her borrow Hugh and Captain Thomas for the day to see if they could locate any of her father's men. She was not content to simply wait in her room and idle away her time behind the still-incomplete walls of William's castle. But even flanked by men and joined by Averill, she felt like she had a target on her back, earning looks both English and Norman as she walked the streets.

Hugh straightened, but his scowl deepened when he saw her and Averill approach. "What did I say about wandering off?"

There was no pleasing the man this day. Isabel did not answer and turned to Captain Thomas, who had finished his conversation. "Any tidings?"

"No, my lady."

She sighed. Despite their inquiries, no one had been able to confirm Julien's death, though they learned he had fought in a contingent ripped apart by the Norman cavalry. The gruesome tales, when pieced together with bits she overheard from Alex and his men, added to her disappointment the conquest had been so brutal. They had not found any more Dumont men, but she did not expect them to stay in London if they avoided injury in battle and evaded capture. Perhaps the ones who were still alive would make it back to Ashdown undetected, a small chance that.

Sunset was not far away and although she was certain Averill would not turn down the chance to see more of the town, exhaustion was starting to creep across the serving girl's face. It had been a long day for all of them.

She met Captain Thomas's gaze. "We should head back."

Without a word, Hugh set off.

"What troubles him?" Averill asked as she struggled to keep up.

"Hugh does not like playing nurse, I expect," Isabel said.

Captain Thomas's lips curved upward, but he did

not say anything as they retraced their steps.

When they neared William's fortress, Isabel spied a young Englishwoman pleading with two Norman soldiers in full mail stationed in front of the gates.

"My boy. Please, have you seen my boy?" she asked in poorly-phrased French. She could not have been much older than Isabel. The Normans sneered at her and shook their heads, exuding an air of self-importance that could only result from the security and superiority they felt on conquered soil.

"Please, I beg you." The woman grabbed the arm of the nearest soldier, a tall man with a healing cut along his cheek, but he shoved her away. She wept as she approached them again. He backhanded her across the face before she had a chance to speak.

She collapsed on the ground.

"I told you we have not set eyes on your spawn." The soldier looked to his partner, a stout man with a round face, and laughed cruelly. "But if you want a babe so badly, that can be arranged."

How dare they! Isabel quickened her steps. She was not blind to the tension between the townspeople and the Norman soldiers, but this was simply too much.

Hugh caught the sleeve of her dress. "Not this time."

"You would let them attack a defenseless woman?"

"If she's making a nuisance of herself, they have the right to discipline her."

She shook him off. "Then you are a greater fool than I thought, Hugh de Roche."

Ignoring his protests, she hurried over and helped the woman off the ground. Isabel faced the two Norman soldiers. "What is the problem?"

The woman fell to her knees, clutching Isabel's skirt. "Oh, my lady, please. My boy has run off. I cannot find him anywhere," she said between sobs.

"And why have you troubled William's men with this?" she asked the woman, though her gaze did not leave the soldiers' faces. Captain Thomas came up next to her, offering silent support. Averill stood wringing her hands next to Hugh, who made no move to intervene.

"Because my son fancies the horses, my lady. He's not yet six and the beasts are all he can talk…talk about." The woman gulped out the words, her face streaked with dust and tears.

"And you think he tried to get into William's stables?"

"Yes, my lady."

Isabel translated the woman's words into French. Enamored by William and his men on their chargers as they paraded the streets of London, the boy probably snuck past the gates when no one was looking or dashed through the servants' entrance. And his mother, being English, would not be allowed past to search for him.

She looked to Captain Thomas and Hugh. Alex's shield bearer held up his hands. "Fine. We'll search for the brat." The shorter of the two soldiers admitted them into the bailey. She hoped the boy was easily found for she had no desire to prolong her standoff with William's men.

Isabel encouraged the woman to stand. She should not have to grovel any more today. A purpling bruise had already bloomed across her cheek.

She turned to the soldiers. "Look what you have done." She pointed to the woman's face. "Is that how you treat a woman asking for your help?"

"How were we supposed to know what she wanted? She sounds like a pig with all her grunting," the shorter one said.

The taller of the two took a step toward her. "Nothing like your dulcet voice."

"You knew she was upset. You should not have treated her so poorly."

He leaned forward like a dog tied to a rope. "She needed to be taught respect." His scabbed-over cut contorted as he spoke.

The shorter one held up a hand. "No one gets in without our say so."

Isabel shook her head. "You can still do your duty without attacking the defenseless."

The tall soldier scoffed. "What would you know?"

Isabel stepped in front of the still-sniveling Englishwoman. "I know William ordered you to use restraint against women and children. And you have done the opposite."

The soldier lunged forward and grabbed her, slammed her up against the wooden wall. Someone screamed. More townspeople gathered on the street, their attention riveted on Isabel's confrontation with the Norman soldier.

"Bitch, you should know when to keep quiet."

Her hand went to her waist, but there was nothing to grab. Her sword and seax were still in her room. Dread filled her as she remembered Alex's request to leave her weapons behind.

A feral grin stretched across the soldier's face. "Who do you think you are, telling us what to do?" His gaze slid over her. "You are just some dressed-up camp follower."

"I am daughter to Lord Bernard Dumont of Lisieux, and you will unhand me this minute!"

The man chuckled and tightened his grip, sinking his fingers painfully into her shoulders. "A Norman? You speak English. You wear these fancy trinkets." He fingered her mother's brooches. He may as well have been touching her skin. He leaned closer. "I bet you even taste English." His gaze locked on her lips. "But I suppose I have to get used to the women here sometime."

Isabel spit in his face. As he wiped the spittle from his cheek, she kicked at his legs and used the distraction to twist out of his hold.

She took a step, mayhap two, before he lunged at her and knocked her to the ground. His heavy weight came crashing down beside her. More screaming rent the air. She struggled to breathe as the brute clawed his way up her legs to pinion her.

How she wished she had her weapons with her. She would run him through without a second thought.

Isabel kicked out, and one of her feet caught him on the chin. He barked in pain. She readied herself to stand, but he pulled her back.

The brute raised his fist to strike. Isabel flinched, helpless. However, the blow did not fall.

Suddenly the fiend was crying out in pain. Alex had caught the man's hand and twisted it behind his back. He gave the arm a hard yank. "What have you done?" Alex's face was tight with fury and some other emotion she did not recognize. "This woman is a lady under my protection, and she is not to be trifled with."

With another twist, Alex released the man and moved to Isabel's side, helped her to her feet. He ranged his hands over her to ensure she was unhurt.

The brute grabbed Alex's arm. "She's no lady, this one. I was merely teaching her manners."

She opened her mouth to retort, but Alex gave her a warning look before he stepped protectively in front of her and punched the other Norman squarely in the face. The man fell back and hit his head against the wall, going quiet.

The other soldier stood at attention when Alex's gaze fell over him. "Who do you report to?"

"Captain Everard, sir."

Alex gave him a tight nod. "I will be informing him of this incident."

The man ducked his head deferentially. "I understand."

The young Englishwoman clutched Isabel's arm. She had almost forgotten her in the scuffle. "My lady, are you well? I am so sorry."

"I am fine—"

"Mama, mama!" A young boy ran up to the Englishwoman, Captain Thomas and Hugh trotting after him.

The woman gathered the towheaded boy into her arms. "My dear! Never do that again."

Isabel shook the dirt from her dress. "Where was he?"

Hugh's mouth curled with disgust. "He was asleep in one of the stalls."

The dark look had not left Alex's face. "Come." He tugged Isabel through the gates and into the bailey. The woman shouted her thanks after them.

They reached her room in silence. Alex turned to Averill, who had followed them into the castle. "Please fetch some wine for Lady Isabel."

The serving girl curtseyed, and Alex waited for the door to close then smoothed the hair away from Isabel's face. Still cupping her cheek, he asked, "Did he hurt you?"

"He tried," she said, avoiding his earnest gaze.

He led her over to a chair. "What happened?"

"The guards were giving that woman a difficult time for asking them to help her find her son."

"And you decided to intervene."

She could not decide if there was censure in his

tone or not. "Yes. I would not stand by and let them ridicule her," she said, thinking of Hugh's inaction.

"Very well. I will speak with Captain Everard. Hopefully we can avoid situations like this in the future."

If all of William's soldiers were like the men she met today, she doubted that very much.

"Any injuries?"

She grimaced. "Bruises, mostly."

"What about your hands?" He grabbed the washbasin and a spare cloth and knelt before her. He gently took her hand and began cleaning it off. The soothing ministrations calmed her heartbeat, which still rioted in her chest.

"When I think about what he could have done, if I had not gotten there in time... Captain Thomas told me what happened, and..." he trailed off, watching her face as tears threatened. "Isabel, what is it?"

She blinked and breathed deep. "I am but shaken."

"Isabel, I swear I will never let another man lay a hand on you."

"Alex, I have lived long in the world of men. This is not the first incident..."

"What do you mean? There have been other times?"

The alarm in his voice surprised her. "Yes, one." Seeing Alex start, she forestalled him. "I got away with my virtue intact, if that is what you are worried about."

"I am relieved you were unhurt, but I would know what happened," he said with a hard edge to his voice.

"So Matilde did not tell you everything?"

"Isabel..."

She sighed. She could put him off no longer. "My father wanted me to marry. Three summers ago, we traveled with the court in the hopes I would take interest in one of the young nobles. Even though my father would abide by my rights as an Englishwoman to choose my husband, he wanted to increase the odds I would find someone suitable. In the end, my father's plan worked, perhaps too well," she said with a shake of her head. "A lord from Northumbria was particularly strong in his courting. After supper one evening, he insisted on escorting me to my chamber, and I foolishly agreed. We ended up near the servant quarters."

She turned away from Alex's gaze. "It was dark, and...he tried to touch me. I was able to hold him off long enough for Kendrick to find us. Fortunately I had my seax, and I take comfort in the fact his face will never look the same." She realized she had fisted her hands in her skirt and took a moment to smooth the tight blue wool. She finally looked up at Alex. "After that, my father seemed content with my staying in Ashdown for the rest of the summer."

"I can imagine."

"Since that incident, I have always carried my sword and seax. I refuse to be caught unprepared again."

Alex set aside the towel and stood. "When I told you to leave your weapons in your room, I did not intend to leave you defenseless. I only hoped to make you less intriguing to my comrades. They might not be as understanding as my men. If I had known this would be the result..." Alex ran a hand through his hair. "Why did you not tell me this before?"

"And give you a reason to find me unfit? You have done all you could to discredit my leadership by suggesting I cannot take care of myself or my people. How could I protest?"

"Isabel, that is not what I—"

With a knock, Averill returned with a flagon of wine.

Alex stepped away from Isabel. "The evening feast will be starting soon. Are you well enough to attend?"

She shifted in her seat and winced at the stiffness of her body. "I will stay here."

"Are you sure? *Non*, you must be. I do not blame you. I must go, but I will bid one of the servants bring you up a tray. I will check on you in the morning."

"I will be fine."

"As I said, I will see you in the morning. I will not leave your side tomorrow."

"That will not be necessary."

"Yes, but where else would I rather be?"

Isabel could not hide her flustered state. She still did not know what to make of him. "I am sure I do not know," she answered primly.

He gave her a sharp look. "Yes, you do. *Bonsoir*."

\* \* \* \*

Smoke and madness.

That was all Alex knew as he fought his way out of the abbey. Angry shouts grew in volume. William was somewhere ahead of him, pushing through the crush of Norman soldiers. Flames swallowed a groaning building across the street.

One minute he and his countrymen were cheering at the sight of the English crown upon William's head. Then he would have sworn they were under attack, given the screams and shouts that filtered into the chamber.

The London townsfolk had gathered in huge numbers on the street outside Westminster before the ceremony—to gawk or protest, he did not know. More men had to be stationed outside to keep the peace. Now, though, there was only chaos.

Alex found Hugh on horseback, trying to hold back the seething tide of Englishmen. He worked his way through the crowd.

"What happened?"

Hugh glanced down at him. "We heard screams inside the abbey. Thought we were under attack."

"What? *Non.* We were only celebrating our new king."

Hugh turned his head and looked at Alex in disbelief. "That was a celebration?"

Alex peered between the jostling bodies and saw William holding out his hands for his men to cease their attack. The crowd gradually calmed, but by now, the fire had spread. William instructed some of his men to assist the English in putting out the fire before returning to the abbey to complete the ceremony.

Afterward, Alex surveyed the damage to the homes and shops lining the street. The acrid tang of smoke and soot lingered in the air. He did not understand why the men stationed outside had decided to set the nearby buildings on fire when they heard the shouts coming from inside the abbey. A stupid, senseless act. And one that further eroded any chance of earning the English people's respect.

When he returned to William's headquarters, he spied Isabel pacing in the bailey, a worried look on her face. Word of the confrontation must have spread. He had asked her not to leave the castle grounds today because he did not want to risk her getting caught up in another misunderstanding between the Normans and the English people. Tensions on the streets had escalated as the crowning ceremony drew near. She had reluctantly agreed. He was surprised she had conceded so easily, but he was not blind to the distrust her countrymen had with a woman so favored by the Normans.

She brightened when she saw him and trotted over as soon as he passed through the gates. "What happened? I heard terrible things." She fell into step next to him.

"A misunderstanding between the Normans and the English townspeople during the ceremony. But worry not. The fire finally burned itself out. Thankfully most of the townsfolk got out of the way in time."

"Do they need help tending the injured?" she asked.

He grimaced. "I do not think so. Those who did not escape the fire will not need the type of care you can provide."

She looked down at her hands. "Oh, I see."

Alex did not know how to dispel the dark look on her face. "It was unfortunate, to be sure," he said as they entered the castle. "And this will not be the last instance of violence between our people. There has been too much loss, and anger has taken the place of grief."

Isabel murmured in agreement but said no more as they walked on.

They came to a stop before a room flanked by Norman soldiers. Isabel looked askance at Alex, but he studiously avoided her. "William has agreed to see us sooner than scheduled."

Before Isabel could find her voice, one of the guards knocked on the door and a manservant appeared. Alex announced himself.

The manservant eyed Alex and Isabel with interest before saying, "The king will see you now. The lady must wait until called."

Alex stepped forward, barely sparing Isabel a parting glance before the manservant shut the door in her face.

It could not be helped.

She had been subdued ever since they reached London, and he was not sure what he could do to lessen her unease. When William had moved up their meeting, he had decided it would be better if Isabel did not know of the change since it would only increase the apprehension she was bound to feel.

Even though they had formed a tenuous truce since he told her of William's intentions, he still did not know her true feelings. His choice to withhold the truth upset her, but he hoped she could see past that. She had to realize, regardless of what she felt for him, things were not going to work out the way she wanted.

Alex knelt before his king.

He just hoped she would not place all the blame at his feet.

# Chapter 17

Abandoned in the hallway, Isabel struggled to keep a placid expression on her face. She inwardly cursed Alex for not warning her their meeting with William had been moved up.

Was this not the moment she had built up in her mind when Alex first pronounced William's interest in her family? Now was her chance to convince the man who had engineered her country's conquest that she, a noblewoman, was competent in all things necessary to keep the Dumont lands prospering. She did not need a man's oversight. Nothing had to change.

She exhaled slowly, doing her best to ignore the guards eyeing her curiously as she waited. William's fickleness was the only thing that could potentially work in her favor, but she feared her request would provoke his anger, not the changes to her fortune she so desperately wanted.

She had known for some time she would not get her way, but feeling it was different. She felt the danger as opposed to just being aware of its existence. It was just beyond the door. She should be grateful. Other Englishwomen were not treated as well as she had been. And no one would be given a husband like Alexandre. Indeed, Alex tempered her protests—she did not want to object too hard and risk having her attraction to Alex replaced by the cold duty to another.

Despite the time she and Alex had together in London, neither broached the topic of William's decision. Alex had been too honorable, she supposed, to bring it up again, and Isabel was too stubborn. Any chance to clear the air between them before William made the arrangement final was gone. It should have made her angry, but all she felt was a profound emptiness, as if she had lost something but did not know what it was. She only knew that it was gone. Like so many other things.

Isabel started when the door opened a few moments later. Alex's face betrayed no emotion as he took her arm and escorted her in. No triumph. No doubt. Did he still want her? She tried to leave her misgivings behind her as Alex brought her face to face with William.

The monarch sat at a small table strewn with maps and legal documents. He looked tired, but his sharp eyes lit up with interest as she entered the room.

Without waiting for Alex's introduction, Isabel curtsied. "My king, I have come to swear an oath of fealty for my family, the Dumonts of Ashdown."

William watched her, amusement dancing in his nearly black eyes, then clapped his hands. "Enough, my dear. Let me have a look at you."

Isabel straightened and tried to smile as the king's gaze wandered over her.

"Well met, my dear, but I will always think of you as that bewitching child who clung to her father's knee."

"I am honored my lord remembers." Isabel heard Alex's sharp intake of breath, but she did not acknowledge it. After all, he had never asked if she knew William, and she had never volunteered the information.

William looked to Alex. "Alexandre, you will forgive me for wanting to reminisce. The last time I saw Lady Isabel, she had just survived her first crossing. Her father could not bear to leave her behind."

Isabel stiffened at the memory, and William's face immediately collapsed into the picture of contrition. "I am sorry. Alexandre told me about your father. He was a good man."

"My lord is very kind."

"Bah!" He waved away the compliment with a stout hand as he would bat a fly. "We should move on to more immediate things." He stood, his stocky frame straightening, and gestured to Alex. "Alexandre, if you would excuse us."

Alex's eyes widened in surprise at the dismissal, but he was too much the picture of good manners to let on. "My lord." He made a quick bow and left the room but not before he lanced her with a look brimming with questions.

As the door shut, William trained his gaze on Isabel. The cool intelligence in his eyes belied his jovial expression.

"You have given Alexandre a difficult time, no doubt." Before she could answer, he started to slowly pace the room. "If I did not have it on such good authority you are an exceptional woman, I would be disappointed. Nevertheless, here we are."

He watched her for a moment, as if daring her to speak, even though he must have known she would not. "Now, I have selected Alexandre as your husband. You have already had the opportunity to measure his quality. However, he has informed me he will defer to your wishes in that matter. Which makes me wonder what happened while he was in Ashdown."

This time there was no mistaking his desire for her to respond. "My lord, I confess I was upset at Alexandre's presence in my home. There were some...misunderstandings."

"Misunderstandings!" He shook his head. "Alexandre may not have handled the situation as delicately as he should have, but he is a most trusted liegeman. He may be overzealous in his actions, but I would not accept less from him. But you, my dear... My expectations of you were very different."

Isabel unclenched her hands, knotted at her sides. She had to explain herself. "My lord, this has been a difficult time for me with both my father and brother dead and my future uncertain. I have tried to be protective of my family's legacy."

"You knew I would not let anything befall you if it were in my power to do so."

Isabel opened her mouth to speak but fell silent.

Understanding spread across the monarch's face. "Ah. You did not trust me to remember you father's loyalty or, worse, trust me to do what is best for you."

Isabel tried to deny it, but he would not hear of it. "Come, come, my child. Do not think me so heartless. I am a warrior, yes, but I am still a man." He straightened, and once more, he was the calculating king who had orchestrated the conquest. "Has Alexandre mistreated you?" he asked in a hard voice.

"*Non.*"

"Hurt you in anyway?"

"*Non.*"

"Do you find him lacking in intelligence?"

"*Non*, my lord."

"Do you find his physical appearance unappealing?"

Warmth spread through her at the question, and she looked down at her hands, clutched together in front of her.

"Come, come, out with it," William urged her.

She raised her head and cleared her throat. "I suppose not."

William nodded. "Then unless you can suggest a better candidate, I see no reason why Alexandre should not marry you. Is there anyone else?"

Her breath squeezed out of her lungs. He was giving her a choice, but Isabel had no one to choose from. There was no one, English or Norman.

There was only Alex.

She closed her eyes. "*Non*, my lord."

"Hmm. I thought not. Then it is not so much Alexandre but marriage then? Willful, no doubt a product of your father's indulgence." He let the silence stretch on for a moment. "Tomorrow then." His voice was heavy with finality. "After Vespers."

The pronouncement was a dismissal, but she was a fool if she did not take this opportunity to speak with her country's new king.

"My lord, do not ignore Wales too long. As Alexandre can attest, we have already forced back two raiding parties just in Ashdown these past weeks. They will not hesitate to press their advantage during this transition."

William collapsed into his chair. "You speak truth, my dear. If England were not given to me by God, I would question ruling a people who not only hated me but were surrounded by such fierce enemies to the north and west." He sighed. "Worry not. I will deploy my best men to the Marches. Including your Alexandre."

"Thank you, my lord." Isabel managed to curtsy and moved toward the door.

"Do not fault Alexandre for being what he is, Isabel. He is a man, but he is a good man. Remember that, my child," he called after her.

It was over, her fate finally and firmly sealed, but she no longer felt the dread she had been carrying with her for so many weeks.

Alexandre waited for her outside. He fell into step beside her. She braced herself for an onrush of questions, but he stayed silent. They nearly reached her room, when she spoke, her voice surprisingly steady. "Tomorrow. After Vespers."

Alex stopped. "What do you mean?"

"Tomorrow we are to be married. That is what you wanted?"

"Hoped for, yes, but I expressed to our king you were not to be forced into the decision."

"I was not."

At her admission, he smiled softly. "My lady honors me." He took her hand and kissed the inside of her wrist, making her tremble ever so slightly.

Isabel glanced about the deserted hallway. "Alex..."

He straightened, and they resumed their walk, but not before he let her see the spark of hunger in his eyes. "You never told me you knew William." His tone held more amusement than accusation.

"I was very young. I did not expect him to remember." She gave him a sidelong glance. "It was after my mother's death. My father needed to return to Normandy to check on his holdings there. Julien had already started his fostering, and without Mother, I think Father felt guilty leaving me behind."

"So you went to Normandy."

She nodded.

"How many more secrets do you have?"

Isabel looked at him before responding. He meant the question as a jest, but the issue of trust fell over them like a shadow. "The number of secrets I have depends on how well I can trust you."

The lingering mirth in his eyes vanished. "And will you let yourself trust me?"

They came to a stop in front of her room. She

opened the door, but paused before entering. Averill was absent, probably consigned into service in the kitchens for the Christmas Day feast.

She turned. "That is not something you can ask, only what you must earn."

Alex followed her, leaned against the doorframe, the casual pose belying the seriousness of the conversation. "Have I not proven myself worthy of trust, my lady?"

The tone was light, but Isabel was not sure she wanted to reopen old wounds. "Things are still so new..."

He nodded. "For both of us." He studied her for a moment. "Very well, what can I tell you about myself to set you at ease? I am sure you still have questions."

She beckoned him to follow her into the room, and once they were inside, he shut the door. "Tell me why you sought to hide our betrothal from me." She faced him. "You said you wanted the chance to court me on your own terms before I learned the truth, but I cannot help but feel it was all a game to see how long it would take for me to fall into your arms."

"This," he said, gesturing between them, "is no game. I admit I did my best to charm you, but I know the alternative would have been far worse."

"What do you mean?"

He started to pace. "Your parents loved each other, did they not?" he asked her suddenly.

"Yes, they did," she replied, unsure why that was important.

"Well, mine did not. My mother's family forced her to marry my father, so the barony would be strengthened. My parents were strangers before they married, and as time went on, it became clear they were not well-suited to one another." He cocked his head. "Though I confess, I am not sure what woman would have pleased my father. The constant warfare made him cruel. My mother suffered his abuses for years, and at some point—I am not sure when—she started fighting back. The strife became too much, and she tried to take her life when I was but your age. My father sent her to a nunnery after that to recover, but it was only a matter of time. The abbess told me she had no will left to live."

"I am so sorry, Alex," Isabel murmured. She had not realized he had experienced such a strained childhood.

"I stayed in Caen for a summer, visiting with my mother at the convent when she was well enough. The abbess took pity on me, and during my time there, taught me my letters. It was a welcome distraction from my mother's decline, and I think the abbess knew that."

He sighed and shook his head as if to clear it. "I am telling you this in the hopes it will explain why I was so resolute in my pursuit of you. I knew we would be bound to each other for the rest of our lives, but I was determined to live a different life from my parents. In fact, I was not certain I would accept William's offer, initially."

He stopped pacing and faced her once more. "It would depend on you."

"And I assume I was not too objectionable."

He chuckled softly. "Your beauty was enough to keep me interested when your manners were lacking. And the more time we spent together, the more opportunities I had to see the possibilities. I hoped I could wear down your defensiveness and get you to see the potential between us."

He paused for a moment and captured her gaze again. Isabel's breath left her in a rush at the intensity of his eyes, burning like sapphires. "The pull between us was another pleasant surprise." His low tone sent a sharp current through her belly. "Isabel, I know you were hurt by my deception, and I am sorry for it, but I hope you can understand it was not done cruelly."

"I think I understand."

He crossed the distance between them, came so close she could reach out and touch him if she wanted. He opened the pouch strapped to his belt and pulled out a pendant on a fine chain. "This is for you. It was my mother's. She gave it to me before she died." He held it up. Torchlight reflected off the translucent stones.

"It is very beautiful." She made no move to take it from him, as it was not her place to do so.

Alex placed it around her neck. "There." He did not back away. Instead, he trailed his fingers along the chain down her neck until they rested on the pendant and teased the warm skin underneath.

Isabel sucked in a breath, swallowing his earthy scent of leather, wood smoke and something she could not identify—it was simply him. She felt his pull, calling her across the last few inches separating them. He was watching her again, something in his gaze speaking to her in a language she did not know.

Then he kissed her, and all uncertainty dissolved.

# Chapter 18

"I just hope Alex realizes that wench is good for only one thing."

"Come, man, be reasonable."

Isabel and her servant had just come from the terce service at Westminster Abbey and were on their way to her room to prepare for the evening's ceremony. Averill breathless beside her, Isabel skidded to a halt outside the stables at the unmistakable voices of Alexandre's men. She crept along the outer wall of the building toward the open door, the men cloistered on the other side.

"Reasonable?" she heard the shield bearer say. "Nothing about the situation is reasonable. I cannot believe Alex plans to go through with it."

"You cannot expect him to turn down William's offer. The king has honored Alex with such a prize. A beautiful woman, and lands to go with it."

Isabel fisted her hands. She was no fool—she knew Alex's shield bearer did not like her. It had not bothered her at first. After all, she had dealt with difficult men before. However, when she became Alex's wife, such blatant disregard would have to be addressed. Mayhap it would eventually fade away before she had to confront the man.

"Her beauty does not excuse her lies," Hugh said. "She is no better than the rest of the accursed—"

"You are being unfair to her. She made a mistake by hiding the truth, but she was scared." Isabel gritted her teeth at Jerome's choice of words, despite the truth they carried. "I grant you, she is a stubborn girl," he continued, "but you must admit she will be an asset to Alex as he tries to gain acceptance from Dumont's thanes and tenants."

"Bah. They will fall in line soon enough once they taste our steel," Hugh said.

"Have you not had enough of warfare?" Jerome asked the younger man. "We joined with Alex to make a new home for ourselves. Without Lady Isabel's knowledge, we risk more fighting. The whole point of such marriages is to weave peace between nations."

"But how can we trust her?"

"Alex and the king trust her. That should be enough for you." Jerome had uttered the words as if he had no doubt of Alex's acceptance of her. Isabel just hoped one day she could be as sure.

"Alex is only eager to bed the wench. I hope he will put her in her place once he returns to his senses."

Jerome chuckled, the sound jarring her raw emotions. "Granted, he has been distracted of late, but surely you can see how well suited they are?"

Hugh scoffed. "She is willful and—"

"And Alex never backs down from a challenge," Jerome finished for him. "And if they cannot find some accord, she will be with child soon enough."

Isabel heard Hugh laugh at that. It was not a kind laugh. Jerome did not need to say once she was pregnant it would be difficult for her to be involved in the day-to-day oversight of the castle. The thought of children settled into her stomach like spoiled meat. She had been fighting against the possibility of marriage for so long, she had overlooked that essential detail. Her mother had died from the complications that had arisen from childbirth. Would that be her fate as well?

Averill tugged on her arm. "Come, my lady.

Ignore them."

The breeze stirred, chilling the tears she did not realize had fallen. She brushed them away and let Averill take her arm and lead the way to her room.

"We will make you beautiful for the ceremony, you will see," Averill said.

Isabel stayed silent as she bathed and submitted to Averill's ministrations. She was dressed in the gown she packed for the occasion, a light blue lamb's wool, the sleeves trimmed with indigo silk. Averill chatted on about the other servants in the castle but Isabel could not be cheered. When the girl finished, she held up the sliver of glass so Isabel could see her handiwork.

She blinked. If the face reflected had not done the same, she would not have recognized herself. She saw her mother's dark brown eyes, her father's pointed chin. Unnaturally pale cheeks and a furrowed brow.

No more. She turned away from the stranger in the mirror and looked down at her hands. Despite her soak, her fingernails had left deep crescents in her palms. She tried to distract herself with happier thoughts, but kept coming back to the stark reality she was utterly alone. Her family gone, her lands not hers any longer.

The enjoyment she found in Alex's arms could not make up for that.

\* \* \* \*

The ceremony had been brief, as many others needed to be conducted. William was shrewd enough to know the best chance at integrating the Normans with the English people was through marriage. Isabel was impressed William personally attended, although he had not lingered once the ceremony concluded. Captain Thomas had been by her side, and, while not surprising, it was comforting to have someone she knew and loved to observe this new beginning in her life. Afterward, they joined the others in the main hall for another lavish feast, but it was lost on Isabel.

She ended up excusing herself early, full of misgivings and annoyed at all the knowing glances skittering up and down the table.

Nothing left to do but go up to her room and wait.

What the night would bring was inevitable, but the knowledge did not lessen her unease. Alex's things had been placed in her room, as his old room was no doubt needed to house another of William's men. Averill would bed down with the other servants until they returned to Ashdown. Someone had also brought up some wine, and an exquisitely made dressing gown had been draped across the bed. No mistaking the intent of those items. She should wear what she had packed, but made the mistake of touching the fabric of the new gown and could not suppress the desire to feel Alex's body through the soft, slippery, translucent silk.

Alex was officially her husband, but did he still respect her now that he had achieved all he wanted? She had nothing left to claim as hers anymore. Not after tonight.

Not after Alex entered the room, carried up the steps by his cheering men, and shut the door behind him with a definitive snap.

As he walked into the chamber, he drank in the sight of the new gown clinging to her body. The men's voices in the hallway fell away as they stood there, contemplating one another. He took a step toward her, but then seemed to decide better of it. Instead, he removed his tunic and laid it over the back of one of the chairs. He loosened the ties of his sherte but left it on as he moved to the table and poured wine into one of the goblets. His eyes found hers as he took a sip, and then he bridged the space between them.

"Here, you should have some," he said almost

gruffly.

Isabel shook her head. Wine was the last thing she needed.

Alex shrugged and drained the cup before setting it aside. He returned to her and ran his hands through the softly curling hair hanging across her shoulders. As he stroked the silken tendrils, she tensed under his warm gaze. He had probably never seen her hair completely unbound, and the thought sent gooseflesh crawling up her arms.

He cupped her face and made her look at him. "Isabel, what is it?" Alex watched her, and she struggled to find an answer that made sense as the silence lengthened between them. "I will not hurt you," he told her as he caressed her neck.

At her nod, Alex leaned in and kissed her forehead. She flinched when he placed his other hand on her shoulder and pulled her closer. He moved his mouth to her lips and teased them open. She obeyed his every move, but did not match them in ardor. Finally, he stopped and set her away from him. He stalked to the table and picked up the wine flagon but set it down before he poured another glass.

"Have I done something wrong?"

A bitter laugh escaped him. "*Non*, you have done nothing wrong. You have done nothing at all."

Heat flooded her cheeks. "I thought I was doing what you wanted me to do."

"*Non*. This afternoon, I married a woman who was flesh and blood. Now I find that woman gone, her fire dampened. I want to know what caused this."

"I do not understand what you mean."

"Why are you holding back? What is wrong? Tell me."

"What is there to tell?" Hugh's cruel words echoed in her ears. "You won. You have what you came for. Why does this matter?" she said, gesturing helplessly to the wooden floor of the chamber.

"Because there is more at stake here than what I joined William to get."

She crossed her arms, the gown sliding against her body. "What are you saying?"

"In you, I found more than I ever expected. I found my complement, my helpmate, yet you still deny it, deny yourself. I thought your acceptance of our marriage would bring us one step closer. But it has not. When I kiss you, I want you to kiss me back as you have before. I do not want your blind submission."

"I have given you all I have, and yet you still ask for more?"

"I do not want cold duty from you, and you know it." The finality in his voice was deafening.

Isabel straightened. "I will not deny you."

"Nor take pleasure in it, I warrant." He remained silent for a moment. "You are too much an innocent to feign your body's response to me." His masculine boast did not match the troubled look on his face as he continued to pace. "I can only assume there is something else amiss."

He stepped closer and pulled her into his arms. "Isabel, Isabel," he murmured against her hair. "Tonight is supposed to be a celebration of our marriage, not another fighting ground. Tell me what is wrong."

Her breath caught in her throat as he surrounded her with his warm body. Why was this so important? He had what he wanted. She tried to pull away, but he held her fast.

"Isabel, please..."

The candlelight illuminated the earnestness etched into Alex's face, and her resolve faltered. She could not bear to be cast aside if he tired of her or

Elise Cyr | Siege of the Heart

relegated her to the solar to care for their children. She thought he saw more in her, but after hearing Hugh dismiss her abilities so easily...

"What is to become of me after tonight?" She barely recognized her voice.

"What do you mean? I will ensure William has no more duties for me here, and we shall return to Ashdown."

"But you are the legal authority there now. You do not need me at all. Tonight is just an exercise in vanity."

"Is that what this is about? You are worried I am going to use you and then cast you aside? You know I would never..." He stopped, watching her a moment. "Perhaps you really do not know. Perhaps I have not made it clear," he said with a hand on her cheek. "You are a part of my life now. Not only am I honor-bound to protect and care for you, but I also need your expertise and your experience managing your father's lands. And I need you to help me earn your people's respect. That way your lands, our lands, will continue to prosper." He paused, his gaze searching. "I also desire you, in a way I have desired no other woman. Surely you know that much."

He had not said the one thing she was afraid to acknowledge, even to herself. Could he come to love her? He needed her, that much was clear. He desired her, but what of love? She was too unsure of her feelings in that realm to fault him for not mentioning it. Such sentiments would only distort the reality of the situation, sentiments that could never be proven. A stray tear slipped down her cheek.

Alex wiped it away, his touch lingering. "Isabel, talk to me."

"I know not who I am anymore."

"You are still Isabel Dumont, which will mean

more to your people than your marriage to me. But you are also my wife, who will share in my fortunes equally. Will you do that?"

She nodded. Again, she was surprised by the esteem he placed in her abilities. He knew if he were to succeed in Ashdown without resorting to violence, he would need her full support. This gave her some degree of power over him, but she was not sure how to wield it, let alone when she would have an occasion to do so. He would be the undisputed man of the house, a lord of the realm, but she would be at his side, which afforded her opportunities for involvement that would threaten lesser men. He would share as much as the dictates of society would allow him to, and she would have to take comfort in that. And she did.

Alex's arms tightened around her. "Will you also allow yourself to trust me?"

"Yes." The word slipped out before she had a chance to think of the repercussions. But it was the truth, and she had nothing to gain by denying it any longer.

The tension seemed to leave his body as he gathered her close and pressed their foreheads together. "Isabel..." he whispered, as if that summed up everything. He cupped her cheek and tipped her mouth to his, blotting away their words with a kiss. She could not reject the sensations he awakened in her anymore.

He explored her body with his calloused hands. She discovered how they felt through the sheer fabric of her gown. Warm, teasing, a touch she had not known she craved until now.

He trailed his hands down her sides. The heat radiated from his fingers and fed into the quickening sparks of hunger deep inside. He pulled her closer, holding her hips against his, and nuzzled her neck, sending waves of pleasure through her. Isabel clung to him for support as he caressed the tops of her thighs through the fabric. He skimmed his fingers across the silky skin of her legs, the touch penetrating her to the bone.

Breathing was harder now. Isabel was not sure what to do. She only knew she wanted Alex to kiss her again. She reached up, tangled her hands in his hair and urged his lips to hers. He groaned. His demanding mouth soon had her awash in rioting intensity as their tongues coiled together.

Alex grew more daring as he slipped his hands underneath her gown and caressed her femininity. Isabel gasped at the intrusion, her hips involuntarily backing away. He stilled but kept her close. His gaze bored into hers, eyes filled with promise. Slowly, he teased the silken curls at the juncture of her thighs. The sensations—wonder and surprise mediated by the newfound pleasure—overwhelmed her. He bit back a sigh as he slid a finger inside her.

As he continued his exploration, soft little cries she had never made before escaped from the back of her throat. He kissed her again, this time teasing the sensitive skin of her face and neck. She arched against him as unexpected yearnings seized her.

The need was blinding.

She needed to move. She needed to do something. She slipped her hands underneath Alex's sherte, reveling in his smooth muscles and the ever-present heat radiating from him. As her hand brushed over one of his nipples, he froze. With a groan, he slipped his hand out from under her gown and removed his sherte in one quick movement. He grabbed Isabel again and reached for her breasts. She shivered as he plucked at each in turn. Then he covered them with his mouth, teased the rigid peaks into aching points through the sheer fabric.

Too much. She clutched at Alex, fumbling with the ties to his braies. He helped her, and in moments, stepped out of the last of his clothes. She barely had a chance to take him in before he grabbed her wrist and placed her hand against his engorged length. His gaze pleaded with her to touch him, and she complied, tentatively stroking his velvety hardness. She marveled as his heat melded with that of her hand.

Just as she found the tip, he roughly set her away from him.

Isabel froze as Alex marshaled control over himself. Then he was pulling her close, grasping her buttocks and holding her against his hard body. Her breath caught as she felt him press against her, seeking to slip between her thighs, his warmth pooling with hers. He yanked at the gown and soon had it off her. The silk whispered as it slipped to the floor. His hands were everywhere at once, drinking in the nakedness she was far too aroused to hide from his gaze.

Alex picked her up and carried her to the bed. He looked down at her for a long moment as she lay against the coverlet, vibrating with need in the candlelight. He enveloped her body with his, gently nudging her legs apart to accommodate him. "You know what to expect?" he asked.

His voice was so distorted by desire, Isabel barely understood the question. She nodded, but not before the first glimmer of real fear seized her. It was too late. Alex plunged into her, leaving her breathless and gasping at the sharp loss of her maidenhood.

Other sensations soon eclipsed the pain as Alex moved inside her. She arched her hips to meet his and felt him sheath himself deeply within her. Never had she expected... She was filled with wonder at this man and his ability to make her feel.

Thrust after thrust, her body ached for release, the

tension tangible. Soon she was lost in the moment, bucking out of control, soaking up all he would give her. With a hoarse cry, Alex emptied himself into her exhausted flesh.

Isabel stared up at the wooden beams crossing the ceiling. She felt so much. The echoes of her release still haunted her body. The physical intensity left its mark on her, and in its wake she felt the overwhelming urge to cry.

Alex watched on as her silent tears fell, gathering in her hair as they slid down the sides of her face. "Isabel, I am sorry I was so rough with you." He smoothed her cheek. "A woman's first time..."

She shook her head, stopping the rest of his words. "*Non.* I just did not realize..." She lifted her shoulder.

"What? What did you not realize?"

"Just that there would be so much feeling. It surprised me." Everything had changed, and she felt foolish trying to absorb the newness of the situation with Alex examining her every word and action. "I am not myself, forgive me."

She wanted nothing more than to burrow down in the blankets, but Alex prevented her. He leaned over her, his breath tickling her collarbone. "Do not hide from me, Isabel. Tell me where your thoughts go."

She looked up and met his earnest blue gaze. "What do you want me to say?"

Alex ran a hand through his hair. "I know not. I just want to know what you are thinking."

Isabel sighed. "You have destroyed my independence," she said softly "And I cannot decide whether or not that is a good thing."

"Isabel, the only thing I took from you tonight was your virginity. Whatever independence you had before marrying was illusory, my dear. As a woman, you would have been subject to your father or brother, had things turned out differently."

"But now my life is dependent on yours, and that dependence makes me weak," she said, her voice catching.

"You must not look on it as weakness. Together, we can be so much more than if we were to continue living separate lives."

Her throat tightened. If she did not speak her mind, she would forever regret the lost opportunity. It was too easy to remain silent and forget her own dreams. To meekly subsume herself into her new role as Alex's wife, and she realized that was precisely what was upsetting her. "I will not let you make me forget who I am, what I want from life," she said fiercely. "I am my own person…"

She took a breath, and in that moment she knew what the real danger was in her relationship with Alex. It was nothing he deliberately did to her, it was just the very fact he was a man and now a part of her life. He would eclipse her. Mayhap not now, but eventually she would only exist through him. And the thought terrified her. "I am losing myself in you."

"Isabel, I was lost the day I met you. I just did not know how much."

She watched him for a moment, trying to gauge his sincerity. Their intimacy was still so new. Perhaps they would be able to navigate the changes their relationship created together. She wanted to think so.

Alex pulled her against his chest. He held her close, his strength fortifying her. "There is so much I need to learn." His reverent tone was a caress to her body, which already prepared itself for sleep.

She forced back a yawn. "You know I will teach you all I know about my lands and people."

"No, teach me about you."

# Chapter 19

Two days passed before Alex made his excuses to William. They set out for Ashdown early on the third day. After the cloying conditions of London, the wooded roads invigorated Isabel. She breathed deeply, and instead of smoke and too many bodies, only smelled horse and fresh air.

They were finally going home.

As far as she was concerned, they had already wasted precious time in London, when it could have been better spent acquainting her people with Alex as their new overlord. Although no longer upset over Alex's deception, she still regretted the fact she had not been able to inform her people of the match and spare them the worry.

She stretched out her neck, surprised by the exhaustion still clinging to her. Everything she feared had come to pass. She was married, and, although the man in question was Alex, she still felt he was in many ways a stranger to her. Would he change overnight and turn into the brutish soldier of fortune she had been convinced she could not escape? Alex rode ahead, in conversation with Jerome and Captain Thomas. His laughter floated back to her and dispelled the chill in the air. She did not think so. Alex was kind and noble in his treatment of her, and she could not stop her cheeks from warming when she thought of the few moments they spent alone.

During their final days in London, he had been

too busy to fully enjoy their marital bed. He had been up before she woke, only to return late in the evening from all the meetings he had to attend. They found time for only one more coupling beyond the first, but the ecstasy she had felt in his arms went beyond all her expectations. Words such as burden or duty she had heard from other women over the years were not accurate descriptions at all. She was learning his body, what made him smile, and coming to enjoy his company. Indeed, she was almost happy, but that seemed dishonest to acknowledge since too many men had died to precipitate such a future for her.

Before they left London, Isabel and Captain Thomas had made a second attempt to locate more of her father's men and reports of Julien, but to no avail. She forced back the disappointment with the knowledge the best thing she could do now was remember her brother and her father's men as they had lived.

When Alex rejoined her, he seemed to sense her preoccupation, but he did not press her. They rode in a comfortable sort of silence for much of the day. As the afternoon hours wore on, it became clear they would not reach a public house before nightfall, having already passed suitable stopping points earlier in the day. They made camp in a clearing well off the main road. Isabel dismounted, eager to stretch her legs. Some of the men were charged with setting up sleeping tents, while the others started a fire. It was not long before the group gathered around the fire to enjoy a hearty stew Averill had prepared, thanks to William's stores from London.

After the meal, when the men started to pass around a wineskin, Isabel thought it best to retire. Brandishing a small oil lamp, she entered the tent designated for her and Alex. Barely five paces in length, it was still much larger than the others. She ducked to keep her head from brushing the ceiling. Only her saddlebags and a few blankets and furs for bedding adorned the tent. The sparse accommodations would have to serve her for this one night, and in a few days she would be back in Ashdown.

She began to undress but stopped when she heard the whisper of canvas as Alex entered the tent behind her. He stole his arm around her waist and anchored her to his front. His warm breath teased the back of her neck.

Isabel froze. "Alex..." She was dirty and tired, and as much as she had come to enjoy their time together, she was in no mood to encourage his caresses.

He trailed kisses down the side of her neck. She could not deny the shiver his mouth provoked but could not let their passion continue when the men and their tents were within earshot.

Isabel tried to pull away, but he held her tight, his hard length pressed into her buttocks. She cursed her corresponding quickening and found herself leaning into him as he cupped her breast and teased the already alert nipple.

"Tell me you are not enjoying this, my lady," Alex whispered into her ear.

She ignored him and the way her body clamored for more. "The men are nearby. They will hear."

He laughed softly. "Worry not. They will drink themselves to sleep."

"Alex..." The note of warning was buried in her sigh as he sought out her sex, his touch searing her through her clothes.

Once more she tried to shake him away, but he clutched her closely. "Do that again, and I cannot be held responsible for my actions," he growled as he pressed himself into her and made her aware of his extreme arousal.

"Your actions are reprehensible," she said, almost breathless, hoping her words would subdue their growing passion.

"Because I cannot keep myself from touching my wife?" He loosened his hold and spun her around to face him. His hands bit into her shoulders.

"Yes."

His nostrils flared. "You want this too." He trailed his hands down her arms and brought them to rest on her waist. "We have not had the time to celebrate properly."

"I... It matters not what I want, only what we should do," she stammered, even as her body throbbed in anticipation.

"We should enjoy the chance to be alone together."

"I will not be humiliated in front of your men."

"Do not trouble yourself over them," he told her, not unkindly. He moved his leg between hers. She stifled a gasp as she fell against him and gripped the front of his tunic for support as his thigh roughly caressed the entrance to her femininity. "There is only one man you should attend to."

The hoarseness of his voice thrummed through her body. She arched against him. Her soft moan was her undoing. Alex must have heard it, known she had been momentarily convinced, and pressed his advantage. He latched onto the bodice of her gown and yanked down, ripping the fabric. He gathered her exposed breasts in his mouth, his demanding suckling only a few degrees away from causing pain. Her whimpers of pleasure were strangled by sudden frustration she had given in. She struggled to pry herself out of his arms.

Her foot connected with his shin. In that instant,

she successfully extricated herself from his arms and unsheathed her seax from her hip. Her mock resistance swiftly became real, surprising Isabel as much as Alex.

She could only gaze uncomprehendingly at the blade in her hand.

"Always the warrior," he said between ragged breaths. "You know I would never hurt you."

She nodded in agreement, but did not change her defensive posture. "I know... I just..." She did not know what to say, even as everything in her cried out for his attention. The desire reflected on his face stole her breath. She was just as excited as he was.

"I did not think you could make me want you more."

She trembled at his words but forced herself to stay calm. Heedless of her shredded gown, she eyed him, ready for any sudden movements. Out of instinct, she had set events into motion when she had drawn her seax. Alex would not allow her to have the upper hand for long. How could she give in, when it was her actions that had brought them to this point?

When Alex lunged to disarm her, she anticipated his every move. Her body was finely attuned to all things Alex. She managed to slip away but was more aware of the way his tunic skimmed against her or the heat of his body, than the strategy she needed to use to successfully evade him.

Was winning the objective? Alex came at her again. This time he gently ensnared her in his arms before they fell against the edge of the tent. He gripped her knife hand. He did not force her to drop it. Instead he just held her, and they stood only inches away from each other, both out of breath from the exertion. She smarted in unrequited need. As she watched him, her surroundings came into sharp relief. His male scent called to her, and she wanted to answer.

She wanted her husband.

The seax slipped from her fingers and fell to the ground. Alex, sensing her surrender, brutally crushed her into his arms. She dug her fingers into his hair and brought his bruising mouth down on hers. Together, they sank to the ground. He held her tightly against him as she straddled his hips. He dragged her skirts up and out of the way, the fabric no match for his insistent hands. As he claimed her breasts again with his mouth, Alex untied his chausses and prepared himself to enter her. It was only once Alex plunged into her that she realized what he had done. She stilled, anchored over him, unsure what to do.

Alex's face was tight with need as he clamped onto her hips, directing her. She shuddered as the friction of their movements cascaded throughout her. Her hips bucked of their own volition, and he gasped in pleasure.

They came quickly with shattering intensity, the rhythm of their bodies too much to bear. All of Isabel's strength vanished. She slumped against him as he emptied the last of his seed within her.

He held her possessively as their breathing finally returned to normal. She waited for him to berate her for her behavior, but there was only tenderness. He caught her watching him, and rolled onto his side, taking her with him so they were still face-to-face.

"What changed your mind?"

Isabel grimaced and wiped off her forehead with the back of her hand. "I could not fight you. The wanting was stronger."

"I am glad for that. Anger, or other strong emotions, often kindles desire." He played with a lock of her hair in an absent-minded manner. "I have a hard time being patient when it comes to you."

"Why?" She had meant the question to be lighthearted but it belied the insecurity she felt when it came to their relationship.

"Why? Because you can heat my blood without even trying. One smile from you and I am lost. And you feel it too, despite how you protest."

"I cannot help it."

"I know." He cupped her chin, forcing her to look him in the eyes. "You are a wild creature, but you are mine. And I will tame you."

For once, she did not take offense at the words. "I worried you would beat me for disobeying."

"Isabel, I will never lay a hand on you." He produced her seax and handed it to her. He watched her slip it back into its sheath. "I have more successful and pleasurable methods for dealing with you," he said with a smirk.

"I am still learning," she said softly.

"So am I." He kissed her, his lips gentle and sure. He finally pulled away with a look of regret. "I shall sit with the men for a little longer. I will join you soon, *chérie.*"

Isabel nodded and barely stirred as Alex stood and covered her with one of the furs. He pressed a kiss to her forehead and was gone.

* * * *

"I thought you already went to sleep," Hugh greeted Alex as he joined the rest of the men sitting around the fire. "Or did you find the bed too cold for your liking?"

A few of the men sniggered, but Alex ignored them and the insinuation. He took a long swig from the wineskin, which had been passed his way as soon as he had taken a seat. "My bed is very warm. I just thought I would take pity on you poor louts."

"We are honored by your company, my lord," Jerome said with a laugh.

"None of that. I am no lord until we reach Ashdown." He took another sip of wine and passed it along. The wine was of poor quality, but it warmed the body against the night's chill. Alex looked around. "Whither Captain Thomas?"

"He has already retired."

Concentrating on the fire's undulating flames, he nodded then let himself relax. The men's voices swirled around him, companionable and comforting. His time with Isabel left him unsettled. What began as vigorous seduction had quickly turned into a battle of wills, and Alex was still unsure who won. When she drew her seax out of habit, his need for her had grown tenfold, and he had struggled to control the manly pride demanding he take her right then. Isabel had given in, allowed Alex's passion to consume her. However, he had been at the mercy of his desire for her from the very beginning. Her defiance, instead of repelling him, only intensified his arousal to the point where he knew of nothing except her.

He had never known such intimacy as when he held her in his arms as they had lain there, spent from their lovemaking. She had consented to marry him, but until he experienced her complete surrender tonight, had not realized she felt the pull between them as acutely as he.

For the past few days, he had wrestled with Isabel's agreement to marry him. Had she come to care for him—the real Alex—or had she only chosen him because he represented a means to an end, a lesser of two evils, someone who was familiar versus some unknown? Regardless of the reasons for her choice, Alex was certain there was more between them than just mere compatibility.

"Don't mind him. He's been impossible since we left London," Hugh said.

"Now, now, he's not even been married for a week," Alex heard Jerome say in return.

Lost in thought, he looked up at his men to find their eyes on him. "What?" Laughter met his ears. Clearly he must have not heard a question directed at him.

With a grin, Jerome pointed at him. "I believe one of the men wanted to know if we would be leaving at first light tomorrow."

Alex nodded. "Yes, I am eager to return. I know Isabel is concerned for her people. And I would hate to have the Welsh attack again while we are away."

"Then it is decided," Hugh said.

Alex looked at men gathered around the fire, at the faces of those who had decided to throw their lot with his. He realized how lucky he was that his men, who had already demonstrated their talent, entrusted their futures to him. It comforted him to know he would not have to completely start anew once he reached Ashdown.

The conversation continued to ebb and flow around him as his men speculated on how things would be once they reached the Dumont castle.

"It will be good to finally have some peace," Jerome said.

"But the fighting isn't over. There is too much bad blood between us," a younger soldier said.

"Bah," Hugh grunted. "The accursed English don't know when to leave off."

"They still haven't caught the rebels that have caused so much grief," another man reminded the group.

"I heard from a Breton in London rebels attacked a contingent of men sent to Oxford to keep the locals from uprising. The men were beaten and left for dead. And the villagers aren't telling who their benefactors were," Jerome said.

Alex remembered seeing the town on a map somewhere. "How far away is Oxford from here?" he interrupted.

Jerome scratched his head. "About a two-day ride. To the southwest."

Alex nodded. "We should be cautious."

"Especially after what Captain Radolf told us in Aylesbury," Hugh said.

One of the men scoffed. "Those English whelps would be fools to set upon us."

"Here's to that," said another, and the wineskin was passed around once more.

Alex smiled tolerantly at their boasts. It was needed for morale, but he had had enough of their antics and excused himself. He picked his way to the tent he shared with Isabel, eager to lie next to her warm, welcoming body. He thrust aside the canvas, and froze.

Isabel and her saddlebags were nowhere to be found.

Where... He blinked back disbelief. He called her name, peering through the trees in the dark. Perhaps she had gotten lost after leaving camp to relieve herself. His shouts brought his men to his side. Quickly, they began canvassing the forest around them.

At some point Hugh took him aside to keep him from barking out any more frantic orders. "The men have been searching for some time now, and there is still no trace of her. Are you so certain she wants to be found?"

"What do you mean?"

"It was common knowledge your bride was not the most eager. I don't think the men would be surprised if she has deceived you."

Hand near his sword's hilt, he took a step toward

Hugh. "Isabel has not run away. I cannot believe you would even entertain such a notion."

Captain Thomas, now awake, joined them. "All the horses are accounted for."

Hugh ignored the old man and matched Alex's aggressive tone. "You have been quarreling with that woman since we first arrived in Ashdown. Why, even tonight you were at it again. We could hear your heated words as we sat by the fire."

Alex's mouth curled bitterly in remembrance. "That was no fight, I promise you."

"She has blinded you from everything. She is no better than the rest of the English. She will—"

"For God's sake, man," Captain Thomas interrupted, "she did not take her horse!" He did not need to say Isabel would never willingly travel anywhere without her mount.

The fact was painfully obvious, but Hugh was too impassioned to moderate his criticism. "Only a fool would trust that wench after her lies about her father!"

"Enough. There is no reason to—" Captain Thomas tried to say as Alex glared at Hugh.

"Sir, sir!" A breathless man-at-arms ran over, unknowingly breaking the growing tension between the men. "Jerome found the beginnings of a trail. It looks like another horse has been this way recently, but it is too dark to follow the trail now. We must wait until daybreak."

Alex glared at Hugh.

"That means nothing," Hugh replied. "She could have planned—"

Captain Thomas spoke up, trying to direct the conversation. "Alex, that is only a few hours from now. They will not be able to get very far."

Alex returned his attention to the man-at-arms. "Very well. See to it we are ready to go at first light."

Hugh shook his head as he watched the man go. "Alex…"

"Not now."

"But—"

"God's teeth, Hugh! Leave off." Alex stalked away, trying to make sense of what happened. With Isabel's scent still pervading his skin and clothes, with the image of her making love to him still firmly entrenched in his mind, he could not believe she left him willingly. He had left her sated and well-loved. She was not in any condition to vanish so completely.

Had some ruffian stumbled upon her as she slumbered and run off with her? Not likely. The presence of Alex's men would dissuade even the most daring. Isabel must have been targeted for some reason. It was no secret to anyone aware of her circumstances, she would be returning this way to Ashdown once their business in London was concluded.

Isabel had never denied her Norman or English ancestry. It was possible some disgruntled Englishman wanted to punish her for being so quickly welcomed by William and his men. Alex thought back to the curses and oaths hurled at Isabel by her people as they had walked the streets of London. So much hatred and distrust plagued the land.

He recalled Hugh's words and all the heated arguments he had shared with Isabel since he had met her. On more than one occasion, she had made it clear she did not trust him or respect his authority. And he knew how upset she was once she learned about their impending marriage. At the time, he thought it was because he had misled her, not that she was actually unhappy at the prospect of being with him. What if she had truly been opposed to him? What if she had devised a means to earn his and William's trust and then found a way to secure her freedom? Isabel had the skills and determination to put such a daring plan into place. His chest tightened at the thought she would willingly deceive him after all they had shared.

Then he remembered the soft look on her face after their last coupling. That made it easier to push away such doubts. Instead, his unease for her welfare grew. Alex hated waiting, but it was foolish to try to track her while it was still dark. The risk of making a mistake was too high to warrant it.

And Alex would not tolerate mistakes. Not when it came to Isabel.

\* \* \* \*

The right side of her body was numb. Cold, too. That was why she hated sleeping on the ground. Isabel shifted and suddenly all the sewing needles in the land were pricking her. She grunted. Past time to get up.

As the stinging pain receded, she cracked open her eyes. Sunlight blinded her. Had Alex ordered the men to take down the tent while she still slept? She smiled, basking in the warm sun on her face. It was sweet of him, but unnecessary. She was made of sterner stuff.

She opened her eyes again, this time better prepared for the rush of light as she sat up. She blinked, and then blinked again as a dull ache throbbed in her temples. Where...

The clearing was silent except for the breeze rattling against the bare tree branches that stretched to the sky. A sick feeling lodged in her stomach. No camp. No tent. No Alex.

He had left her. Left her behind to fend for herself. She had been such a fool. After everything they had shared... Why?

She bowed her head as tears blurred her vision. Then she saw the ropes loosely linking her wrists and ankles—just enough mobility she had not felt the restraints until now. Her seax, which she had strapped to her waist after her tussle with Alex, was gone. Belatedly she thought of what she was wearing. Alex had been none too gentle on her riding dress, and she had drifted into sleep without a thought to modesty. Now, though, she was clothed in her traveling cloak, which sheltered her against the cold air. A blessing, given her state of dishabille.

Her head shot up, and she reevaluated the clearing. Her gaze landed on an unfamiliar horse, stocky and piebald, tied to one of the trees behind her. Not the mount of a man of consequence. What was going on?

A twig snapped underfoot. Alone no longer. Her heartbeat thudded in her chest. Should she pretend to sleep or confront her captor? Before she could decide, booted feet tramped closer.

"Here, you. Thought you'd still be asleep."

Isabel twisted and spied a man entering the clearing. Just as his mount confirmed, he was a peasant or craftsman at best. The man looked strong and alert, with a short, sturdy blade fastened to his belt. Was it just him or were there others hidden in the trees?

She forced air in and out of her mouth. "What is going on? What have you done to me?"

"You stay quiet like a good lass." He turned to his horse and rummaged through the saddlebags. The jangle of jostled supplies filled the clearing.

"You cannot treat me thus! Untie me at once!"

Despite the ropes, she struggled to her feet. Dizzy, her head throbbed with each beat of her heart. What was wrong with her?

The man finally troubled himself to come over. "Here now, stop that. I'm supposed to bring you back in one piece."

His touch was harsh but impersonal as he made

sure the ropes were still secure. She tried to pull away but her motions were slow and clumsy. Handling her as easily as if she were a child, he forced her to the ground with an ease that made her gut lurch. He sank to his haunches next to her and produced a leather pouch held closed by a length of twine.

Pleas would not affect him or promises interest him. Resignation shrouded his features. This was a man who had seen too many battles, too many betrayals. He would not be swayed. Whatever he had been hired to do to her, he would see it through to the end.

He placed a kerchief around his face, protecting his nose and mouth, and opened the leather bag.

"How dare you!" Her voice held the imperious quality she used with her servants.

For a heart-stopping moment, he stilled. Then he acted as if he had to remind himself what he was supposed to do. Pity glimmered in his brown eyes briefly, but then he shook his head as if to clear it and brought closer the bag. It likely contained a concoction of herbs that would drug her into oblivion. Again. The only explanation for her sluggish reactions.

"If you know who I am, you know I will kill you for this injustice," Isabel said quietly.

He placed a firm hand on her mouth, preventing her ability to avoid inhaling the aromatics.

The air suddenly became oppressive, and she could feel herself slipping. Buzzing filled her head, as though she stood next to a beehive in high summer. Colors leached together, culminating in darkness. Her mind became heavy and full of slumber.

Before she gave into the inevitable, she heard the man speak again. "He told me you might say something like that."

# Chapter 20

A long way off, she heard voices. The words did not make sense but they floated around her mind nonetheless. Her head had stopped aching, but the cloying aftereffects of the herbs still clung to her. It must have been days since she last had eaten solid food, and her bereft stomach lurched unpleasantly.

She moaned, and suddenly the voices were closer, more insistent, pressing on her. She opened her eyes to darkness. A blindfold muffled her face and constricted her sight.

"Shh...not so fast. Gently now." The voice was much closer than she had expected, and a momentary tremor swept through her.

"No good in coddling her," a man cut in. "I want answers out of her when I return."

Something brushed past her. The sensations were lost amid her body's protest as someone helped her into a sitting position.

"There."

The first voice was so familiar, yet she could not place it. Someone stroked her hair as if trying to soothe her as she struggled to get comfortable. She found herself wishing it was Alex, but he could not help her now. Her errant thoughts were only a dream.

"Isabel, wake up. You must eat. You need your strength."

She heard the words, but the voice affected her at a visceral level. The recognition was blinding. Shaking, she tried to push herself away from the arms holding her. "No..."

Hands kept her in place in spite of her feeble attempts to escape.

"Isabel, calm down. All is well."

"It cannot be..." She could feel the blindfold being loosened and was terrified of the sight before her. Panic filled her senses.

"Be not afraid. It is your brother, Julien."

Even though she had recognized his voice, his touch, she was still not prepared for seeing Julien crouched before her. Bewilderment jolted through her. "How is this possible? I thought you were..."

"Dead?" he finished with a grim smile.

Isabel stared askance at him, unsure if he was just a product of her drug-addled imagination.

"Here, eat this. Then we talk."

The bowl of broth he proffered seemed real enough as she inhaled its aroma and took the first bite he directed into her mouth. She sat there awkwardly with her hands tied behind her back, her brother spoon-feeding her as if she were still a child. She digested not only the soup but also the fact she had found what she thought lost.

A few weeks ago, she would have been ecstatic to find Julien again, to learn he had survived the bloody conquest. Now, with her aching head and chafed wrists, she did not know what to think. He looked older, and exhaustion covered him like a cloak. The brother she had grown up with was still there but now shared the body of a world-weary stranger.

As the broth nourished her body, she glanced around at her brother's companions inhabiting the meager camp. They appeared to be disenfranchised Englishmen, and she observed a handful of bond slaves among them. The men's hands tended to linger on the hilts of their swords in uneasy comfort as they stamped around the camp. They no doubt fought against the Normans at Hastings but took to the countryside after Harold fell, an act of self-preservation to allow them to fight another day. Despite being among her people, Isabel could not shake the feeling something was terribly wrong. She did not belong here.

Once the last of the soup was gone, Julien set the bowl aside and looked at her in silence.

She was consoled by his gaze and hoped the circumstances belied his relief at being reunited with her. Just seeing him again was a balm on her soul, easing the guilt and pain, which had plagued her for far too long. But, she was beginning to cramp and could not wait any longer to fracture the moment. "Are you going to untie me?"

An apologetic look stole over his features. "Not yet." He casually glanced over his shoulder. Surely the men around camp were too occupied in their own endeavors to overhear their exchange. Julien finally turned back to her. "Father bade you to stay in Ashdown," he said in French.

It took her a moment to absorb the accusing tone he had levied at her. "How could I stay there when William would have our family greet him in London?"

He shook his head. "Still, your actions have made it all the easier for some Norman cur to take advantage of you."

"I have only done what William wished of me," she said, not sure why she needed to defend herself.

Julien sneered. "And how many men did you sleep with before you secured such a favorable future? You should have been married off to a nice Englishman well before now. I argued with Father to get you settled on more than one occasion. But you were always too stubborn. And now you have let yourself be defiled by these conquerors."

She knew the signs, knew that he was impassioned with English rhetoric and imbued with a false sense of superiority. Her temper rose to match his, but she found the emotions sapped too much of her strength to show him just how unjust his words were. She wanted to shake some sense into him, but everything about the situation prevented her. She was speaking to Julien the rebel, not her brother.

"You forget our namesake. There was never any danger to me, to us, from them. Only our loyalties needed to be confirmed," Isabel said through her teeth.

"I was not about to let those Norman fiends take our country from us. They had not the right..."

"They had the Pope's blessing," she said quietly.

He faltered for an instant before he found the thread of the argument he had memorized by now. "Rome does not command us." The response was firm, but it could not fool Isabel.

"You have already lost. Just look at you and your men. You are nothing but animals in hiding. Julien, you would have been spared if you had not—"

"Had not what? Fought for my king, fought for the glory of my country? I did my duty, something you and our father never could understand."

"Julien..."

"No, Isabel, you need to listen to me. I saved you from the Normans, saved you from having to sell yourself like some common house whore to those men."

"But I have already been married off. It is too late to speak of saving."

Her somber tone brought a frown to his face. "I tried to stop it, stop them from taking you, but you were always so closely guarded, even on the road to London."

"What do you mean?" He watched her, patiently waiting for her to puzzle it out as he had when they shared their lessons so long ago. Isabel shook her head, trying to make sense of his words. "Are you saying you organized the raid against Alexandre's men?"

He gave a short nod. "I was surprised at how fiercely you were protected." He quieted, then softly, he began again, his voice full of condemnation. "I heard how you yourself fought against my men."

"How could I have known..." He had tried so hard to reunite them and prevent her from having to fulfill William's plans. At that moment, though, with Julien's grim gaze on her, the brutish men surrounding them and the coarse ropes cutting into her skin, she would have fought against her brother's men all over again had she known this awaited her.

His words interrupted her thoughts. "You know not how it felt to think you had to marry a Norman to secure your place. It disgusted me I left you to such a fate."

"How did you find out?"

He gave a bitter laugh. "William is still too much in thrall over his victory at Hastings to realize there are still so many who would defy him. When Kendrick joined our band, he had some interesting things to tell me."

Everything fell into place as his words faded into silence. Kendrick... His wistful gaze as he rode through the gates of her father's castle was still vivid in her mind. "Is he here?" she asked, surveying the other men more closely. If Julien knew this much about her activities, what did he make of Alexandre?

Julien shook his head. "He and some of the other men journey to one of the local towns for supplies."

Isabel could not suppress a frown. "Do not tell me you have resorted to blackmailing the countryside for food and supplies."

The flare of anger in her brother's eyes stole her breath. He clenched his fists. She wondered if he would smack her for such brutal censure, but there was nothing. "We will be the ones to rid this land of the thieving Normans. And the English people know that," he finally said.

Tears welled behind her eyelids. She felt so helpless, not for her situation but for her misguided brother and his men. They would die before accepting a different—Norman—way of life, and she could do naught to stop it.

"I am sorry I was too late."

The sincerity in his voice wrenched her heart. "It is not so hopeless as you make it sound. Alexandre is a good man, and he cares about our people."

"Bah, he has only poisoned your mind against your country, against your own blood. Just like *Maman*, spreading her legs for some Norman whoreson," he said with a harsh eye on her still-torn clothing not completely hidden by the folds of her cloak.

Mortification swept through her but she fought for control, concentrating on the ugliness of his words and not the hurt they caused. "Blame me not for finding a few moments of pleasure in all this chaos. I had no one to turn to, and William's demands left me no choice."

Something must have gotten through to him for he let the matter drop and switched to English. "We will talk no more on it tonight. You are with us, and we should take comfort in being together again."

"Julien, you do not know how difficult it was when I learned you and father were dead."

"I know, little sister, I know, but I am the one who is going to take care of you now. So worry not."

"But Alexandre and his men…"

"They will not waste their time searching for you. You are not worth the trouble."

She slowly nodded but his callous words only kindled her secret fears. After all, Alex had already achieved what he had hoped for when he fought for William. Worse still, what if he assumed she ran away? He knew of her temper, her reluctance to marry, her desire to protect her people. He would think on those things and decide she was up to her old tricks again. Mayhap this would be the last straw.

She shifted her stiff limbs, relishing the pained movement so she did not have to ponder the pain in her heart.

"And the ropes?"

Julien's gaze slid away. "That is not my decision."

"What do you mean? You lead these men, do you not?"

"It is complicated. I will talk with Alric and try to get him to understand." Isabel was certain she would have been freed if her brother were in charge—even if he still questioned her loyalty. Not for the first time, she wished she knew him better, knew the man he had become. He looked over his shoulder, and then to her. "Now, you need your rest. I will be with you again in the morn."

He was right. She could feel the fatigue bearing down on her frame. He leaned in and pressed a kiss to her forehead, the gesture confusing her all the more. Julien helped her lie down on her side and pulled a worn blanket over her. With a soft touch on her shoulder, he was gone.

\* \* \* \*

Alex reined his horse to a stop, and his men followed suit. They had reached Chalgrove, a small village raided only a few days ago, according to reports. Alex commanded Hugh to accompany Captain Thomas as they visited with the English townsfolk to see if they could glean any more information about the attack. After a short perusal of the town, Alex and the rest of his men sought out the nearby monastery, where they hoped the abbot knew enough French to help them along.

They had spent the last two days combing the land for the trail Isabel's captor had taken, but it soon disappeared, leaving them with few options. They were close to Chalgrove when they heard about the raids from a merchant they met along the road. With nothing more to go on, they decided to see if anyone in the town was knowledgeable.

Flanked by two of his men, Alex entered the monastery, preceded by a timid cleric. Incense flooded his senses. Grimacing, Alex turned the corner, matching their guide's movements down another dim, stone corridor. The cleric finally led them into a small chamber where the abbot sat at a desk.

He looked up from an illuminated tome, his brow wrinkled in irritation. "Well? You just missed them. Heading west toward Bampton. But a half-day's ride."

"I beg your pardon?"

The priest tented his fingers. "William's man, are you not?"

"Yes, we are trying to find—"

"The men who attacked the village. Yes, yes. I know all about that."

"You do? Who are they?" Alex asked.

"I will tell you what I told Captain Radolf." The priest rubbed his temples. "They stole only supplies. Tenant farms to the north were hit hard. Some young soldier who William sent here was killed when he tried to interfere."

"I see." Raiding supplies and livestock was one thing. Killing the king's men was another, and Alex could not hold back the concern that flared up when he thought of Isabel in the hands of those murderers. "Have there been any other sightings?"

He shook his head. "You will have to find Radolf to learn more."

What if the two incidents were not linked? Was he so desperate for the truth, he was forcing connections where there was only coincidence? If so, getting involved in the search for the rebels would distance him from his true goal, finding his wife.

The priest cleared his throat. "There is naught more to tell. Be off with you now...unless you wish to unburden yourself of some coin?"

With a reluctant grin, Alex dropped some gold pieces in the proffered offering plate. "And you said I could find Captain Radolf to the west?"

"Yes, yes. They left this morning."

"I thank you."

The monk waved him off, and the same cleric led Alex out of the building.

Alex gulped in deep lungfuls of fresh air after escaping the incense that filled the monastery. Jerome waited for him in the yard, Averill standing next to him, wringing her hands.

"What did they say?" Jerome asked.

"A group of rebels came here for supplies, and a force of William's men are in pursuit."

"Captain Radolf?"

"The very same."

"What good fortune!"

Alex shook his head. "Not if the incidents are not related."

"But we have nothing else to go on."

"I am well aware." He looked at Averill.

The serving girl had burst into tears when she learned of Isabel's disappearance. And the honest reaction helped ease his lingering doubts as to whether Isabel had left him willingly. Although the girl was not accustomed to hard travel, she had not complained once when he and his men abandoned plans to return to Ashdown in order to search for Isabel.

"If Isabel has indeed fallen in with the remnants of Harold's army, how will she be treated once they learn who her father is?" he asked the girl, setting aside the idea Isabel had to have been targeted for some reason.

"I know not, my lord. I have served the Dumont household since I was a child, and I am not familiar with—"

Alex raised his hand. "Your best guess then."

"Isabel's brother Julien was Harold's man." The girl swallowed. "Mayhap that will be enough to keep her safe."

Safe. From what? He ran a hand over his face. He would not think of that. It had only been two days. There was still time.

"What are your orders?" Jerome asked.

"We join Radolf."

\* \* \* \*

Someone nudged her side with a booted foot, waking Isabel from sleep none-too-gently. She grimaced as Julien's face invaded her vision.

"Can you stand? A walk will help."

The soup the night before had done wonders, and her muscles nearly screamed at the prospect of some exercise.

Julien extricated her from the frost-covered blankets but left her ankles hobbled. She was relieved when he moved to untie her hands behind her back, but those thoughts were dashed when he bound them together in a more comfortable position in front of her body.

Julien led her around the camp in silence. In the new dawn, many of the men still clung to the last few moments of sleep. Last night, she had not been able to make much out of her surroundings in the dark, especially considering her weariness, the residual effects of the herbs in her system and the surprise of finding Julien back in her life. In the morning light, however, her brother's exhaustion was even more apparent. Pain etched his face and affected his carriage. Stiffness marred his step. He must have been injured at some point and either the wound had not yet healed or not healed correctly.

"Where did you get hurt?" Her brother was not the type of man to let an injury hold him back.

Julien ignored her as he helped her pick her way around the perimeter. She could see him working out his answer in his head and suddenly knew he was worse off than she had thought. Finally, he faced her. "No matter. It's only a scratch."

"You should know better than to lie to me. How long have you been feeling ill?"

"Since some Norman slashed into my stomach." She winced at his tone. He ran a hand through his hair and sighed. "I stopped him, all right? Stopped him from killing me. I managed to take cover with some of my men who knit me back together. By then it was too late. The Normans claimed their victory. So here I am."

He would not meet her eyes. "I'm all mended," he said through his teeth. "Worry not, little sister."

"That is no mere scratch. Let me look," she said softly.

"No, Isabel, I already told you—"

She came to a swift halt, and Julien stumbled slightly. Anguish wrapped around his features at his abrupt movement.

Isabel shoved aside his tunic, ignoring his protests and the awkwardness of the ropes holding her wrists together. Sooner than expected, Julien gave up trying to prevent her perusal.

Crisscross scars interrupted the smooth skin across his lower belly. This was no trifle. His insides had been nearly gouged out. The wound had indeed closed, but the discoloration and swelling spoke of something far more ominous. Isabel did not miss the pained intake of breath Julien made as she gently probed along the wound. Fear settled into her heart as she measured with her fingers what had to be one of the worst injuries she had ever seen.

"Julien, tell me they used yarrow when they dressed this."

He must have sensed the panic behind her words, for he pushed her hands away and dragged her down the path, a hand firmly directing her by the elbow, the other covering his stomach with his tunic once more.

"I cannot tell you, for I do not remember."

If he had not been driven into unconsciousness by the injury, any attempts to sew him back together would have knocked him out. Now, though, he was far too active, given his weakened state. Being forced into hiding and traveling the countryside did not leave much room for respite or proper hygiene. "You should take more time to rest. You are still healing and—"

"I have healed enough."

"But—"

"Enough! Naught can be done at this point. The men here, they are my men and they need to be led if we are to ever take back what is ours. I cannot do that from a sickbed."

Tears stung behind her eyelids. He knew it was bad. He did not need her to confirm it.

"If these are your men, then who is Alric? Why do you need his approval to let me free?" she asked.

The tension building in her brother's frame told her he was close to losing his temper, but she could not afford to waste any more time wondering what was to become of her.

He looked up at the bare tree limbs splayed overhead. "Alric of Evesham and some of his men joined up with us after Hastings," he said with reluctance. "They have been useful on some of our raids and in identifying people who will harbor us. But when he learned of our father, he would turn the men against me, thinking me no better than those conquering barbarians." He faced her. "And he has nearly succeeded. With my injury, I can do naught to challenge him. So to keep the peace, that is why I do not tempt him further by granting your freedom. And even if I could untie those ropes without fear of recourse from him, I am not sure I would. How would I know you would not go running back to the bed of your Norman lover?"

What could she say to that? Finding Alex was indeed first and foremost on her mind, assuming he still wanted her. She had a place in the new country William was trying to build, a place her brother and his companions would condemn her to hell for. Men like her brother would not give up their aspirations for independence. She understood their sentiments, but she could not condone them when the country was in desperate need of peace.

She shook her head. "Julien, you know not the trouble I caused Alexandre and his men when they came. He probably thinks I ran of my own free will and has lost whatever trust he held for me. If I were to return to him, there would be no warm welcome."

Julien must have sensed her melancholy, for he

stopped their progress, forcing her to face him. "Do not tell me it is true?"

She looked up at him in surprise, not understanding his implicit question or the sharpness of his tone. "What?"

"Do not tell me you actually care what this man thinks about you! He is a thieving Norman who killed your people in cold blood."

"I know who he is better than you." She tried to shake off his hands, which suddenly gripped her with frightening intensity.

Julien sneered. "Don't even try to defend him. Or yourself. You, who rejected every Englishman who would have you."

"That is not fair! You know I could not accept any of the men presented to me. Before we recount their arrogance and abuses, remember that they would expect me to be happy with naught else than knitting in my solar and dandling children on my knees. I would rather die than live with those kinds of restrictions."

"And what makes you think this Norman is any different?"

"Because he wants me to be involved. He seeks out my advice and respects my opinion."

"No doubt this was all before he bedded you," Julien said with a harsh laugh. "He trapped you, make no mistake. Now, with us, you have an opportunity to start over."

"You may be indifferent to your change in fortune, but I cannot be. I will not leave our people, Matilde, or even Captain Thomas. By remaining with Alexandre, I can help our people transition to William's rule, protect them and make the changes as painless as possible."

He scoffed. "Too late for such noble sentiments, sister. By your own account, you've already lost

Alexandre's trust. Even if he were to come galloping to your rescue, your very presence here with me and my men casts further suspicion on you."

"Yes, but how will those thoughts change when he realizes I have been kept a prisoner here this whole time? He may be Norman, but stupid he is not, Julien, and you would do well to remember that if he comes."

"If, Isabel...if." He shook his head, lips curled in disgust. "I still cannot believe you have come to care for this man. To him, you are merely a spoil of war, naught more. And yet you stand here defending him. I will hear no more about this, do you understand? You are with us now, and naught will change that."

Isabel held his angry gaze for a few heartbeats before turning away in defeat. She did not want to fight with Julien when she had been granted a second chance to be with him. However, his assumptions about her relationship with Alexandre, while not surprising, still troubled her and fed into her doubts. Mayhap, before this had happened, she and Alex had a chance to actually be happy. Now, though, she could not even be sure he would try to find her.

She changed the subject. "What about Father?"

A look of pain flooded his face. He gritted his teeth and met her gaze. "He rests at St. Bride's. I was able to convince the clerics to properly see to his body." He pressed his lips together momentarily. "He asked me to watch out for you, and I gave him my oath. I carry his sword now." He pulled the broadsword halfway from its sheath, enough for Isabel to recognize the pommel and scrollwork at its base.

Isabel absently wiped her eyes on her cloak with a shrug of her shoulder. She was too heart-sore to mourn her father again. She let her brother finish leading her around the camp before he returned her to her nest of blankets.

"Do not forget your oath," she whispered.
He left her without another word.

# Chapter 21

One of Captain Radolf's scouts intercepted them before nightfall and led Alex and his men to their makeshift camp in a small forest clearing. Since Aylesbury, Radolf's ranks had swelled to nearly two-dozen Norman soldiers.

The captain greeted them, "What brings you here? Last I heard you were headed to London."

In the dark, Alex had difficulty deciding whether or not Radolf was surprised to see them again so soon. "That is correct. We just came from there but a few days ago on our way back to Ashdown to the west. However, the Lady Isabel, who traveled with us, disappeared that first night on our return trip."

"Was this the pretty lass who was with you when we met at the inn?"

"Yes. We tried searching for her but the trail went dead outside Chalgrove. We heard rumors of the rebels and thought they might be involved."

"So you think she was kidnapped?" He was silent as he mulled things over. "How do you know this woman did not run away? She is just an English wench, no?"

Captain Thomas tensed beside him, but Alex trusted the man enough to hold his tongue. Alexandre leaned forward. "Lady Isabel, daughter of Lord Bernard Dumont of the Dumonts of Normandy, is not just an English wench. Nor did she run off, that I'm certain. Someone took her away…from me."

The captain's eyes widened at Alex's possessive claim, but he made no comment as he continued to survey Alex and his men.

Captain Thomas cleared his throat. "We were told by monks in Chalgrove you were tracking the rebels who attacked them."

The captain nodded. "True enough. We have been close to catching the fiends a number of times, but they know this terrain, this land, too well. They disappear on us no sooner than we see them. But we're getting closer, aren't we, boys?" he asked heartily of his men around him.

Alex waited for the men's eager affirmations echoing around the clearing to die off before speaking again. "How many are there?"

"It is difficult to tell," Radolf said with a sigh. "We have received reports survivors of the English army are traveling to the coast, sailing north to Norway rather than acknowledge William as their king. But many have stayed behind, hiding themselves in the English countryside like the animals they are. They split up, attack multiple towns and villages simultaneously, and retreat in different directions if challenged. Look at this."

He pulled out a rough map of the area indicating the raids that had taken place over the last few weeks. "You can see almost all the attacks have taken place south of Oxford in roughly a twenty-five mile radius of here." He pointed out the village of Bampton. "They must have connections with some of the locals to keep them supplied. We think they have someone spying on us as well so they can stay abreast of our movements. But they are getting careless, and it won't be much longer before we'll get them."

Alex spared a glance at both Hugh and Captain Thomas. Hugh's brow furrowed as he studied the map.

Captain Thomas gave him a nod subtly endorsing whatever Alex decided to do. Although there was only one real choice. Alex faced Radolf. "By your leave, we would offer our services in locating the rebels."

The captain let out a mirthless chuckle. "I see no reason to refuse your request, but I must tell you there have been no reports of a woman traveling with the group."

"I understand, but right now, these outlaws are our only lead in locating Isabel."

"May I ask why this woman is so important to you?"

"William granted me Dumont's lands in exchange for marrying his daughter."

Comprehension dawned on the captain's face. "Well, then I hope it is not a fool's errand. Your men should rest now for we will break camp just before dawn."

\* \* \* \*

The midday meal came and went, and Isabel strove to ignore the hunger plaguing her.

"Here, eat this."

Isabel looked up, momentarily blinded by the sunlight that backlit the person before her. She gradually made out the rangy body and golden beard. "Kendrick?" Her voice creaked from disuse.

"As you see," he said with a small smile. He quickly glanced over his shoulder, then dropped a crust of bread into her lap.

She had given up hope of being fed. "Thank you for thinking of me." Her polite words did little to cover up the greedy way she snatched the bread and stowed it under a fold in her cloak. There was still so much to ask him, how he had come to be there, but he seemed uneasy they would be caught together.

"Are there others here?"

He shook his head and moved a few feet away but not out of hearing distance.

"You told Julien where to find me," she said quietly. She was not sure if she should condemn or thank him.

Kendrick looked at her then. "Yes, but—" He walked away from her as a group of Englishmen came toward them.

Her disappointment at his disappearance was only partially mitigated by the bread she had hidden away. No doubt Kendrick brought her food of his own free will and was worried he would be caught at it. Everyone, including herself, was uncertain of her standing. She was still a prisoner, despite her brother's protection.

Nevertheless, she relished the nourishment the bread afforded and did her best not to call attention to Kendrick's gift, taking stealthy bites when no one was looking.

Toward mid-afternoon, judging by the position of the sun in the sky, more men converged in camp as their duties were completed. As far as she could tell, her brother's companions were separated into groups responsible for different tasks, with the bondsmen relegated to more menial work. Some collected firewood and kindling, others concentrated on hunting and food preparation. Some served as outlooks on the outskirts of camp. Still others sharpened axes and arrowheads, which spoke more of their intentions than anything else.

With the day's work behind them, the mood around camp lightened. One knot of men became involved in a game of dice while other groups of men played draughts. Drink was passed around and the men became boastful in their talk and bold in their play. As it grew darker, the campfires blazed higher, and meat was placed on spits, the smell reminding all that supper was near.

Isabel shrank as far away from the firelight as she could. Given her tenuous status, she did not want to attract undue attention even though everyone was probably aware of her presence in camp. It was only a matter of time before someone latched onto it, like a dog worrying a bone, unwilling to leave off.

She found herself watching a particular group of men who had returned from a day of hunting. They immediately gorged themselves on the available ale before launching into a game of draughts nearby. She heard their wild boasts from where she sat. They would soon exhaust all the insults they could throw at each other, and then she feared they would ridicule whatever else was at hand—her.

"And that's another for me," bragged a hulking brute of a man with beady eyes nearly lost in his fleshy face. "You know, if you keep losing, we're going to wonder whether you are man enough to wield that axe of yours."

The resulting guffaws did little to lessen his younger opponent's embarrassment. "Fool, I am more a man than you. What was it I heard? You needing to blindfold a woman before she'd have you?"

"Nonsense," said the first. "A lass need only see my manhood to know the bliss she'd have rutting with me."

"So then it wasn't rape I saw between you and that maiden at the last village?"

"No, it wasn't," the first man said, anger in his voice. "It was, how do you say...spirited lovemaking. Spirited lasses always bring the best out of ye."

"No honor comes from taking what is not offered," the younger ground out.

"Oh no—all this talk about honor. You wouldn't

know honor if it slapped you in the face."

"I am not the one having trouble finding willing lasses."

The words pushed the first man over the edge. Their companions seemed to realize the imminent confrontation and took up positions around the two men to keep them from attacking the other.

The first easily shook off the men holding him back by the shoulders. "Then let's put those words of yours to the test. If you can't make that creature over there bed you, the rest of your purse is mine."

"Fool, that woman is off limits, and you know it," the younger man said with nary a glance at her.

"That woman's off limits," the first mimicked, his face flushed with drink. "From what I've heard, that trollop has willingly spread her legs for those rutting Norman dogs. It's time she learned what a good Englishman can show her."

The men had come closer now, inexorably drawing her into their circle.

"In fact, she is already trussed up, so it should not be too hard." The first man grabbed her wrists and hauled her to her feet. She did her best to hide her dread, willing her features to remain impassive.

The younger man looked at her with a mixture of pity and disgust. "That's your way, not mine."

"She has already known a Norman devil's bed," the first man scoffed. "She deserves nothing more." He tugged again on her ropes.

Isabel forgot how to breathe as the men pressed closer.

"She deserves your respect," her brother interjected.

Isabel sagged with relief at Julien's timely arrival and tried not to show emotion. She would not give these men the satisfaction they had succeeded in needling her.

Hoof beats echoed. The men shifted uncomfortably around her. The mysterious Alric must have returned. Even Julien looked upset at the leader's arrival. The man in question rode straight toward them, two men-at-arms following. Dark brown hair touched his shoulders and his full beard helped mask the bitter lines of his mouth. He carried an axe, like Julien and many of the other Englishman. As he swung down from the saddle, Isabel could see Hastings had left him unscathed. He handed off his reins to one of his men. She was certain his intelligent gaze had not missed the confrontation or the cause behind it as he surveyed the camp.

"My, my, Dumont. Surely your sister knows better than to keep company with these men."

At his words, the first man released his grip on her. Without his support, she struggled to stay upright, her shackled feet precariously balancing her. Julien grabbed her by the shoulder as she started to sway. Before he removed his hand, he squeezed her in what she hoped was a comforting if not cautionary gesture.

Seeing their leader had trained his gaze on Isabel and her brother, the rest of the men crept away to rejoin the others around the fire, no doubt eager to avoid any censure for their actions.

Once the men were far enough away, the Englishman spoke again. "Forgive them. Most are simple farmers and do not know how to give a lady proper respect."

"I am sure I am not worthy of such respect in their eyes...or yours," Isabel said.

He was silent for a moment, and she ignored the way Julien tensed beside her. "Indeed, your forthrightness should surprise me not, from what your brother told me, but I find myself amused nonetheless.

269

Forgive me, where are my manners? My name is Alric of Evesham. Welcome to our camp." With a flourish, he gestured at their surroundings.

Isabel remained unaffected by the display while Julien stood awkwardly silent next to her. "My brother told me to ask you whether I can have my ropes removed."

"Did he now?" Alric flicked an inscrutable look at Julien.

"Am I a prisoner?" Isabel asked, which brought his gaze back to her.

He gave a short laugh. "A prisoner? No. We went to a great deal of trouble to rescue you from those Norman brutes."

She raised her wrists, displaying the corded rope. "Then these are?"

"Merely precautions. We don't want you getting overexcited. There is much to be done."

"You do realize, I cannot be ransomed. As my brother can attest, our father's legacy has already been passed on in marriage."

"Where do you get such ideas, my dear? Your brother informed us of your plight, and we were eager to rescue such an innocent from Norman corruption."

Isabel studied him, put off by his honeyed words and his too-handsome bearing. His tone was a counterpoint to the sharp look in his eyes and tightness in his jaw. No wonder Julien did not want to provoke him. He was not a man who would forgive easily.

"Enough talk. I'm hungry," Alric said.

He led Julien and Isabel to the fire. Men cheered or raised their cups as he passed. He took the central seat, bidding Isabel to sit beside him. She did not miss the way her brother winced as he stiffly sat cross-legged on the ground nearby. Alric gave the signal for food to be served, and a bondsman brought over meat and bread. Isabel was hard-pressed to keep the food from spilling on her, but she managed to feed herself with her hands tied, nonetheless.

"Dumont, I'll need you and Kendrick to take two men to Burford to get some supplies. Leave after you have eaten your fill."

Julien gave her a harsh look, bidding her to be silent, before he turned to Alric. "As you wish."

"I'll expect your return in two days' time."

Julien grunted in acknowledgment, and Isabel's hopes sunk. Days of hard riding would further impede recovery from his injury. Julien's presence was the only reason she was being treated fairly. If she protested his assignment, she might weaken him further in the eyes of his men. Deep in her gut, she knew the next two days would be the hardest yet without Julien or Kendrick around.

When her brother finished eating, he drew her up beside him and led her to her blankets.

"Julien..."

"Behave, little sister. I'll be back soon." A bitter laugh bubbled up inside her, but all Julien offered in return was a quelling look. Then he was gone.

* * * *

The next morning, a stranger jostled Isabel awake. "Who are you?" she asked blearily, trying to get her wits about her. A thin layer of frost covered her blanket. Daylight had just broken, and she could hear the men beginning to stir.

"I'm hurt you don't remember me, lass."

Isabel shook away the rest of the sleep still clinging to her and reassessed the man before her. He was the man behind her kidnapping, the one who brought her here in the first place.

"You!" She threw herself out of his grip.

"Not so fast, lass. Your brother bade me look

after ye while he was away. If you don't like it, then you won't mind if I send Alric over instead."

Isabel stilled, recalling the rebel leader's steely gaze. She wanted no part of him.

The man snorted. "Thought not." He guided her to her feet and led her outside the camp so she could relieve herself. He also gave her the opportunity to walk about a bit to work out some of the stiffness from sleeping on the ground. Throughout it all, she refused to speak to him.

Just before they returned to the camp, the man pulled her off the path between two bushes. For what purpose? Her stomach lurched when she realized she could no longer make out the campfires. She tried to shake the man off, but he held firm. His hand on her chin forced her to face him.

"Alric will be looking for an excuse to use you against Julien." He let her go once he had her attention.

"What is your name?"

"Osbert of Tamworth"

She nodded. "Well, Osbert, somehow I doubt I'll be able to prevent Alric from doing what he sets his mind to."

Osbert backed off. "Just remember there is only so much I am willing to do for a Norman whore."

Isabel flinched at his words but did not protest as he pulled her back on the trail toward camp. He deposited her at her blankets before he returned to his duties. She understood his warning for what it was, but she knew Alric was both cunning and determined.

If he wanted to use her against her brother, she was in no condition to protest, being half-starved, weaponless and without companions.

# Chapter 22

The rest of the day passed uneventfully. Waiting for the men's return was Isabel's only occupation. Once Alric arrived in camp, he again requested her presence next to him during the meal with a sharp tug on her ropes. His touch sent warnings throughout her body.

Isabel watched Alric closely while they ate. As much as she disliked him, his ability to converse with the men and garner their respect was impressive. He wielded his silver tongue well, and it became increasingly clear how this man was able to wrest control of the rebels from her brother. When Alric spoke, the Englishmen listened.

The meal over, the men moved on to their idle chatter. Isabel had grown stiff, and she longed to move about before she retired for the evening. Without her brother there, though, she felt even more vulnerable.

"It is time you upheld your end of the bargain," Alric said, his words pulling her out of her reverie. She was keenly aware of the way his gaze had fallen on her periodically throughout the supper, a man assessing his prey.

She stiffened. "What bargain? What are you talking about?"

He chuckled at her, indulgent, as if she were a child. "You were in London. You have seen William and his men. I have many…questions. And you must earn your keep."

Knowing looks passed between the men sitting closest to them, and menace lay behind Alric's words.

"After all, we went to all that trouble to rescue you." The hard stare he leveled at her felt as though he could see through her worn clothing to the flesh they adorned.

What little meat and bread she had eaten turned to lead in her stomach, but she would go to hell before she let him know how much he sickened her. "Pray then, explain why you are still treating me as a prisoner?" She raised her bound hands so they were framed by the firelight.

"Because you are not to be trusted. Not yet," he said with a smug glance at the rest of the men. "Come."

He grabbed the rope holding her wrists together and pulled her up until she stood unsteadily on her feet. She looked out among the smirking men, seeking, then finding, Osbert. For an instant, her gaze collided with his, but he studiously looked away when Alric dragged her forward.

"I won't let you do this," Isabel said as he escorted her from the campfires and his men's prying eyes.

A muscle in his cheek twitched before he forced another smile. "You are in no position to argue." His fingers tightened into the flesh of her upper arm, emphasizing the annoyance he felt.

"My brother—"

"Is not here. And you would do well to listen to me." He left the threat unfinished, hanging over them, as they moved further from the firelight to the edge of the woods bordering the camp. "Tell me what you know about the Bastard."

Where could she start? She resisted the urge to throw up her hands. "You will have to be more specific."

The moonlight glinted off his bared teeth. "How many men does he have?"

"In London?" Isabel tried to recall the conversations she overhead between Alex and his men, but she had been so preoccupied with her situation, she had barely listened at the time. The Normans were in control. That was all that mattered.

Alric gave a cruel tug on her wrists, and she nearly tripped. "Five thousand, maybe more. I am not certain. I am only a simple woman and cannot remember—"

His harsh laugh cut her off. "Come now. You expect me to believe you learned nothing, sharing a bed with one of William's favorites? You may have fooled your brother into thinking you are an unwitting victim in all this, but I know better. Now tell me what you know, and I will consider letting you live to see your brother when he returns."

"What do you want me to say? Harold's army was all but destroyed by the Normans. And although you and my brother wish it otherwise, your little band here is not enough to take back this land."

Alric spat and walked faster, Isabel hard-pressed to keep up with the rope around her ankles shortening her strides. "Mayhap not yet, but the day will come."

"Your fine words might convince your men, but they do not change the fact the Normans outnumber you. Why, beyond the men I saw in London, there are other contingents sweeping the land for rebels, the remnants of the English army."

Alric glanced back at her, his face indistinct but no less menacing in the dark. "Ha. If that is true, then there is naught to fear. The bastards will never be able to find us. This is our land."

"Not any longer."

He said nothing as he came to a halt near the tree

line. The campfire was a mere speck by now and the full force of night had settled over them. She stopped a pace behind him.

He finally spoke, keeping his back to her. "The English people are strong. They will not tolerate a foreign ruler."

"You did not see the London townspeople," Isabel said softly. Alric cocked his head at that. "They are bitter, angry, yes. But what surprised me most is their resignation. They honestly feel God has abandoned the English people."

Alric spun toward her. All she could make out was a brief glimmer of his eyes. "I refuse to believe God would punish us with Norman conquerors."

"But the Pope—"

"The Pope is William's puppet, naught else."

What more could she say? She flexed her wrists. "Return me to camp. I have answered your questions."

He was too still. She barely made out his breaths over the sudden acceleration of her heart.

"Ah, but I still have one more question." He grabbed her by the hair and tilted her head back. "Why would a good English girl give herself to one of those thieving Normans?"

She swallowed a cry. "I had...no choice."

Alric laughed, low and bitterly. She imagined a cruel grin stretched across his face. "We all have choices. For example, I could choose to take you back to camp this instant." He gave her hair a sharp tug. "Or I could lower myself to take a Norman whore as my own and make it all the easier to keep your brother in line."

Her stomach twisted as his breath wafted over her face.

"Now what do you think I choose?"

When he leaned toward her, Isabel lost herself to

instinct, slammed her knee up and out, striking his groin. It was not a direct hit, as her bonds still restricted much of her movements. His startled groan was her reward.

"You stupid bitch." He struck her across the face with his fist.

He had bloodied her lip. The metallic taste sent a rush of panic through her. She spat at him as he came after her again. She managed to twist out of his reach, thanking God the bond slaves had kept his ale cup full at supper. It gave her a small measure of hope. If Alric had been sober, she feared she would not be able to evade him for long.

He swung out again and caught her with his fist, sending her scrabbling across the wet ground. Reaching out with her bound hands, she searched for a sharp rock or stick, anything to repel him. He lunged as she closed her hand around a stone. Grabbing her hips, he swung her around to face him. She did not resist his power, instead using it as momentum as she locked her arm and drove the stone into his temple.

He grunted and toppled back, dazed, leaving her enough time to move away from him. Too soon he was back on his feet. He lurched forward, and his weight dragged her with him to the ground. She pushed her hands up and locked the rope between her wrists against his windpipe, trying to keep him away from her.

He groped her even as she struggled. She tried once more to buck him off her, but her body was weakening. Alric managed to grab her wrists and force them away from his neck. No… She could not bear the thought of having his mouth on her, but his face moved inexorably closer. Their harsh breaths mingled.

She had no more strength to fight back. She closed her eyes against the coming onslaught.

Instead, she heard a dull crack. Alric's dead weight fell against her, squeezing whatever air she had left in her lungs. She opened her eyes in disbelief and saw Osbert silhouetted before her, a heavy tree branch in hand. She shoved Alric off her and got to her feet, unsure of what she should do.

She struggled for breath. "I...thank you."

"Don't thank me. Thank your brother," Osbert said curtly. "Here." He held out her seax. She snatched it from him and sliced through the ropes shackling her hands and ankles.

Rubbing her wrist, she turned to Osbert, the man who had captured her only to help her escape. She opened her mouth to speak, but he forestalled her.

"Begone with you."

Without sparing Alric a second glance, she ran.

\* \* \* \*

She fell to her knees, her overexerted muscles unable to carry her any longer. Days of not eating well had taken its toll. Each labored breath echoed the pain in her chest, which tightened whenever Alric's words and actions slithered to the forefront of her mind. Her skin burned where he had dared to put his hands on her. She still felt the press of his beard against her face. She shuddered.

It started to rain, softly at first, saturating her clothes and skin and the woods around her. Isabel pushed wet hair out of her face and took stock of her surroundings. Only a stone's throw away, a dense tangle of trees would provide better cover. Alric would have men on horseback after her once he recovered. Despite her protesting muscles, she settled herself deep within the copse, doing her best to ignore the way the trickling rain and still-frozen ground stole her remaining warmth.

She gave a small prayer of thanks for the drizzle.

It would make tracking her much more difficult, concealing her scent and shrouding her from view. As the stitch in her side lessened, she evaluated the cuts and scratches she had sustained on her flight through the woods. At least she had not turned her ankle on any of the slippery tree roots and stones she had passed over. She could feel the swelling around her right eye and lip where Alric hit her. The rest of her would be covered with bruises, for the tender spots were already making themselves known.

It was not long before she heard the horses crashing through the bracken, sticks snapping with each step, and the men's shouts as they were forced to cut a path through the woods. Searching for her. Isabel tucked into herself as tightly as she could and covered herself as much as possible with her travel-stained cloak. She held her breath, willing the seconds to slip by, as she heard the horses—many more than she expected—pass her hidden den on either side until they were lost in the night.

Alone once more, she gulped in greedy breaths. What if the men doubled back? She dared not stay in one place for too long. Isabel rose to her feet and fought her way through the brush, searching for a tree to scale so she would not be underfoot if the men came back through. She moved as silently as possible among the branches. A misstep would surely bring them upon her. After she had put a good amount of distance between her and her last hiding spot, she found a tree large enough to hold her.

Peering into the darkness, she strained to hear anything over her clamoring heartbeat. She held still for a long moment, and then relaxed. Still alone.

After hiking up her skirt, she dug her numb fingers into the sodden bark. May she have the strength...

She had barely begun before she started to slide down, her palms tearing to shreds on the rough surface. Gritting her teeth, she adjusted her grip and pulled herself up the rest of the way by sheer force of will, seeking purchase with her booted feet. The effort made her dizzy, and once she made the first limb, could do nothing except breathe in and out, clenching and clasping her sore hands. She needed to get a little bit higher before she would let herself rest.

Climbing was easier now, the branches closer to each other than to the ground. She finally stopped at the apex of two larger limbs where they branched out from the trunk. Without a thought to the decomposing leaves and lichen softening her perch, she closed her eyes and bid her body relax into the rough bark cradling her. She had almost fallen asleep, when a loud snapping shattered the silence.

Isabel started, having forgotten where she was, and fingered the necklace Alex had given her. She smoothed the length of chain as she surveyed the darkness around her. What could have made that sound? Had Alric's men found her? Yet there was only silence.

Her panicked heartbeat slowed. She knew she should stay alert. In case she needed to find another place to hide. She would only close her eyes for a moment. Just one moment...

\* \* \* \*

Isabel hit the ground in a rush, landing on her stomach, unable to breathe.

She had dreamed she heard triumphant shouts. A low-level buzzing had filtered into her consciousness and insisted she wake. At first, she thought she had merely fallen out of the tree in her sleep, too exhausted to keep from slipping from her perch. The rough hands that grabbed and forced her upright told her otherwise.

Awareness slowly trickled through her as she assessed the team of Alric's men, who had dragged her from her hiding place, which was now visible in the dawn's early rays. She still smarted from her impact with the ground. Blinking back her disorientation, she moved into a crouch. The amusement on the men's faces told her they thought her a fool for even attempting to escape, but she had to try. She would accept no less.

She waited, willing one of the men to make their move. The man closest to her reached out, and she lunged away. Before she could catch her breath, Alric was suddenly there, grabbing her by the shoulders, destroying any resistance she was capable of.

He slammed her against the nearest tree—her tree, the tree that had kept her safe in the night— crushing her chest into the rough bark. Hard body pressed into hers, he kept her in place while two of his men took position on either side and held down her arms, preventing her from moving.

Alric removed himself with a growl. "There is no way to escape this time, Isabel." He ran a hand through her hair before suddenly pulling it taut and forcing her to look at him. "There is no one here to stop me from teaching you a lesson."

She heard him pacing behind her. What was he doing?

"You've been allowed to run wild for too long. It's time you learned your place." A sharp crack punctuated each word. A whip? A branch? She twisted around and saw the supple stick in his hands.

Directly behind her now, Alric traced the stick over her body and down her back. She knew what kind of man he was. All this was to see how far he could bend her before she would snap like a sapling in its first summer storm. He chuckled at her involuntary shudders. "You are not worthy of your English blood," he decreed.

Even though she had expected it, the first lash surprised her. She struggled to breathe through the biting pain unfettered by the clothes separating the stick from skin. He struck again. The pain sharpened, deepening the inroads of the first strike. Her neck arched back involuntarily with the third switch, her teeth clenched to resist the burn. The men struggled to keep her still as the fourth came down.

It went on, and she could hold back her screams no longer.

# Chapter 23

With the additional men, Captain Radolf's forces were able to cover twice as much ground as they attempted to ferret out the rebels.

As they traveled, it became increasingly clear just how much the English despaired of the Norman's presence. Despite the trouble in Ashdown, at least Alex had not felt the blind hatred aimed at them now. Thanks to the Dumonts' mixed heritage and household, he had been largely protected from the anger and turmoil many still felt. In London, the Norman presence overwhelmed the English townsfolk, making it easier to ignore their resentment. The countryside was different. He was painfully aware there were fewer of his countrymen to help him face down the palpable hostility he encountered in each village. Even Captain Thomas was shunned when attempting to facilitate their efforts by serving as translator.

Shouts pulled Alex out of his thoughts. Hugh and another Norman galloped into camp, his shield bearer barely checking his animal before he dismounted and ran over to Alex.

"We've found something."

Captain Radolf stepped forward. "The rebels?"

Riveted on Alex, Hugh barely spared Radolf a glance.

An inkling of hope spread through him. "Isabel?"

"We don't know. One of the merchants in Cricklade said a tenant farmer come into town to trade complained of a woman's screams near dawn but a day ago. The villagers were alarmed and made sure all the womenfolk were accounted for. None were missing. I got directions to the farmer's to see if there's more to his story. We haven't gone yet as I thought you'd want to join us."

"Indeed. Good work, both of you." Alex turned to the Norman captain. "With your approval, we would like to investigate this further."

Radolf laughed. "By all means. I would be a fool to stop you."

"Thank you. Hugh, fetch Captain Thomas. No doubt he will want to be there as well."

Hugh nodded.

Alex went through the motions of saddling his steed. Anticipation rushed through him, despite his doubts. It might be any woman, but, that no one was missing from the village kindled his optimism. This report, however unlikely, was their only clue in locating Isabel, and, given the rumored patterns of the rebels, they would have passed through here around the time the English farmer heard screams. If it were Isabel, what did the screams portend? Alex tried to keep from tormenting himself with images of Isabel being tortured or raped, as they were the only scenarios in which he could see his wife crying out in fear or pain. He prayed to God he was wrong.

"Alex, we're all ready," Hugh called out. The men waited on their horses.

He nodded in acknowledgment, mounted swiftly and followed Hugh and the others. The ride to the tenant farm was shorter than expected. The farmer waited for them as they rounded the turn in the road, taking a defensive stance in front of his home. The approaching hoof beats must have alarmed the old man.

Alex bid the men rein their horses to a walk and signaled for Captain Thomas to greet the man in English.

He did not attempt to understand their conversation. He had been in England long enough to pick up a few words here and there, but they spoke so rapidly he was not able to discern any of the terms. The Englishman relaxed as Captain Thomas conversed with him, occasionally pointing toward the woods closest to the hut.

"He said it rained two nights ago, and toward dawn, he heard the screams coming from the woods. They only lasted a few moments before it grew quiet again," Captain Thomas reported.

"How does he know they were a woman's screams and not a man's? If the storm was particularly fierce, perhaps it was only thunder that woke him."

Alex waited as Captain Thomas relayed the questions to the farmer.

"He says both he and his wife were woken up by the noise, but it was not repeated, and they had no way to learn the truth. However, they both agreed it was a woman's cries."

Alex took a better look at the territory, surveying the forest just beyond the farmer's fields.

"Thank him for his time," Alex said, tossing Captain Thomas a small pouch to give to the man. At his signal, the rest of the men directed their mounts to the woods.

"Look for anything out of the ordinary. Torn clothing, footprints, broken plants. The screams would not have carried far, so keep close to the outer perimeter of the forest," Alex said as he maneuvered his horse between the trees.

Even if they did come across something, there was no way to know if Isabel or the English rebels were involved. Too much time had passed.

After searching the eastern edge of the forest, Alex heard eager shouts. He followed the cries westward and met up with Hugh and another of his men, who clutched something in his hands.

"Well, what is it?"

Hugh nudged the young soldier. "Show him."

"Here, sir." The man-at-arms placed the object in Alex's hand.

He looked down. A scrap of fabric reminding him of the color and texture of Isabel's cloak cushioned his mother's pendant necklace. He clenched his fist over the items and slowly raised his head to meet their waiting faces.

"Where did you find this?"

\* \* \* \*

Isabel woke with a start—her body had cried out in warning—only to be hampered by the secure leather thongs around her wrists and ankles and the rope tying them together. She gagged at the ill-tasting piece of fabric tightly secured around her head. She adjusted to the bonds, slow to recognize the pain everywhere at once. Her right eye was nearly swollen shut, and her back and sides ached where she had been hit.

Twisting her head around, she winced as the rebel camp greeted her eyes. Osbert, unconscious with a large contusion along his temple, was trussed up beside her. Isabel felt a pang of guilt he had been caught, but the thought left her when Alric suddenly thrust his face into hers, a savage grin stretching across his face.

"Well, well, my lady. I am so glad you've woken."

Isabel tried to turn away but he clamped down on her shoulders and forced her to look at him. His breath licked her cheeks. She winced as the ground dug into her bruised back and pain flared through her once more.

"I hope I need not remind you how I punish those who disobey me."

She narrowed her eyes, and Alric's smile widened.

"You should have let me sample you." He traced his hand over her curves then rested it on her breast, despite her struggles to avoid him. He smirked. "But you have given me something better with your little stunt, and you have my thanks."

Isabel grunted as he finally removed his touch and stepped away from her. She did her best to still her rampant heartbeat and struggled to bring more air in through her nose. Alric had not gone far enough away for her liking. She still felt his eyes on her as he conversed with one of his men nearby.

Another soldier-at-arms rushed past her and kicked up dirt into her face as he headed toward Alric. "Sir, Dumont and his men will be here any moment."

"Excellent. Bring them to me at once."

Isabel swore to herself. She would be used by Alric as leverage against her brother.

Julien could not argue for her release. Not when Alric and the rest of the men would find him unfit to lead if they thought him sympathetic to her, especially since she had tried to escape and injured some of the men in the process. Her unease deepened as booted feet tramped closer. Isabel wanted to see how Julien had managed on the excursion despite his injury. Her brother and Kendrick stood before the rebel leader, dusty and tired. Neither man looked her way. Julien was pale and sweating despite the chill in the air but held himself proudly. What did it cost him to meet Alric's gaze head on as if nothing was wrong?

"We brought the supplies you requested," he reported.

"How many bows?" Alric asked.

"A dozen, plus the two bushels of oats and four sacks of flour."

"Good. What tidings do you bring?"

Julien shared a glance with Kendrick then said, "Only more rumors of a group of Normans searching for rebels."

"They were last seen in Bampton," Kendrick added.

Alric shrugged. "No matter. They have proven to be poor hunters."

"Their numbers have grown," Julien said. "I think it would be wise if we break camp and—"

"No. These curs are no match for us. We will stay here until the weather improves. At least another week."

Kendrick spat on the ground but said no more.

"Where is my sister?" Julien asked.

Alric's eyes sparkled in the waning afternoon light. "Did you not see her? She is over there with the other prisoner." Alric pointed toward her, smirking.

"Prisoner?" asked Kendrick as he finally faced her.

"Sadly, yes. She tried to escape—"

"What have you done to her?" Julien demanded, raking her with his gaze. Isabel felt helpless as he stared, knowing the impossible position he was in. He turned and faced Alric. "I care not if she tried to escape. You had no right to injure her like this!"

"No right? Even if she wasn't a Norman whore, she deserves every hurt I gave her for attacking me— her and that bondsman of yours."

"Osbert would have no reason to attack you..." Kendrick looked at Julien and searched his expression. "Unless..."

Red mottled Julien's face. He took a step toward

Alric. "You bastard. How dare you touch her!"

Kendrick grabbed his arm and held him in place. "Julien, don't," he said as the older man struggled with his temper.

Alric smiled. "I'll touch the wench any way I please, Dumont. Although she's looking poorly right now."

Isabel's brother pulled away from Kendrick and stalked closer to Alric. "It's finished. I'm taking Isabel and my men away from here. You and yours can go your own way."

"It's too late for that now. We need to be united against the enemy. I can't have you and your men breaking ranks over some woman," Alric stated, coolly appraising Julien's reaction.

"You do not deserve our loyalty," her brother bit out.

"Loyalty? I only need your compliance, willing or no."

Julien scoffed. "I have heard enough. We are leaving. Kendrick, gather the men."

Kendrick nodded and moved away as Julien turned his back on Alric and approached Isabel. Behind her brother, she saw Alric loose his axe. No... She should not be surprised Alric was so base as to attack Julien without warning. She shook her head to alert to her brother but he only looked confused.

Something must have made him realize what was happening. He stopped, eyes wide, and reached for the axe strapped to his back. Kendrick shouted in warning and with a muttered curse, Julien released the axe from the worn leather straps.

Alric swept his axe blade toward him with all his weight thrown into it. Julien met the strike and pushed Alric off him, pain wrenching his features as he twisted away.

"Alric, only you would be so cowardly as to fight an injured man!" Kendrick shouted before two of the rebel leader's men restrained him.

Alric waved him off with a sneer and came at Julien again, this time with speed behind him. Julien deflected the blow. His foot slid along the ground at the effort.

Her brother brought up his elbow and jabbed it into Alric's face, enough to force him away. His stance ready, Julien held his axe in his hands before him and waited for Alric's next move.

Alric came at him again, no doubt fueled by the knowledge Julien was weakening. He prepared to strike her brother's left shoulder. At the last possible moment, the rebel leader switched tactics, demonstrating a surprising amount of skill, and struck the opposite side.

Julien could not react to the change in time. Alric's blade sank into his padded surcoat. The blow forced Julien to his knees with a deep-seated groan. Alric knocked Julien's axe aside and brutally kicked him in the stomach. He collapsed and was still.

"You bastard! You knew of his injury. That will kill him more surely than a knife to the heart," Kendrick cried out.

"Silence the whelp!" Alric commanded. His men rushed forward and quickly gagged Kendrick and hauled him away.

Alric leaned over her brother's prone form and unstrapped her father's blade from his waist. A guttural growl was all she could manage through the gag as Alric greedily snatched up the priceless sword to replace his worn, secondhand steel. If she ever had the opportunity, she vowed to recover the blade.

Alric met her glare, a twist of a smile on his lips, and then he too was gone.

\* \* \* \*

The evening meal was long past when Julien finally stirred, and she curled around so she could see him. Face ashen, he struggled to breathe. It took a long moment before he finally looked as if he recognized her. Isabel's hands had been secured around the front of her body to aid her in eating, and no one had bothered to replace her gag when she had finished.

"Little sister," he gasped, "I am—"

"Speak not. Save your strength." Her voice was sharper than she intended in the falling dark.

A ghost of a smile graced his lips. "Too late." He struggled to sit up, but the effort was too much for him. His breathing was wet, his brow damp. He cleared his throat. "I did not want this for you. I am sorry."

"Julien, be quiet. I mean it," she said as if scolding a child. "There is no knowing how badly Alric hurt you."

"I know."

The grim tone of his voice infuriated her. How could he be so calm? Had he already given up? She wanted to reach over and shake him. "There could be damage internally. You could—"

"Isabel, I know," he said more forcibly. "I did not join with Harold unprepared for what war could bring." He began to cough.

"Please, just rest," Isabel pleaded.

Julien shook his head as if he meant to argue with her, but the coughing fit would not leave off. Blood trickled down the corner of his mouth.

Helpless, Isabel watched her brother wheeze, his inhalations troubled and slowing. She would not sit there and watch him die. "Alric, I demand to see him!"

Faces around the campfires turned her way in the dark.

"Leave off, wench," one of the men yelled. "Here,

here," cried another. Their voices echoed across the camp.

"Devil take you! I must speak to Alric now!" Isabel's frenzied cries brought the rebel leader, Kendrick and other interested onlookers to their side.

"Alric, please let me tend to him," she begged when Alric came near. "He could die."

The rebel leader stood there, looking back and forth between Julien and her, amusement lighting his eyes. "How nice. Such sisterly concern. Too bad I cannot trust you."

"If you will not release me, then let me tell one of your men how to treat his injuries."

Alric laughed at her before taking another long look at Julien. Blood slipped down to his chin as weak coughs still shook his frame. "My men have their own responsibilities. And they don't include nursing a traitor back to life."

"I will tend to him," Kendrick said as he stepped forward. A bruise had formed along his cheek, no doubt from his scuffle with Alric's men earlier, but otherwise he appeared to be unhurt.

Alric stared at him before finally nodding. "Very well, but you know what will happen if you defy me. When you are done dealing with this mess," he said, nudging Julien's leg with the tip of his boot, "I would have you rejoin the bondsmen in their work."

Kendrick bowed his head. "As you say."

Alric and his men stalked back to the campfire.

She shifted closer to her brother, hating the bonds that prevented her from helping him. Kendrick would have to be her hands tonight. "Make sure Julien is lying flat. Good. Now, I need you to see if there is maythen, and some mint leaves or the root of masterwort in the supplies. You know what to look for? You will need to crush the herbs between two stones and let them steep in hot water."

In those tense moments as Kendrick left to locate the ingredients, Isabel did all she could to avoid dwelling on her brother's plight as he lay beside her. He had finally gone quiet. She shifted, trying her best to get comfortable on the hard ground. The rebels' laughter ebbed in the night air. When Kendrick returned to her side, the campfires had become glowing embers. He ground the herbs into a paste and added it to the bowl of steaming water he had set beside him.

Once the mixture scented the air, Isabel told him it was time to wake Julien to see if he would drink the brew. Julien roused enough to haltingly choke the infusion down. He grasped Kendrick's arm and held the bowl to his lips.

"Will it help?" Kendrick asked later in a small voice, after he helped Julien lie down again. Her brother fell to sleep almost immediately.

Isabel shook her head. "I know not. It will help him to rest and soothe what ails his stomach, but I am afraid he is too injured to fully recover. That does not mean we should not try."

Kendrick nodded. "We must hope God will see fit to spare him." He turned to face her. "Can I get aught for you?"

"No." What she wanted was not in Kendrick's power to grant. "What did Alric say to you earlier?"

A thin smile was barely discernible through his golden beard. "He said if I worked with the bond slaves, I would be allowed to live."

"That is ridiculous. You are a free man, no matter what Alric says."

"I will do the work so long as you and your brother are under his control. It is a small price to pay to keep you safe." He ran an agitated hand through his hair. "I wish I stayed silent on what William intended for you. Julien thought he was rescuing you, but I know he did not want to make your situation worse."

"I know." She sighed. "Part of me is glad I am here with him, nonetheless," she said with a glance at her brother's slumbering form. "Everything suggested he fell at Hastings. Losing both Julien and my father... I thank God I got to see him again, whatever happens."

"Are you happy?" Kendrick's voice was uncharacteristically soft. She looked at him in surprise, trying to bite back the sharp retort that she was miserable, angry with Alric and herself for her capture and terrified her brother would simply waste away beside her. As she met his earnest gaze, she realized that was not what he meant. He was talking about Alexandre. Just like her thoughts, everything seemed to come back to Alex.

Unsure what she could say that would be true to her feelings for Alex but respectful of her friendship with Kendrick, she could only stare at Kendrick. His gaze faltered under hers, and she knew her inability to speak confirmed she was forever lost to him.

"Kendrick..."

"Isabel, I understand. When I saw the way you were with him, I knew. Worry not. He will come for you."

Isabel scoffed. "Alex no doubt feels he made a lucky escape from me and thinks I abandoned him to join the rebels."

Kendrick shook his head. "I cannot believe that. Even if he did feel betrayed by you, Alexandre strikes me as the type of man who would seek out the truth." He paused, barely restraining a grimace. He cleared his throat. "He is an honorable man, Isabel, and you love him for it."

She did not deny it. She could not. It was true, and she struggled in silence with the knowledge. Alex had laid siege to her heart, and his absence made her realize just how much she had come to care for the Norman knight, how much she wished she had let him know what she felt before they had been torn apart.

"Do you really think he will come?" she finally asked, hating the quaver in her voice and the vulnerability in her heart. She had given up so much when she married Alex. Regret filled her at the thought of never seeing her husband again.

"Isabel, I saw the way he watched you. The pair of you are the closest thing to a love match these accursed circumstances could ever allow. He would take your disappearance to heart and strive to uncover what happened—" He raised his voice when she would argue with him. "I know because I would have done the same thing. For you."

Tears welled at his words, but Kendrick's face was devoid of sadness, only calm with acceptance.

\* \* \* \*

Alex heard Radolf's men charging through the brush before he saw them emerge in the clearing, a struggling Englishman between them.

Captain Radolf strode forward. "What do we have here?" He grabbed the captive's hair and raised his head so it could be seen in the firelight.

"We caught him trying to sneak into camp," one of the men reported.

Alex growled as he recognized the golden locks of Isabel's friend, Kendrick. "Get Captain Thomas," he snapped at Hugh, who stood nearby, before coming to stand next to Radolf.

Kendrick's gaze found his, and Alex was surprised to see the relief in them. "Kendrick of Ashdown," he said. "I did not expect to see you again so soon."

"You know him?" Radolf asked.

"Yes. One of Lord Dumont's men," he said with a snarl.

Kendrick tried to shake off his captors but to no avail. "Call them off," he grunted.

"He speaks French?" the Norman captain asked in wonder before his expression hardened. "You are in no position to make demands."

Kendrick ignored Radolf, his gaze steady on Alex's face. "Call them off if you want to know about Isabel."

Alex locked his hand around Kendrick's throat in that instant. The young man flinched but Alex was too enraged to care. "What have you done to her?"

"Naught, I swear it," he rasped out.

"We found this on him." One of Radolf's men brought forward a small knife. "He had no other weapons."

"Isabel's seax," Captain Thomas said behind them.

Alex spared a glance over his shoulder to see that the captain and Hugh had joined them. He lessened the pressure on Kendrick's trachea.

The Englishman's gaze burned into his. "That is correct. She is being held by the group of rebels you have been tracking."

"How did she come to be captured?" Alex demanded.

Kendrick's gaze faltered. "Her brother learned of her fate and sought to prevent it."

Alex sneered. "And you had nothing to do with that."

"Julien is alive?" Captain Thomas came forward and laid a firm hand on Alex's shoulder. Alex reluctantly released the Englishman. "You must tell us what happened," Captain Thomas said.

Alex looked at Captain Radolf in deference, who

grudgingly nodded. The Normans relaxed their hold on Kendrick. Alex stepped back, taking Isabel's seax from one of the guards to inspect for himself. He recognized the blade's scrollwork and wrapped handle instantly. He returned his attention to Kendrick. "Speak."

"After I left Ashdown, I fell in with a group of Englishmen—"

"You mean rebels," Hugh corrected.

Kendrick eyed him with dislike. "You could say that. Isabel's brother, Julien, was with them."

"We thought he was dead," Captain Thomas said with a glance at Alex.

"Yes, I made inquiries on Isabel's behalf. Reports said he was killed in battle," Alex added.

"He very nearly was. He was badly hurt at Hastings, but his men helped him escape, and he recovered. When he learned Isabel was to be married off"—his mouth worked bitterly—"he bid his men to get her back. We watched the road to London, knowing you," he said with a nod to Alex, "would bring her to William eventually."

"So it was you who attacked us on the road?" Hugh asked.

"Yes, but we did not succeed. Julien was disappointed and decided on a different strategy."

"Was Isabel aware of this plan?" Alex asked quietly, afraid to learn the answer. He knew her brother had contacted her after the battle at Stamford Bridge. Did he contact her again without him knowing?

Kendrick shook his head. "No. Julien thought he was saving her, but he realized his actions just made things worse for her."

"How do you mean?" Captain Thomas asked.

Kendrick sighed. "One of the rebels discovered Julien's Norman heritage and discredited his leadership. Julien lost control over the men to a man named Alric. He has been the one attacking the local villages and killing the Normans stationed there."

Radolf scoffed. "And we are supposed to believe you and this Julien fellow are innocent of wrongdoing?"

Kendrick glared at the Norman captain. "Our sins are less severe, yes."

"You said things got worse. How?" Alex demanded.

"Alric ordered Julien and me on a mission, leaving Isabel alone at camp." Kendrick's gaze followed Alex as he began to pace back and forth in agitation at his tale. "Alric tried to attack her, but one of Julien's loyal men prevented it. Isabel managed to escape, but they found her the next day and brought her back to camp. When Julien and I returned, Julien fought with Alric when we learned what happened. Alric won, using Julien's injury against him. Now they are both captives."

Alex whirled and faced Kendrick. "Then why are you here? Why have you not helped them?"

"Don't you think I tried?" the Englishman snapped. "Alric knows you are close to finding them. I came to let you know what happened, and to help you, if you will let me."

"How can we believe you?" Hugh asked with contempt. "You made no secret of your dislike of us."

"Hugh is right. Why should we trust you?" Alex said.

Kendrick compressed his lips. He looked up, and Alex could see raw pain and real fear warring for dominance. "Because you know I could not live with myself if something happened to Isabel. I already feel responsible for setting these events into motion."

Alex watched the Englishman. He was telling the truth.

He relaxed his stance. "What can you tell us?"

# Chapter 24

Alex did not trust himself to help with strategy as Radolf and his men made plans to strike the rebels. His mind was too full with news of Isabel. He stood well outside the ring of firelight in the now quiet clearing where they were camped.

"You heard what they said?" Hugh asked.

Alex nodded, too caught up in his thoughts to manage conversation.

Captain Radolf sent his two best men to scout ahead to confirm Kendrick's story. The camp was stationed but a few miles away, and the scouts skirted the site in the darkness to see if it could be breached. While they had been able to identify only thirty rebels or so, they had a developed network of sentries, making scouting time-consuming and difficult. The men were exhausted with the effort. They had to hike an additional two miles through the forest to avoid being seen by the lookouts, and they waited until well after midnight to return to the Norman camp.

It was clear from the scouts' report Kendrick had told them the truth, yet Radolf had insisted they wait until dawn before striking. It made tactical sense, but Alex had not been feeling particularly sensible for some time now. The men had also spied a woman among the Englishmen, bruised and bound, with golden brown hair and a grayish blue cloak. Alex's stomach clenched at the tidings. Hearing the scouts' description of Isabel's condition destroyed any doubts he had let cloud his heart as to her conduct in all this. She had not left him willingly, and for now, it was enough.

The last few days spent alone had sharpened his attachment to her. He missed her warmth beside him as he drifted off to sleep, even though they had only had a handful of nights together. He tried to recall the smell of her, elemental and feminine, that would linger in the air when she had moved past him, but they had been separated for too long. It was not merely lust, and it had not been for some time. It was the comfort she gave him, the passion she inspired in him, it was simply her. And he wanted her back.

Alex sighed, and Hugh shifted his feet awkwardly beside him. Hugh had not repeated his criticism of Isabel in the days they had spent searching with Radolf and his men. His shield bearer had been uncharacteristically subdued in his interactions with Alex ever since. He wished he could simply forget Hugh's words, but Alex would not tolerate any more suspicions of his wife's loyalty.

Finally, Alex cleared his throat. "Isabel's safety is our priority tomorrow. I do not want your personal feelings to get in the way of that. When this is over, you may leave my service if you cannot—"

"*Non,*" Hugh said quickly. "I want to stay with you. I misjudged Isabel, and I am sorry for doubting her."

Alex eyed him, wary, and then nodded. Hugh must have worried about how things were left between them the last time they spoke like this. "I am glad. I have valued your service to me."

Hugh looked relieved. "I am honored."

Alex was content to leave things as they stood. Hugh would not be the first man to question the motives of the English people. Something he would not soon forget as a new lord. He ran a hand over his face.

"Come on, we need our rest since it looks like we will be using our swords in the morn," Hugh said with newfound confidence.

Alex reluctantly followed Hugh to their sleeping gear. He prayed to God to pardon his actions on the morrow, for he knew he would not hesitate to kill all who stood between him and his wife.

* * * *

"Wake up, little sister." Isabel started at the sound of her brother's voice, weak but recognizable amongst the din of camp being broken.

"Julien, you should be resting." Isabel pulled herself out of the cramped position she had fallen asleep in.

Her brother shook his head with impatience. "Never mind that. Alric ordered the men on the march just before dawn."

"Perhaps he finally realized the sense of your advice." Isabel glanced around the clearing. Men were indeed packing up their sleeping blankets and tents, stowing cooking utensils and supplies onto wagons and fitting their steeds in the early morning light.

"No. He would have stayed here just to spite us, if that was his only motivation. I heard one of the men on duty spied something strange when he was patrolling. Alric is worried it was a Norman scout."

Isabel perked up, finally managing to push the sleep from her mind. "Do you think they found us?"

"From the way Alric has been shouting out orders, it would surprise me not. That and one of the men went missing."

"Who?" she asked as she looked around. Osbert was no longer tied up with them. "Your man, Osbert?"

"No, he woke last night while you were sleeping, and Kendrick convinced Alric to release him."

"Then who?"

"Kendrick himself has gone missing."

"No! That does not make sense."

"Kendrick could not be accounted for after he left us last night."

"I do not understand. He said he would serve Alric so long as we were kept safe."

"Kendrick is no coward. Perhaps he learned about the Norman scouts and went for help. And," Julien said in a somber voice, "I hope for your sake your Alexandre is with them."

"Julien..." Isabel did not want her brother to draw her into another discussion of her Norman husband. She simply did not want to fight with him anymore.

"No, Isabel. Let me speak. I heard you last night, talking with Kendrick."

Her cheeks heated, and she looked away in shame. "Those words were not intended for your ears."

"It does not matter. You care for the man, that much is true. He fought to protect you, married you and showed you a respect that many a conqueror would have scoffed at. Here, you have been subjected to every sort of villainy I would protect you from. Can you forgive me for trying one last time to be the older brother you deserve? I only want what is best for you."

Isabel's breath left her in a rush. She had not been sure what her brother was going to say, but it was not this. "Yes, I forgive you. How could I not? You are my brother, the only family I have left."

Julien stared at her for a long moment. "Thank you for that, Isabel. Now I can rest easy."

"Nonsense," she said. "We will both see the end of this."

Julien weakly shook his head. He was tiring. Coughing, he lay down, and the sound broke her heart. She cringed as she sat there helplessly, still bound hand

and foot and largely ignored by the Englishmen who went about their work.

They were packing up the last wagon when shouts rang out in alarm. Arrows pelted the rebels, emanating from the surrounding forest. Harsh cries filled the little clearing.

"I cannot tell who they are fighting," she said as the rebels readied their weapons and scattered to take cover. She tensed as the next round of arrows crept closer to their location.

"It will not matter for long," her brother said. "They will soon be upon us."

She desperately wanted to stretch her muscles and touch the handle of her seax, as she would have been able to do under different circumstances. The worn leather wrapped around the grip had always brought her comfort. Here, she could only watch and pray she and Julien found an opportunity to escape in the melee. Julien had more color than he had the day before, but how well he recovered from his injuries was in God's hands. She did not trust herself to carry him to safety in her weakened state, but she refused to leave him behind.

Another wave of arrows sailed through the air as warhorses broke through the tree line. Unfamiliar but unmistakably Norman men wheeled their steeds around the camp as the rebels surged forward to meet them with their axes and swords.

Despite her bonds, Isabel crawled closer to her brother so she was positioned between him and the nearest combatants. One of the Normans had been forced to dismount when an Englishman cut the straps to his saddle. He blocked the swing of the axe with his shield, and then dove to the ground to avoid the next sweep of the axe aimed at his head, losing his helmet. As the man rolled away, kicking up dirt, Isabel could have sworn he was Alex's shield bearer.

Before she could be sure, Alric appeared at her side, his face darkened by something stronger than anger. He carelessly slashed at the ropes and leather bindings at her feet. His blade caught her leg, and she flinched, the folds of her skirt offering scant protection.

He pointed to her brother. "Get him up."

Isabel's cramped muscles protested, but she knelt by Julien and helped him to his feet.

"Come on." Alric growled into her ear, pressed her father's sword into her side.

Isabel pulled her brother's arm across her shoulder to make it easier for him to walk as Alric led them to a secluded spot among the trees, away from the fighting. Isabel helped Julien sit, a tree at his back to keep him upright.

Alric forced the flat side of the sword into her side again lest she forget his presence. "Who are they?"

She glanced at the men fighting only a few yards away, and then faced him. "I know not."

"Look again," he snarled. He shoved her closer to the battle, the sword still pressed against her.

"They are Normans."

"Do you know them?"

Just as the words of denial were ready to leave her lips, she saw him. The awareness coursed through her. The residual aches and pains and the dull fear she had been struggling with since her captivity were thrown into sharp relief at her shock of seeing Alex hack his way through Alric's men. She did not recognize the primal, yet determined set of his face, but it was surely him, and a frission sliced through her at the prospect of being reunited with her husband.

Alric must have seen something in her expression or spied the tremors flaring through her. He tightened his grip, biting into her skin with his fingers, as he spun her around to face him.

"You recognize them." Fury mottled his face.

Isabel shook her head, too dazed to utter a denial.

With a growl, Alric snapped his hand around her neck, held her still and began to squeeze. "Whore, tell me. Are they your Normans?"

Isabel's pulse hammered against his thick fingers. The pressure of each breath sputtered through her trachea. "Yes," she managed to say. "You should run like the coward you are," she said more strongly. She was feeling lightheaded, but instead of worrying, felt an overwhelming urge to laugh. Absurdity bubbled up her throat as black spots appeared in her vision.

His fist connected with her cheek, and she was suddenly floating, and then rapidly falling, to the forest floor. She could no longer make out Julien's curses as her eyes drifted shut.

\* \* \* \*

Alex's sword sliced through another Englishman's tunic. Blood streamed through the tear in the worn woolen fabric. With a brutal kick, Alex pushed the man away from him and his horse as the Normans forced their way deeper into the rebel camp.

When they came crashing out of the trees, he spied Isabel almost immediately. Exhaustion marred her profile, and he could make out dark smudges on her face. Were they bruises or merely dirt? She had stationed herself protectively over a man with the same chestnut hair. His eyes narrowed as he examined the man who must be her brother, the reason his wife had been taken from him in the first place.

Alex's attention was divided as he dodged and ducked blows, guiding his steed between the fighting men. The next time he was able to safely look back to where he first sighted Isabel, she was gone. For one cruel moment, he thought he had imagined her presence. He had been so heart-sore and desperate to see her, perhaps his eyes had tricked him. Frantically, he scanned the area. He found her, just before she, her brother and another man disappeared in the far trees.

Isabel's comrade fought nearby. "Kendrick!" he cried out. He hoped the younger man could hear him over the din of clashing swords and axes, iron striking iron. Kendrick looked up the second time Alex called out and made his way over to where he was holding his ground.

"Isabel and her brother have been taken into the woods," Alex shouted just before he blocked an axe blow with his shield. He grimaced as the force of the impact jolted into his shoulder.

Kendrick had just pushed back another opponent before he turned to Alex again. "I'll go after them." He started to extricate himself from the fiercest part of the battlefield.

"No, wait!" It was too late. Alex wanted to be the one to see to Isabel's safety, but he knew the other man had the better chance to reach her. Alex was still mounted on his horse and in a much stronger position to hold his own against the rebels.

He briefly surveyed the field. Captain Thomas, Hugh and the rest of his men were scattered but effectively managing the rebels' attacks. For the most part, Radolf and his men were on foot and working together to corral a handful of rebels, backing them up against a pair of wagons.

One of the rebels snuck alongside his horse. Alex barely caught the movement out of the corner of his eye, just as the man sliced through the straps of his saddle.

Gripping his sword, Alex braced himself for impact with the ground.

\* \* \* \*

Isabel struggled to consciousness. She had forgotten something important, but her eyes would not obey her commands to open. She lay there in a stupor as someone stroked her hair. Her brother. Alric, Alex, the rebel camp... It came back in a flurry of images.

Julien's face was impossibly close as she came to. "Easy now." He helped her sit up.

Kendrick appeared over her brother's shoulder. Isabel flinched in surprise at his sudden appearance. "She seems well enough," he said.

"Alric?" she asked, still getting her bearings.

"He left a few minutes ago to join the fighting," Julien told her.

"Where?" Isabel followed their gazes to the clearing where the Normans battled with the few remaining Englishmen. Some had fallen, and Isabel suspected many of them had fled into the safety of the woods.

Two men ganged up against Captain Thomas, who was a good distance from the other Norman soldiers. Kendrick, too, must have realized the Dumont captain was in trouble. A silent looked passed between him and Julien, and then Kendrick sprinted to Captain Thomas's aid.

Isabel sought out Alric. Her breath caught when she saw his opponent. Alex.

"That's him, is it not?" her brother asked before descending into a coughing fit.

Isabel nodded. "Help me to my feet." She was still weak and rattled from Alric's rough treatment.

Gingerly, her brother helped her stand. He winced at the effort, and Isabel felt guilty for causing him more pain. She gripped his arm and swayed against him as she waited for her head to clear. "I am ready."

They trudged closer to where Alex and Alric stood squaring off against one another. Blood of previous combatants spattered Alex's hauberk, worn over his coat of mail, but Alric was relatively fresh, having avoided the bulk of the fighting, even though it appeared he had lost his axe at some point. Her father's blade caught the sun as the rebel slashed at Alex.

Isabel stumbled as her brother steered her around a fallen soldier. Julien swore to himself, and Isabel snapped her head up. Alric's sword caught Alex's arm before he could pull away and avoid the brunt of the attack.

Isabel quickened her steps, Julien laboring beside her.

By now, most of the English lay injured or had disappeared into the woods, and only Alex and the rebel leader were still engaged in combat. At the other side of the field Thomas's aggressors had been chased away. Kendrick helped Captain Thomas to his feet.

"You fiend!" Alex cried as Alric nearly clipped his shoulder with his sword.

Her gaze returned to Alex. After a few more blocks with his increasingly scarred shield, Alex became more aggressive, backing Alric up with each thrust of his sword. Isabel was unable to look away, convinced Alric was tiring as he evaded Alex's attacks with less dexterity than before.

Julien pressed her hand and pulled her thoughts away from the fight. "Isabel, forgive me."

She turned to him. What was left to forgive? "Julien?"

He took a deep breath and lurched over to where Alex and Alric remained in heated combat. Without her brother's support, Isabel tumbled to the ground, surprised by Julien's behavior. Frantically, she pulled herself into a crouching position, frustrated her body was so unwieldy and weak.

Julien staggered toward the combatants,

approaching Alex from behind.

A savage grin stretched across the rebel leader's face. Alex blocked the man's next sword thrust and pushed him back a pace, giving himself the chance to take a stab at his upper thigh. Alric jumped back, barely escaping the tip of Alex's sword as he advanced. His next swipe knocked the other man's sword to the ground.

Alex took another step toward his English assailant. Instead of hanging his head in defeat, Alric just smirked.

Julien quickened his pace, and his cryptic words came back to her. She stiffened at the thought that he would go to such extremes. That he would attack a man from behind—risk his life—simply because Alex was a Norman, because Julien could not bear the thought of his sister married to a brutal conqueror. It mattered not that by now Alex had forced Alric's sword away and was the victor in their fight.

Time slowed down as Isabel stared forward, tears slipping past her cheeks. She thought she had gotten through to him. She thought Julien understood her position and the depth of her feelings for Alex. However, she could not ignore the despair that filled her or the alarmed faces of the onlookers as they watched Julien explode upon the two men.

English, Norman...the designations mattered not as the three men converged upon one another. All she could do was scream.

# Chapter 25

"No!"

Isabel's sharp cry drove away all thought. Alex took his eyes off the rebel and twisted his body to locate her.

He was suddenly thrown forward. The rebel he had been fighting produced a small knife in all the commotion. Alex toppled to the ground, and he could feel a slight whiff of air against his skin as the blade sliced past him. The man who had shoved him did not fare so well. Alex looked up to see the knife lodged in the breast of Isabel's brother.

Taking advantage of the confusion, Alex scrambled to his feet and knocked his attacker unconscious with the hilt of his sword, before moving to Julien's aid. Isabel's brother must have realized the rebel would have stabbed Alex if he had not intervened.

He laid the man down after removing the blade. Julien gripped the front of his hauberk and pulled Alex close with surprising strength. "Take care of her," he whispered roughly before collapsing.

Shaken, Alex waved his men forward to tend to him. Isabel had not moved from her spot on the ground a few yards away and looked stricken. He fell to his knees before her and rested his hands on her shoulders. Though she seemed not to see him, she was here, within his grasp. At last. Struggling to find something to say, he drank in her presence.

She blinked, her gaze slow to find him. A sob worked in her throat. "I did not leave you."

He had to strain to hear her voice. "I know." He cupped her cheek and ran his fingers along the cuts lining the side of her face. He wanted to tell her how much he had missed her, how much he wanted to hold her and touch her, but her brother's condition was more pressing.

"Come, see to your brother," he said with no small amount of reluctance. She looked up at him in surprise but complied as he helped her to her feet and led her to Julien.

As she knelt over her brother's body, Alex caught Hugh's grim look. Alex had no idea what Isabel's reaction would be to her brother's death. He watched as they spoke softly in English, clinging to one another. Captain Thomas and Kendrick stood by, offering silent support.

When Julien's words slowed and his hands slid from hers, Isabel placed one last kiss to his forehead, and then straightened. With dry eyes, she marched over to the man Alex had been fighting with. She yanked the sword belt off him and collected the blade Alex had knocked free during their fight. She wiped the sword off in the grass before she strapped it around her waist.

"My brother's sword, my father's before his," she explained softly. "Kill him," she said to Kendrick, nodding toward the unconscious rebel. The Englishman stepped forward without hesitation, and Alex realized his last combatant must have been the heinous rebel leader who had threatened Isabel. She turned away as Kendrick slit his throat.

The day blurred past. Men were buried, others needed bandaging. Isabel was tireless, checking the injuries of each man. Captain Thomas had suffered a large cut along his side, but he was in more pain than

danger. The rebels had knocked Hugh around during
the battle as well. An axe blade had nicked his upper
arm and a blow to his temple still bled freely. Under
Alex's watchful eye, Isabel knelt before him and saw
to his injuries as she had done for everyone else.

Alex only succeeded in getting Isabel to rest once.
He cursed her stubbornness, when it was so clear she
was exhausted. Unable to watch her push herself any
longer, he grabbed her elbow and directed her away
from the others so they could have some privacy.
While he shared some bread with her, he inspected the
cuts on her wrists and face. He was unhappy with the
way she rushed the food down and the weight she had
lost since her abduction.

She gently pushed him away when she had
finished. She had not spoken to him since they had
buried Julien, and he had not pressed her. They were
together, and it would have to be enough until they had
time for themselves.

Alex and his men helped Captain Radolf in
assessing the stores and supplies the rebels left behind.
Radolf's men would take the bulk of the foodstuffs and
weapons, but little else was of use to them. They
burned what remained in case some of the Englishmen
returned.

"That is the rest of it," Radolf said. "When I make
my report to William, I will be sure to tell him of your
contribution. We would not have been able to take
them on without your help."

Alex nodded in thanks. "I am glad we could be of
service."

"Well, you found what was lost," he said,
indicating Isabel, who talked with Kendrick while they
watched the flames of the bonfire. "I had my doubts
she would turn up."

"I am thankful she did." Alex faced Captain

Radolf. "Safe travels."

"And you," Radolf replied, gripping Alex's forearms in farewell. He and his men mounted their horses and left the clearing, and soon only the crackling of the fire could be heard in their wake.

Alex joined Isabel, still uncertain how he should treat Kendrick. The other man looked wary at his approach but moved a respectable distance from his wife. Isabel faced Alex, and for an instant he thought he saw a glimmer of relief within her dark brown eyes.

"Alex, Kendrick and Osbert will not be returning to Ashdown with us. I told them they would be welcome, but they have declined," she said.

"We will travel to Norway. Too much has changed here, and they still hold to the old ways. I think we would both like the opportunity to start anew," Kendrick said.

Alex nodded, unsure how he should feel. "Norway is a fair distance from here. Are you sure you do not wish to reconsider?"

"No. Osbert has some distant relations there who will help us get settled."

Alex faced Kendrick. "Thank you for your loyalty to Isabel. Godspeed."

Kendrick's face was unreadable as he met Alex's stare, but it only a lasted a few seconds before he turned to Isabel and gave her a short bow. He looked as though he wanted to say something more, but the Englishman only held Isabel's gaze briefly before he turned away. He met Osbert, and they put their gear into a small wagon they would use to travel to the coast.

Isabel sighed and slipped closer to Alex, and he wrapped an arm around her waist. They watched the wagon fade into the forest. Alex pulled her tight against him, inhaling the scent of her hair and relishing in the warmth beneath his hands. "Are you ready to go home?"

As she looked up at him, a small smile brightened her watery eyes. "Yes."

\* \* \* \*

"We will need a bath brought up as soon as possible," Alex ordered when they reached the public house. He secured two rooms, one for him and Isabel and the other for Hugh and Captain Thomas to share. The captain was still in pain as Hugh helped him to their room, but Isabel thanked God his injury was not life-threatening. Jerome and the rest of the men would sleep in the stables overnight.

Averill hovered near Isabel as Alex settled with the hosteller. The girl had stayed behind in Radolf's camp during the fight, and once reunited with Isabel, had been eager to see to her mistress's injuries.

With the arrangements finalized, Alex took Isabel's arm. When Averill moved to follow them, Alex forestalled her. "I will tend to Lady Isabel. We are not to be disturbed."

Isabel managed a small smile for the dispirited girl before Alex led her upstairs to the biggest guest room the inn had available. Isabel gratefully sank down into a simple chair, and Alex stood by as the inn's servant brought in buckets of warm water for the wooden tub they placed in the center of the room. Isabel was quiet, watching the water swirl and slosh as each bucket was added.

After the last heave of water, the serving wench curtseyed clumsily. "Just tell us when ye be done, miss."

Isabel nodded.

With a click of the door latch, she and Alex were finally alone. She stood up, disconcerted to find herself trembling and her breath shallow.

Alex was quickly at her side and ran his hands up and down her arms in comfort. "Come, let me help you."

He reached down, unbuckled her sword from her waist and took a moment to look at it. Her old blade had been well-made, and this one—her father's—was even finer. He slid the sword back into its sheath and set it on the nearby table.

Alex turned to her, plucked her cloak from her shoulders and put it aside. He froze when he saw the dress she wore underneath. Gently, he smoothed the torn fabric, the touch sending a jolt through her as she recalled the last time they were together. Every acute detail. The warmth of his skin, his scent and the way he had fired her blood.

He must have felt it too, for he pulled his hand away as if burned. She took a shaky breath. Such thoughts would only complicate things between them now. She waited as he reached down and grabbed the edge of her dress. He pulled it up, and Isabel slipped out of it with little effort. He repeated the process with her shift, grimacing when he saw the cuts on her shins and her knees. Her chest was largely unblemished, with only a few stray bruises along her sides.

He led her toward the tub. She gripped his arm tightly as she stepped in, a hiss of pain the only sound escaping her when she made contact with the steaming water. Her motions still clumsy, he helped guide her down into the bath. With his arms wrapped tightly around her, she felt the intake of breath jolting through him. He must have looked down at her back for the first time, at the mass of bruises that no doubt ran down her spine.

"*Jesu*! What did they do to you?"

Isabel grunted. "Punishment for escaping." She twisted toward him. "It does not hurt me much anymore."

Raising his brows, he softly trailed his hands down her back and saw her wince. "Liar. I should have killed the brute myself."

Alex pulled off his overtunic and pushed back the sleeves of his sherte before sinking to his knees next to the tub. The serving girl had left behind some pieces of cloth, and he grabbed a small scrap and soaked it in the water. He took Isabel's hand and started to wipe away the dirt and grime. She was quiet as he continued his ministrations, traveling up her arm before moving on to her other hand. When he reached her chest and neck, he kept his touch from lingering too long in any one area. He then came to her face, and he cupped some water in his hand and poured it over her brow, wiping away the dirt and dried blood with his fingers. An unknown look shone in his eyes as she watched him.

Smiling reassuringly, he trailed his hand over her cheek one last time before he turned his attention to her back and carefully worked his way down over her bruises. When he was done, she dunked her head, slowly kneading her scalp and hair. She finished and moved to get up. Alex was at her side with a hand on her elbow and another larger piece of cloth to wrap herself in. He led her to the bed and then went over to their gear. He rifled through her saddlebags they had managed to recover and pulled out her comb. She took it gratefully and started running it through her hair.

Alex removed the rest of his clothing and got into the tub, not wanting to waste the water. He hastily performed his ablutions, dried off and put on a pair of braies. He called for the serving girls and had the tub removed. They also brought up a tray with some bread and cheese and left it on the table. Isabel sighed when he shut the door behind the last servant, knowing there would be no more disturbances.

Alex joined her on the bed. Her drying hair started to curl around her temples. He fingered it then pulled the comb out of her hands. "You should eat something."

She nodded in agreement but did not move from her seat.

He set the comb on the table, grabbed a piece of bread and placed some cheese on it. He handed it to her, and she dutifully took a couple of bites. Alex ate as well, including what she could not finish. When he was done, he returned to the saddlebags and pulled out a clean shift for her. She stood. He pulled the towel away from her body and helped her slip on the gown.

Isabel smoothed the shift into place, relishing the clean clothes. She looked up at Alex's face, at a wrinkle in his brow that had been there all day. She wanted to say something to dispel it, but could not find the words. Instead she stepped toward him, and he wrapped his hands around her as she hugged him close.

She pressed her cheek against his warm chest. "I thank you," she breathed.

"I am sorry we did not find you sooner."

She shook her head and pulled away from him. "We cannot change what happened. I was grateful for the chance to see my brother once more." Her gaze fell to the bed. "But I am also glad I do not have to spend another night on the ground," she said with a small smile.

His mouth quirked. "Indeed." He stepped away from her and dug out a necklace from the pouch on his belt.

Isabel gasped when she saw it. "I thought I had lost it."

He smiled. "You did, but when we found it, I knew we were closer to finding you," he told her as he clasped it once more around her neck. She ran her hand over the chain and pendant in wonder.

"Come," he said with a nod toward the bed.

Together, they sank onto the rope mattress. After blowing out the candle, Alex lay on his back, gathered Isabel in his arms. Her chin rested on his shoulder. Absently he picked up her hand, lacing their fingers together.

As her eyes adjusted to the dim light the brazier in the corner of the room cast, Isabel concentrated on their breathing, noting the rise and fall of Alex's chest. Sleep pulled at her, but Alex deserved some answers before she gave in to her exhaustion.

"I know you have questions, and I will tell you what I can."

She saw a frown crease his face briefly before it disappeared in the dark of the room. "I know enough of what happened, but now you need rest," he said. Kendrick had probably already provided him with most of the details regarding her captivity.

"Only if you are certain."

"Sleep," he said, his voice gentle to soften the command.

She nodded, and for a time all was well. In the warmth of Alex's arms, Isabel slept soundly, the dread and discomforts of the rebel camp now behind her.

She woke sometime later in a panic, still not convinced she was safe. It took a moment for her to control her erratic breathing as she stared, uncomprehending, around her, at the man lying next to her—Alex—his profile unmistakable despite the dimness. She shuddered in relief and curled into his side.

He came for her. He really came. She had not dared to believe he would, and even though they were now together, had he only done it because it was expected—the honorable thing to do—or was there a deeper meaning to his actions? Their time apart had crystallized her feelings for him, but she had no inkling as to what Alex felt. For her.

Their marriage was the result of the conquest, and now their reunion was precipitated by even more bloodshed. What kind of a future could they hope for?

Alex woke to the muffled sounds of Isabel's sobs dampening his chest. "Come, *chérie*, do not cry."

Isabel sniffed, too upset to be embarrassed by her tears. "I did not mean to wake you."

He pulled her closer. "All is as it should be," he said. "We are together, and tomorrow we will be in Ashdown."

"I know. I can hardly believe I am with you again."

"You know not how glad I was we were able to find you before..."

"Before it was too late?" Isabel supplied.

Alex nodded. "I kept envisioning horrible possibilities," he said with a sigh. "I feared for your safety."

"I was fearful as well." She closed her hand over his arm that anchored her against him. "Even though I was reunited with my brother, it did not take long to realize he could not help me. Kendrick could not help me." She took a breath. "And... I feared you would not help me." She looked down in shame at that, more tears slipping down her face. "At night, every cross word, each of our fights, filled my head. All the lies, all the awful things I said."

He cupped her cheek. "Isabel, do not—"

She ignored him. She needed to unburden herself of all her sins, her doubts...everything. "And I despaired. Why would you want me back after that? Even if you did, it was Julien who pointed out it looked like I ran off of my own accord. Given our past, it would not be unreasonable for you to assume as much."

Alex sighed. "You are right. I did doubt. I thought on those same things and made similar assumptions." His tone was heavy with regret. "But then other things did not make sense. Like why you left without your horse, the fact that you were leaving your people behind to fend for themselves..." He cleared his throat. "And the soft look on your face when I left you that night."

Isabel knew what he meant, and hearing him talk about that intimate moment with such reverence nurtured the anticipation coiled around her heart.

"Those things gave me hope," Alex continued, "hope I would find you again." He tightened his arms around her.

She sniffed. "When I saw you fighting Alric's men, I knew all would turn out. Even when you were fighting against the devil himself, I did not doubt... Not until Julien left my side."

Alex tensed beside her.

"Like you," she continued, "I first thought he was going to attack you from behind. Kendrick explained to me later Alric always had a seax hidden in his tunic to use as a final defense. My brother knew that and sought to prevent him from surprising you with such an attack," she explained. She shuddered as she remembered the short, sharp knife so like hers that had been removed from her brother's body as Captain Radolf's men scavenged the rebel camp.

Alex nodded. "Your brother—"

"I hated myself for doubting Julien's intentions, especially since we came to an understanding of sorts in the end."

He was quiet for a moment. "I am sorry he did not live," he finally said.

"Even if he had not been stabbed, his injury would have surely killed him. I cannot help but feel I lost him all over again."

"You had to deal with reports of his death only to find him once more so he could die before your eyes. I am amazed by your strength in all of this."

She laughed and was surprised at the bitterness she heard. "Do not be. It is not strength, but merely survival."

"Hmm..." Alex was not convinced. "Either way, we are together once more."

"I know. And I am glad."

He pulled her close again. "I am so sorry I could not protect you from this."

"As you said, we are here, together. I may be bruised, but I am not broken."

"For which I am eternally grateful," he said with a growl.

He leaned over her and peered at her face through the darkness. Her breath caught at the serious look on his face.

"When you disappeared, I realized how much I had lost," he said. "It was not just your knowledge of the English people, the language or even your father's holding. It was you, all of you. I love you, Isabel...I just did not know how much."

She closed her eyes as astonishment and hope and...love streamed through her. Her heartbeat picked up as she recognized the truth of his words.

"I knew it was a gamble when I joined with William," Alex said, "but I never expected such a fortunate outcome. Yes, I was hoping for lands, but I got so much more. You are reward enough, even without such trappings."

Isabel opened her eyes and took a calming breath. "Alex, I love you, too. I just hope you can still trust me—trust us—after all that has happened." She was so afraid that despite all they had shared, all they felt for each other, the differences between them would prove their undoing.

"With my life."

Relief flooded through her as he gathered her up in his arms.

When he finally kissed her, it seemed as though she had been waiting for that moment since they last parted. It started out innocently enough, a reassuring press of lips that ensured she wasn't dreaming. Then the scent of him hit Isabel just as his tongue teased her lower lip, and she was ensnared.

She parted her mouth for him, reaching for his neck and drawing him closer. His arms were unintentionally digging into her bruised back, but she did not care. This was right. The way it should be.

Too soon, Alex eased them apart. "My lady, what of the men?"

"What do you mean?" she asked, irritated by the question. She hummed with repressed need, and she wanted nothing more than to get lost in more of his kisses.

Alex smirked at her knowingly. "They could hear if we continue..."

Her cheeks heated as her words from so long ago were flung back at her. "You...you are a bad man," she said with as much indignation as she could muster.

He grinned. "As you say."

Isabel pulled him closer so she could whisper in his ear.

"I care not."

As a lover of history, I am constantly fascinated by accounts of how one person can have a profound effect on events. This story started with one person as well: William Malet, who was an English advisor to Duke William as he prepared to cross the channel and take England for his own. I wondered at how an Englishman could come to help a Norman take over his homeland, and figured there must be others in England who would be in a position to help Duke William in the conquest, given the charged political climate.

Thus, Isabel's father, Lord Bernard Dumont, was born, a man with conflicting loyalties who could ease the way for Duke William's rule. He never makes an appearance and we never really learn what his choice would be between Normandy and England, but I hope his presence is felt throughout the book.

Bringing history to life with adventure and romance is my passion. To learn more about the history and the resources I used to write *Siege of the Heart*, please visit my website http://elisecyr.wordpress.com/

Thank you for reading.

*To my husband. Thank you, always.*

## Acknowledgements

This book evolved over the course of many years, and I'm grateful to a large number of people who helped me along the way.

First, special thanks to Eric, Lori, Gilly, Laura, Rachel, Andy and Sandra for all their suggestions and feedback on multiple versions of this story.

I also want to thank my editor, Paige Christian, along with Mary Murray, Renee Rocco and the rest of the Lyrical Press staff for their support and assistance in the publication of the book. I'm so glad it found a home.

Finally, thanks to my family for their love and encouragement. It has helped me more than you know.